Going the Distance

Going the Distance

edited by
Alan Beard

TINDAL STREET PRESS

First published in 2003 by
Tindal Street Press Ltd
217 The Custard Factory, Gibb Street, Birmingham, B9 4AA
www.tindalstreet.co.uk

Typesetting: Tindal Street Press Ltd

A CIP catalogue reference for this book is available
from the British Library.

ISBN: 0 9541303 5 9

Printed and bound in Great Britain
by the Cromwell Press, Trowbridge, Wiltshire

Acknowledgements

Thanks are due to Alan Mahar and Emma Hargrave at Tindal Street Press. Also grateful thanks to all Tindal Street Fiction Group members past and present for their stories and feedback, and for helping me to keep sane over the years. Also cheers to Clare, Chloe and Grace, my mum, dad and sisters, and my mate Pete Dickens.

Contents

In the rather daunting marketplace of fiction writing persistence and continuity do count for something – and going the distance is therefore an achievement in itself. The first fortnightly meetings of Tindal Street Fiction Group took place in the community room of a junior school back in 1983; and they're still going. As a founder member I feel proud to have set this machine in motion and helped sustain it. People have come and gone in that time, but the focus on producing and reading stories has always been consistent. *Going the Distance* (twenty years' worth edited by a distinguished story specialist and long-time member) is proof of more than mere survival; it is testament to the quality and talent of an extraordinary coming together of writers.

Alan Mahar

Introduction

Going the Distance celebrates twenty years of Tindal Street Fiction Group, a remarkably successful collective of writers that meets fortnightly in Balsall Heath, Birmingham.

Many of these stories, then, are set in the West Midlands, but the reader can also expect to visit places such as Trinidad, Colombia, Canada, Wales, Essex, Liverpool and even somewhere called London. There are stories set in offices, pubs, bus shelters, tower blocks, bedsits, antique shops, swimming pools and strip clubs. The characters range from teenagers taking their first frightening steps in the adult world to the middle-aged embarking on new and tricky relationships. In these stories an alcoholic drinks himself into a new country; in another, a man finds himself the only guest at a bizarre party. In Colombia a woman's stolen car is stuffed with flowers and she decides to leave the country; in Trinidad parents fear their teenage daughters being corrupted by glumbo glisaes, young men in league with the devil. A grandmother sails out for her final journey, while a semi-literate father mourns the death of his daughter. Ghosts, torture, violence and drugs feature in some; in others, a child worries about having her tonsils removed, and a pub quiz team try to work out a winning strategy. Variety, not only of subject matter and setting but also of style and approach, is assured from Tindal Street

Fiction Group writers, reflecting the diversity of their backgrounds and experience. The youngest here is twenty-six, the oldest seventy-three: all are accomplished. Their stories are as strong and sharp as any you'll find, and properly celebrate twenty years of quiet achievement for TSFG.

The commitment and respect shown to the short story by these writers is not, however, reflected in English literary culture as a whole: the short story appears to be in crisis in England. Story collections are seen as hard to sell and writers are often discouraged from practising the art. This is in sharp contrast to, say, the USA, Canada and Ireland where short stories are not only considered worthwhile but are rewarded: published, discussed, read. Competitions, magazines, 'best of' compilations abound. Jhumpa Lahiri, on the strength of one collection, is not only recognized but mobbed by adoring crowds when she returns to Bengal. In Russia, story collections regularly sell out; in the USA prestigious journals such as the *New Yorker* and *Atlantic Monthly* have stories at their heart, while innumerable others carry fine examples and sell widely. In the UK, space disappears as magazines fold and good collections are neglected. Mainstream publishers produced just thirteen collections by UK writers in this country last year. (See Debbie Taylor's article, 'Endangered Species', in *Mslexia*, issue 16, Jan–March 2003.)

Last year an Emergency Summit was called at the University of Northumberland to tackle this perceived discrimination against the form by agents, publishers and booksellers. And as a result the Save Our Short Story Campaign has been set up to revive the story's fortunes, to increase the number of outlets, events and competitions for short fiction. A new research fellowship has been established; a website created; annual anthologies planned. Let's hope these initiatives lead to a growing, sophisticated readership eagerly awaiting new collections and anthologies, valuing stories for themselves and not just as tasters for forthcoming novels.

So, in this context, it seems appropriate to celebrate a twenty-year anniversary with an anthology of stories from TSFG because, although some are novelists and poets too, all group members are storywriters, intensely interested in and excited by the (good) short story. The story's possibilities tantalize and we all chase the elusive perfection a story seems to want and mustn't quite achieve. We are drawn to the form's intensity and focus and the variety of its effects, which can be as subtle and long lasting as a novel, but also have an immediacy and an enchantment difficult to sustain over the course of longer material. At TSFG meetings there are no rules or manifesto to conform to – we all look for the story that delights or grips or stuns with its beauty, economy or vitality; the one that sticks with us; is more than the sum of its pages. Attending meetings is like subscribing to a good literary magazine, two stories a month, and it is a privilege to be in on the first readings of so many fine examples of the form. OK, not every piece works. Some come back again and again for further comments and adjustments, some never quite make it, but many do, going on to be published or broadcast, a feat cheered and discussed – and the whole group gains confidence and learns from that individual's success.

Tindal writers got the exposure they deserved, slowly at first. In the 1980s stories appeared in *London Magazine*, *Iron*, *Panurge* and *Sunk Island Review*. Then in the 1990s *Critical Quarterly*, *Bete Noire*, *Malahat Review*, the *European*, *Main Street Journal*, *Metropolitan*, *Ambit* and *Fantasy Tales* among many others were added to the list. Stories were broadcast on BBC Radio 4 and appeared in anthologies such as *Best Short Stories*, *Telling Stories*, *Heinemann New Writing*, *Signals: London Magazine Stories*, *Darklands* and *The Mammoth Book of Dracula*. They were winning prizes such as the Tom-Gallon, and *She/Good Morning* awards. Collections came out from Alan Beard (*Taking Doreen out of the Sky*) and Joel Lane (*Earth Wire*), along with novels from Alan Mahar (*Flight* Patterns), Lane (*From Blue to Black*), Jackie Gay (*Scapegrace*) and Gul Davis (*A Lone Walk*) – which also won the JB Priestley Fiction Award, and Annie Murray began a series of novels with *Birmingham Rose*, followed by *Birmingham Friends*.

The 'noughties' – so far – continue in the same vein: appearances in anthologies and magazines such as *Pretext*, *Neonlit*, *The Ex-Files* and *Groundswell*, second novels from Mahar (*After the Man Before*), Lane (*The Blue Mask*) and Gay (*Wist*), and more from Murray (including *Poppy Day* and *Chocolate Girls*). Julia Bell joined the ranks of novelists with *Massive* and will follow it up with *Out There*. TSFG members have also been editing short-story anthologies, among them *Hard Shoulder* (another award-winner), *England Calling* and *Birmingham Noir*.

The 1983–2003 anniversary seems a natural point to mark this long-term success. Members suggested stories they'd like to see in an anthology repre-senting the group's staying power. We certainly wanted to acknowledge past landmarks; for example, Godfrey Featherstone's innovative and moving piece had to be included in any celebration of TSFG. However, we also wanted to show that the group is still going strong – indeed in its most productive phase yet.

The reader will find, therefore, highlights from the first three TSFG self-published anthologies: *Tindal Street Fiction* (1984), *The View from Tindal Street* (1986) and *Mouth* (1996), along with other stories published in magazines from 1980s and 1990s, but the majority here date from the last five years and show the group flourishing. Seven are published for the first time.

We can confidently say that here in Birmingham the short story is valued. Loved even. The critical success of the Tindal Street Fiction Group anthologies contributed to the setting up of a separate organization – Tindal Street Press. Since its inception, the Press has shown a dedication to raising the profile of the short story. *Going the Distance* is the sixth anthology that it has published. Anthologies by black and Asian writers, women and young people, for example, demonstrate the talents of authors who deserve space, recognition – and a readership. A third of the Press's output has been devoted to airing 117 new stories by a hundred different writers, two-thirds of whom are new to publication. Proof indeed of a commitment to the form in the face of increasing indifference elsewhere.

If you're looking for a place where the short story is thriving and gaining an audience, then I'd say look to Birmingham.

Alan Beard
June 2003

Going the Distance
Gemma Blackshaw

DONNA KITE DID IT HERE. It says so in Tipp-Ex on the Braintree to Chelmsford line bus stops. There are ten stops in each direction, and I've seen it in every one. That's twenty times she's done it, at least. Twenty times can't be right. Donna hasn't got a boyfriend. But I'm not gonna argue with her.

You don't argue with Donna Kite. She wears make-up and everything. She lost her virginity when she was ten. She's telling the truth because she wears a tampon and everyone knows you can only wear a tampon after you've done it. I haven't done it. But I've seen people doing it on the TV. I get *Cocktail* out from Titles Video to watch Tom Cruise and Elizabeth Shue doing it. It's a Rate Fifteen. I'm sort of in between thirteen and fourteen; actually, I'm nearer fourteen. I put on Mum's Traffic Red lipgloss and turn up my denim jacket collar so the video man will think that I'm old enough to do it. Mum doesn't do it. She doesn't get out much. And we don't live on the Little Waltham council estate like Donna. Mum says if you live on the council estate you can't get enough of it.

Dawn Haliday, Sandra Harthard and Tina Boyce have all done it with Donna's brother behind Riverside Leisure Centre. They go on a Wednesday night, which is under-18s night. Donna's brother drives them around in turns on his new Honda motorbike. They don't wear helmets. Their hair is crunchy from mousse, staying stiff around their shoulders despite doing sixty down the Chelmer Valley Road. They've got perms and highlights and everything.

Mum says they look like slappers. I don't know what a slapper is. I'm not gonna ask her because last time I asked her what a word meant she took my Madonna *Like a Virgin* record away. It was fuck. Donna says it all the time. Mum said it once when she saw Dad and Rita in Sainsbury's together. – Fuck him, she said through clenched teeth. – *Fuck him.*

I tried it out on the fish and chips man after school. I tried it out because Donna was behind me in the queue. I could hear her scuffing her shoe up and down while I decided on a 75p cone or a 95p cone.

I said, I'll have a fucking 75p cone of chips with extra salt and vinegar and a sachet of sauce, please.

He didn't say anything. He just gave me a wink, leaning over the counter when I dropped the change on the pavement. Mum says he's a dirty old man. That I'll pick up God knows what from that place. It's a kicked-in van with K9's: COULD YOU MURDER A BURGER? painted on the side doors. Blokes stop there late at night to smoke cigarettes round their cars, leaning across the dusty bonnets with their stereos on Essex FM and girls in the back seats. The man who owns it has an Alsatian chained to the litterbin. It wears a muzzle and everything. You can get cheese burgers and hot dogs and donner kebabs there but I usually just stick with chips because I don't want to get too full up. I eat them one by one on the way back because I'm not allowed to take the bus and having chips makes the Broomfield Road go faster.

Past the Esso garage, the BP garage, TC News, Broomfield Casualty, the Wimpy Homes development. I don't mind it in the summer when everything smells of concrete, litterbins and petrol fumes and all you can see are brick-layers, stripped and shining, on the building sites of new estates. Essex is a built-up area. Basildon Council rejects in bomber jackets and sovereign rings come down on the A12 for work at Marconi Radar and never make it back up the motorway. Mum says we've got Melbourne flats for people like that.

– Why couldn't she have stayed in Melbourne flats? she says.

I usually count the different makes of car on the main road as I walk back. Boy racers burn it up and down with their hands gripping the steering wheels and their arms locked. There's none of that casual elbow on the wound-down window stuff. They drive like they're in the Smash City arcade booth. Foot flat down on the accelerator knocking up a ten-second lead on Nigel Mansell. Everyone drives fast in Essex. Doesn't matter what you're driving. Second-hand Saabs, Escorts, Cortinas, Montegos rev it up towards town. Fords are popular in Essex. Mum's got an Orion but she doesn't drive it any more.

I pass the hot, greasy cone from hand to hand as I cut across the Esso garage until the chips at the top cool down. I'm thinking about maybe getting a can of Tizer for afters when Donna Kite comes over in her Shoe City slingbacks. She stands in front of me with her arms across her chest. She's got an underwired bra on. I'm not allowed a push-up bra. Mum says it will give me ideas.

– Give us one, she says.

I hold out the cone. Donna sticks her fingers into the chips, turning them over until she finds the fat ones. The cone burns the inside of my hands while I hold it still for her but I don't say anything. She lifts one out and licks it carefully, all the way round, never taking her eyes off it. Her gold hoop earrings clink against each other. She's got

17

two piercings in each ear. You get a deal in Ratner's if you get two piercings in each ear.

– Ta, she says, throwing the chip to the ground. – You comin' to get the bus with us?

It's the first time she's ever spoken to me. Girls like Donna don't have to say much. They have what Mum calls *presence*. – Like Lady Di, she says, except Donna's hard as nails.

Mum says that's what comes of living in Church Close. That they're a different breed in Church Close. That they're at it like rabbits.

Donna links her arm through mine, her free hand fingering a thick gold chain with a kicking lady's leg dangling down her Aertex shirt. I'm trying to walk with my tits out, looking sideways at her pierced ears. And I think about saying to Mum that Donna's got hers done so why can't I? But I decide against it. Stuff like that doesn't go down well. Mum wears clip-ons.

It's just me and Donna in the Chelmer Valley bus stop. We wait for the 144. There are cigarette ends, Twix packets and cans of cola around our feet. There's a slight breeze. Flyers for Double Glazing at Zenith Windows, buy now pay later, skip across the road.

It's one of those hot days when the sun hits you square in the face, the crunched-in doors and hubcaps of passing traffic reflecting bright light into the bus shelter. There are no clouds. There are never any clouds in Essex in July. It said in the papers that the South-East is becoming a dust bowl. Like Arizona or something. The heat shimmers across the tarmac and I can hear the clank of metal and cement mixers on the nearby building site.

I'm swinging my legs back and forwards, in and out of the sun and the shade, until I remember about the hair and tuck them behind my school skirt. Mum won't let me shave my legs. She says there's plenty of time for all that.

Donna gets hers waxed. She says her older sister's a beautician. I've seen her working behind the Max Factor counter so that must be right. I want to be a beautician. Mum says there's plenty of time for all that. She says that quite a bit.

Donna lights a cigarette inside the orange lining of her satin jacket. She pulls the smoke in and holds it there, eyes closed. She exhales. The smell thickens with the heat and makes me feel sick.

She says, I goes to Sandra at break, you don't live on the estate, do ya? I've seen ya looking at us. D'ya wanna get in with us or something cos I've had a word with the girls and we was thinking that maybe you're all right. Your dad went off with Rita Shore, didn't 'e? She still cleaning?

– No, I say.

Donna puts her legs up on the rubbish bin. They're milky, thin blue veins curling over her thighs. She says, I never seen your mum. She go down the White Hart?

– No, I say, she doesn't get out much. She has a lot to get on with in the house. You know, ironing and stuff. She listens to the radio a lot while she does the ironing, I say.

I'm thinking how I'm gonna explain to Mum that I'm half an hour earlier than usual when Donna puts her arm around my shoulders. I want to pull away but I don't. I can smell her chip breath. I think, what's she gonna do? I start to sweat underneath my bottom lip, under my tits. Her hair is hard with hairspray against my face, all four fingers covered in gold rings to the knuckles. Big rings that Mum would call nine carat crap.

She says, I told Sandra that you're all right. You should be riding up the back of the bus with us. Fuck walking it!

She smiles so I smile back at her and smooth my skirt over my knees.

– You know me bruvver Darren, well he was saying that you'd be really good at it. You can tell, he says. By the way

19

you walk and stuff. He reckons you must've done it. 'Ave you ever done it?

– Yeah, I say, I've done it. I've done it loadsa times.

Donna holds her hand up to her mouth in case anyone's listening. A woman with a shopping trolley turns to the timetable and runs her finger down the bank holiday bus list. She looks a bit put out. I get embarrassed when grown-ups look a bit put out.

– D'ya like it? Donna asks.

I smile and look across the road. She laughs.

– Darren told me to ask ya if ya wanna do it with 'im. D'ya wanna go out with 'im? she says.

I shield my eyes from the sun moving round the top of the bus stop. I'm still looking across the road at the washing line in someone's drive and the sheets are so white they hurt your eyes.

– Yeah, I say, yeah, I'll go out with him.

– Why don't ya come out with us tonight? Just down K9's. Meet ya at the bus stop?

I'm just about to say I'll have to ask Mum first, when I see myself standing next to Darren's motorbike in Mum's Bourgeois mascara and my new pixie boots at the top of the Broomfield Road.

– All right, I say.

I sit next to her on the back seat of the bus, holding the rail in front of me to stop my arms from shaking.

Mum is in her nightdress at the kitchen table when I let myself in. She's listening to 'Lady in Red'. It's her favourite song. She's got her hands around a cup of coffee. Mum doesn't drink out of mugs. She thinks they're common. There's a stack of ironing in the clothes basket at her feet. Piles and piles of the sheets that match the curtains that match the cushion covers. She's taken to washing the bed linen every day. She strips the covers off, then throws them down the stairs, then ties them into a big knot to take them into the utility room to unknot, sorting out colours from whites and pouring white deserts of Persil Colour into the Hotpoint. Dad bought the washing machine for her birthday last year.

She looks up at the kitchen door as I come in. Her hand flies up to her bare neck. She stands with a scrape of the chair against the blue and white tiled floor and immediately starts to wipe the breakfast bar. She said she wanted the French look when we got the fitted kitchen. We went to the showroom in town every Saturday morning for two, three months before she could decide on the cabinet colours. She turns to the sink and washes up her coffee cup, rinsing it under the tap, taking the excess water off with the blue and white striped towel, staking it in line with the others on the draining board, drying her hands, going to the drawer for Atrixo hand cream and digging it into her nail-beds.

– You're back early, she says.

– There was a staff meeting, I say, we got let out before the bell. I can lie really well. You've gotta make it automatic for it to be convincing.

– Oh, she says.

She walks quickly over to the radio and switches it off. She turns around, smoothing the creases in her nightdress, pushing her hair back behind her ears. She smiles quickly, brightly.

– I was just about to get dressed, she says. – I've been so busy. Hoovered from top to bottom. Managed to get your washing and ironing done. I don't know where the day goes. I thought, oh I'll just give the floor a quick wipe while I'm down here before I pop something on, and look it's quarter to four. I don't know where the day goes. I honestly don't. Be down in two secs.

She runs up the stairs, her thin feet slapping the carpet. Kids are playing on their BMX bikes outside. They crash

21

into people's gates and front-garden beds. I was never allowed to play on the street. Mum said it was in case I got run over. Hayley Wood got run over and lost her hair from the shock. It would grow back and then fall out again.

– Do you want to be like that? Mum would say. – Do you? Do you? So I had to invite kids over for tea instead.

Mum comes down in a skirt and blouse. It was so quick, she must've had the clothes all laid out on the bed. She's ringed her eyes in Emerald Evening pencil and matching mascara. She smiles and blinks rapidly at me.

– Right, she says, how was your day?

I mostly make it up. She's not listening to any of it. She never listens to any of it because she's taking the Marks & Spencer Shepherd's Pie out of the fridge and removing it from the silver-foil tray and putting it in a brown glass dish because she thinks they look cheap but they're so convenient when you're on the go all the time. Mum likes to do things fast. To keep busy. She says there's plenty of time to sleep when you're dead. So she's clicking over to the freezer drawers and back and running the veg underneath the hot tap to make it thaw out quickly. Plastic bags full of veg she's prepared in bulk beforehand and then sectioned off into individual meals for one. And then there's a plate of food and a jug of gravy next to a dish of green peas and diced carrot with a separate spoon and a paper napkin folded into a triangle underneath my fork.

Meat and two veg on a laid table. She still hasn't got out of the habit. Weird thing is, I don't think Dad was over-keen anyway. He was buying tuna salad in Sainsbury's last time I saw him. He wasn't even meant to like tuna salad. She sits in front of me and watches me eat. And she talks about her phone call with Auntie Helen, and about switching to skimmed instead of semi-skimmed milk, and the programme on the radio while she had a quick coffee and a biscuit. She talks non-stop like this every evening.

And then she frowns at the pleats in her skirt and says that this synthetic material creases so easily. Falls out of shape. You'd hardly know it was from Bolingbroke & Wenley.

I can hear Mum putting the dishes away downstairs. Mum says, trouble with modern housing is that the walls are paper thin. You can hear everything. Donna says she can hear her mum and Barry at it all the time. I never heard Mum and Dad at it. Not even at weekends. But then, Dad never said much anyway. I mean, he's a quiet kind of bloke.

Mum has her first drink at five thirty. – Just the one, she says. – My treat, she says. The glass she uses stands next to the bottle of Gordon's Gin in the lounge cabinet. It's the only glass left out of the twelve we got with Dad's petrol stamps.

– Good crystal, he'd say, bringing a glass home every week until we had a dinner-party set.

I came home from school one day and she was sitting at the kitchen table with one in her hand and the others smashed around her feet. She said she'd dropped the tray. – Damn tiled floor, she said, and rushed to get the dustpan and brush.

It's *Dallas* night on TV. I wait for the music to start and then I go into her bathroom. I sit with my back against the toilet, my legs cool on the cork-tiled floor and go through her make-up bags and toiletry bags, turning up all the lipsticks and trying them on the back of my hand. I pick out the Bourgeois mascara and the Traffic Red lipgloss. They're my favourites. Then I go to her underwear drawer and get out the bright red bra that fits me now. I try it on whenever she's watching *Dallas*, walking in front of her fitted wardrobe with the sliding mirrored doors.

She said she wanted proper storage, deep drawers, long and short hanging spaces, open shelving for all her shoes. She got sections made for her tights and Dad's socks and pants and everything. I leaned against the doorframe as she emptied out his stuff and packed it in the weekend bag. She put his socks inside his shoes and folded all his shirts with the arms underneath so they wouldn't have crease marks. I couldn't believe that. I mean, I really couldn't believe that.

I ease the stiff drawer of her bedside table open and reach in for her red leather jewellery purse, unzipping the third section for her clip-on earrings. She bought them in Debenhams at the opening of the Joan Collins' Costume Jewellery sale. – These'll put a bit of sparkle in your life, the saleswoman said. – Don't you look stylish?

The lights are off in the lounge. The TV screen colouring the furniture. Mum sits with her legs underneath her so all I can see are the toe seams on her American Tan tights. She clinks the ice cubes in her glass. The sound is on loud so she doesn't hear me open the front door and stick my Adidas bag outside. She doesn't unfold her legs to an upright position and give me that quick, alarmed smile. I hate it when she does that. When she makes out that I've given her a fright. – God, she'd say, you made me jump out of my skin. Sneaking up on me like that. Catching me out like that.

She's just sitting on the sofa, watching Sue Ellen hit JR Ewing. Watching her make a tit of herself at Southfork in a diamante Stetson. Tomorrow Mum will phone Auntie Helen and they'll talk about Bobby in his slim-cut leather jacket. Rita's bought Dad a leather jacket. He was wearing it in Sainsbury's. She smiled and smoothed her hand over the shoulder.

– Romford Market, she said, you can get all your leather in Romford Market.

I wondered how much leather you needed. I wondered if Dad did it with her in his leather jacket. – He's a different man, Auntie Helen says.

I turn the collar down on my new denim jacket with the Madonna badges on the sleeves that I bought in Trend Fashions. I stand just outside the light coming from the TV so Mum can't see I've got my tight jeans on.

– Mum, I say, Mum, I'm off out.

She holds a hand up to the side of her face. – At this time? she says. – Where are you going?

She stands up, switches the main light on and turns off the TV.

– What are you all dressed up for? she says. She swallows, hard. – You can't go out looking like that, you can see everything in those jeans.

I look away at the blank TV screen and chew my bottom lip to keep it steady.

– Where are you going?

I look down at the carpet. – I saw Dad after school, I say. – He was waiting for me in the car park. He wants to take me out for fish and chips.

Mum turns away and picks up her glass. – You've just had dinner! Why can't he pick you up from here? Why couldn't he phone here and ask you?

She shakes her head and starts to laugh and before she gears up for another go I say, really quickly, I didn't think you'd mind. I haven't seen him since Sainsbury's and that doesn't count because I only ran into him and he was busy and you were there. And it's just gonna be me and him tonight. He said it was just gonna be me and him.

It comes out so quiet that I can hear the TV screen prickling with static. And I think that it's been two and a half weeks since Sainsbury's. Since I saw him in his new leather jacket. – A different man, Auntie Helen says.

Mum flashes her quick, bright smile. She's good at them. She turns the TV back on but I know she's not concentrating because she puts it on channel 9 so there's just a grey fuzz on the screen.

– Don't be too late then, she says. – I want an early night. I've got a busy day tomorrow.

– Yeah, I say, all right.

I pick up the Adidas bag and swing it over my shoulder. I let myself through the gate, cut across Broomfield Park in the direction of the school and wait for ten minutes. Then I run in the opposite direction when I know she'll have stopped looking out of the window and I cut down to the public loos at the bottom of the playing field. Inside, it stinks of piss. There's a dirty sanitary towel by the metal sink and the soapbox tap drips onto it. The flecks in the grey concrete sparkle. There's a skid mark on the toilet seat and wet paper towels on the slippery floor. I go into the cubicle and get into the rest of my gear, peering into Mum's compact mirror to put the Bourgeois mascara and Traffic Red lipgloss on. And all the time I'm thinking about that scene in *Cocktail* where they do it on the beach and she's saying, don't stop I'll die if you stop. The zipper on my jeans cuts into my skin. Mum said they were too tight in the shop.

– You don't want to look like a tart, she said. She pulled the matching boob tube off over my arms and folded it up on her lap. – I hate town on a Saturday, she said. – Put your clothes back on. We're going.

I walk past the park benches surrounded with dry, cracking mud. Essex is totally flat. Stretching on in front of you with no real landmarks so you never feel like you've covered distance. Like you've moved on. So I'm just heading towards Church Close, past the back of the shop parade, the kicked-in phone boxes, the White Hart beer garden, the bit of land being sold to the council for a youth club. The air is thick with pollen from the green belt fields divided with hedges growing over rubbish dumps and tin cans. You can cut your feet on all sorts round here. Mum says it's about time they cleaned the place up. That those prefab buildings should be razed to the ground. That we should get a nice French restaurant instead of a Burger King.

I cut down onto the main road so I can approach the bus stop at an angle where they can see me. And then I slow right down and look dead straight in front of me. I don't want to catch their eye at a distance. Then you've got to fix a smile for five minutes until you reach them. And it's awkward like that.

– All right, Donna says.

– Yeah, all right.

You don't say hello when you live in Essex. It sort of comes with the area. People in Broomfield say all right; people in Melbourne say watcha.

– That's typical, Mum says, what with all the single mums and druggies in those flats. Watcha back more like.

Rita's from Melbourne.

Darren doesn't say anything. He's checking the exhaust on his Honda motorbike leaning on its stand in front of the bus stop. He's got a leather jacket on and it creaks as he moves his arms up and down. It's elasticated around the waist and padded on the elbows and shoulders so when he stands up he looks like an Action Man. He holds his bike helmet against his hip and scuffs the toe of his trainer in the road. I stand with my weight on one foot and my arms crossed like Donna does. Mum saw her in town once. – Just look at the state of that, she said, she'd make mincemeat out of you.

He says, D'ya wanna get some chips or something?

– Yeah, I say, all right.

He gets on the bike and jerks his head back for me to get on behind him. My jeans cut into my thighs and when I look down I can see the white stitching pulling between the seams. I should have worn them in a bit. The bike kicks forward and I grab at his waist, trying to get a lever on the leather jacket with my sweaty hands. We drive to the BP garage and turn round the petrol pumps. The bike's doing sixty as we pass Donna smoking cigarettes and waiting for the others in the bus stop. I have to hold one leg out because the exhaust pipe's hot, burning the inside of my ankle if it touches the metal. He's accelerating past all this traffic, revving up behind lorries and people on pushbikes. And I screw up my eyes against the dust, feeling hot blasts of air over my face and arms, smelling the petrol fumes coming out the back and thinking this is just like *Top Gun*, this is just like that bit in *Top Gun*. And I run that 'Take My Breath Away' through my head and wonder if Rita says that to Dad when he's wearing his new leather jacket. She's into stuff like that. She was hoovering the stairs when Dad came home from work early. Her bum stuck out through her tight skirt with the ripped split up the back. Her face was red and puffy from the heat when she turned round to let Dad get through.

– Cor, she said, your dad's like a film star, in'e?

Dad used to drive her back to Melbourne flats in his company car so she could save on the bus fare. She always sat in the front.

Darren doesn't offer to buy me any chips and I don't have much dinner money left so I just get a can of Lilt, tapping the top with my nail to stop it from fizzing when I pull the ring tag.

– Nice bike, I say.

– Yeah, it's a five-speed fuel injection. I wanna trade it in for a Yamaha. I've put an ad in down Two Wheeler.

He holds his cone of chips and ketchup up and says, D'ya wanna go and eat these down the park? He takes my hand, walking slightly in front of me. I've never held a man's hand before, except Dad's and that doesn't count. We head past the swings and see-saws to the benches and public loos. There's dog shit everywhere. We sit on the bench nearest the Gents. It's dedicated to the pupils of Chelmer Valley Comprehensive from the PTA. I guess they couldn't stretch to the swimming pool everyone put down on their end of term forms. I can't cross my legs in these jeans so I sit with them slightly apart and stare at my pixie boots. When we finish the chips he puts his hand on the top of my leg and says that he likes the ankle zips on my jeans. I start to laugh because I'm not exactly sure what else to do and then he puts his left hand up my vest and starts to squeeze my tit.

He says, D'ya wanna go in the loos? His voice is slow and thick. Thick as two short planks, Mum would say. And then we're in the end cubicle and he's pulling my trousers down and putting me up on the toilet cistern so our heads are level. And he puts his face in my neck and my arms around his shoulders and pulls my knickers to the side. And I look at the white of his knees against the grey concrete walls as he says, Fuck, fuck, fuck. And I think, this is what the word must mean, I s'pose.

He drops me off at K9's and I walk back down the Broomfield Road, past the Esso garage, the BP garage, TC News, Broomfield Casualty, the Wimpy Homes development. I don't mind it in the summer. I dump my Adidas bag outside and check the zipper on my jeans. Mum's in the kitchen with the radio on. It's Essex FM's *Love Hour*. She's changed back into her nightdress. She looks up as I come in and takes her glass to the sink. She's got her back to me.

– How was your dad? she says.

I look down at my suede pixie boots, at the dust from the road on the toes.

– Yeah all right, I say. – We had chips.

Julia

John Gough

Julia had no option but to chuck David out of her office. They'd been talking for over four hours, including lunch, and she was tired. He'd even gone into his sad adolescence. OK, so she'd asked about it, but, God, all that stuff about his father dying and how Liverpool only existed for him in his memory – couldn't he tell he was boring her?

She'd shivered when he mentioned his father, went all goosebumped, and so it was then that she said, 'I'm sorry, David, I'm going to have to chuck you out. I've got so much to do and you've got your train to catch.' Nothing registered on his face, no embarrassment, just a quick smile, and a thank you for the time and the chat and the ideas.

As he got up to go she offered him the usual bland exit statements, like, if there's anything else you want to know then don't hesitate to give me a call; and then she left him to go on his own down the stairs from what had been the servants' quarters and were now her office. For most of the time she sat there on her own, making trips to talk to people who worked on the floors below. In fact, wasn't that why she had invited David down, to show the others that she could also entertain business visitors, and that she didn't always have to chase them?

Although she'd sent him out, she couldn't resist looking

out of her window. He was crossing Gordon Square and moving in and out of the shadows of a late autumn afternoon. She watched as he appeared to flick something from his thumb towards a bin. Did it go in? He didn't break stride and continued walking quickly towards Euston. She turned away only when he was out of sight.

It had to be the effect of straining her eyes to focus on him. She blinked and rubbed her eyes and sniffed.

Her phone rang. She dropped the handset as she tried to answer. She should've known it was her boyfriend, Ian. He usually called at about the same time every Friday just to tell her how shit his day had been. The number of times she'd told him to give up teaching.

She could feel him sidling up to it, asking silly questions that he knew the answers to, before popping the one that had been on his mind all week: Annabelle's party and did she still want to go. Julia sighed and, as he talked on, the arguments she'd heard from friends dropped down like song titles on screen credits. 'You Never Get Perfection' by Sarah MacGowan. '(He's Your) Little Domesticated Darling' by Frances Cox. 'He's Got Your Rhythm' by Natasha King. And so on. He was tidier than her. More considerate. She could've penned her own song title as a riposte, but Ian interrupted her creativity.

'So you still want to go and swank around with those pretentious types?'

'Please yourself,' she snapped. 'Pick me up at eight thirty. And if you change your mind, then let me know so I can get a taxi there.'

She knew that threat would cement his resolve. He was paranoid about her getting a taxi on her own. Every taxi driver was a potential rapist. The lift would be helpful, though. He wouldn't drink at Annabelle's party, simply clutch his glass of orange juice and lemonade or the organic apple and mango he'd bring with him.

She said she was still busy and ended the call, blowing a kiss down the receiver to placate him. She returned to the window. The sun had disappeared behind the houses and the sight of leaves falling in the square made her shiver. Goosebumps again. David was getting on his train by now. She'd really had no choice but to tell him to go.

That didn't change the fact that she was still being unfair.

OK, so she admitted it now. He hadn't blabbed on about his father. Nor really bewailed his adolescence. What had really sealed his fate was when she told him she wasn't going to get married. That was her first public admission of what had felt like a terrible secret. Her parents were already talking of the wedding they'd waited for years to plan, and there was she was, about to provoke their disapproval again. But he didn't react, he simply nodded and stared at her, as if he could look right in, and it was at that point she'd gone shivery and told him to go. She'd had no choice. She didn't drop such intimate secrets casually, certainly not to a man she hardly knew, and for him not to react was so unnerving as to be nearly unforgivable.

She turned away and sniffed again. There was the party to attend to.

She threw herself into Annabelle's party. Ian accompanied her, but she soon left him in the hall as Annabelle took her by the arm, saying, oh, you must meet Giles, or Simon, or Amanda, or John D.

John D?

'And what does the D stand for?' she asked, looking up into his tanned face, already darkened by his thick eyebrows.

'Daniel,' he replied. 'The firstborn males are always John D. It's a family tradition.' His voice was surprisingly mellow and transfixing. 'And what's your middle name?'

'I don't have one,' she lied. 'It's a family tradition.'

He inclined his head and raised his glass. 'Here's to family traditions, then.'

He was exotic. A star earring. Long hair. He lectured in media studies part-time but his real love was making short films. He explained patiently what they were about: mainly highlighting life's strangeness and absurdities. Later, out in the garden, the autumn air not yet cold enough to reach through the fog of wine, he offered her his thick spliff and she dragged deeply and coughed, afraid for a moment that it was something stronger than she'd been used to. It was some years since a boyfriend had inducted her in the ways of smoking weed. Ian had never smoked.

Their talk and the spliff mingled as smoke. She tried to steer some of David's observations and analysis of *Billy Elliot* in a straight line down her tongue. They'd talked about the film over lunch, something about the price of individuality against community. John D was impressed. 'Very structural,' he said, blowing out more smoke. 'We should get together sometime to talk some more.'

'Name your day,' she said. As the spliff dwindled, they kissed smoky kisses and then she left him abruptly, clutching a date to her memory in case it should flutter away in the cold.

Ian took her to his flat. His on Fridays, hers on Saturdays. At first she couldn't stop laughing as he tried to take advantage of her. His touch actually felt quite sensual as he carried on despite her laughter. And then she got the spins of the kind she usually felt on fairground rides. The only stop-off point was the toilet where she heaved and heaved, until she realized Ian was still there, rubbing her back and offering to wipe her face. He helped her back to bed where, as reward for his consideration, she promptly fell asleep.

*

David's email arrived days later, at lunchtime, while she was eating a prawn sandwich. She'd forgotten that she hadn't forgiven him for not reacting to her grand secret, and replied with the sandwich in her mouth. So I suppose you want me to visit the uncivilized provinces? she wrote. His response was immediate. Had he been waiting to pounce on her reply? Was he eating his sandwiches at his desk like her? She agreed a date and time before checking on the trains.

She hadn't been north for a long time. Leicester was hardly North, as touchy people from 'the real North' would remind her, but it was north enough for her. And York University, where she'd been a student, was practically the Artic. Her memory of the place was that it was always really cold in the winters. And when it snowed, even the drifts in the town centre were high enough to bury cars. She'd let herself fall back into one when she was drunk. The glorious sensation of letting go into softly fresh snow. Looking up at the snowflakes as they fell and melted on her eyelashes. Trouble was, she couldn't get up when she started to feel seasick. And then, when she did get out, she proceeded to vomit into the snow. Her friends eventually came back for her. At least her puke had melted into the snow. She did that a lot at university: drink and puke. Her reputation used to make her shudder.

Had she already told David she was a disappointment to everyone? Was that another secret she'd let fall? She put aside the prawn sandwich and thought of what she might say. The conversation started. 'I was a management trainee for M&S,' she said. 'That's impressive,' he replied. 'When I left it started going downhill,' she went on. 'Of course,' he agreed, and then he waited, as she faltered at first. She spoke for longer, about how it had all been so wrong, and how despite going to boarding school she'd been just too anti-everything. How she'd been carpeted by the store manager for having the temerity to say, let's just chuck it out. How dare you say, chuck it out? And the worst thing, towards the end, was how she used to cry on the shop floor when all the decisions she had to make became too much and she couldn't think. When she resigned she packed in her boyfriend. He was a trainee with Arthur Andersen. I mean, God, what was the point of marrying someone like that, a bloody accountant? And my parents, God, my parents, and my brother, they were so disappointed it was incredible. Julia, they all said, people don't just resign from M&S, dear. And getting married, what about getting married to someone sensible?

A knock on the door brought her round. It was Parvita.

'Oh, sorry, I thought you were talking to someone,' she said.

'Oh, no, there's just me and a prawn sandwich,' Julia replied, smiling.

When she approached the reception she saw David listening to someone, his face its usual blank attentiveness. She tried to seem nonchalant and announced who she was to the receptionist. 'We don't usually see people of your sort, you know,' he said behind her, and when she turned quickly she saw his face transformed by a smile.

'There are loads of eateries around,' he continued. 'But I've got one in mind.'

She followed him down to the River Soar and its waterfront. The Italian restaurant looked incongruous next to what was left of a breaker's yard. The red wine was so easy to drink that she knocked back three compared to David's one. 'I do this when I'm nervous,' she said, and then regretted it as he paused and smiled.

'You're not nervous, are you?' he asked, and then steered her to safer ground. He complimented her work. Thought it sounded great. All those training packages she was developing and selling. She looked into the bottom of her glass, at the collection of sediment, and then blinked as she looked up. He offered her a tissue and she made a show of blowing her nose, as if a sudden irritation had made her eyes run.

Swans drifted down the river. She asked about his children, but hardly listened to his replies. The pasta arrived. She was grateful for something to occupy her hands, her mouth. He asked about her gap year, after she left York.

'Oh, it was awful,' she said. 'I went to India and then Malaysia and just hated every minute of it. I got ill and went like a stick. Did me no bloody good at all. M&S thought the travel experience had changed me and that's why I didn't fit in, but that wasn't the reason at all. I only travelled because my friends were. It was the thing to do. In fact, everything I've done has been a complete disaster.'

'Not everything,' he said gently, reprovingly. 'Surely not everything.'

'Haven't you ever felt like a failure?' she asked.

He turned his head and cupped his chin. 'No,' he said after a while. 'Maybe frustrated sometimes, that I wasn't getting where I wanted to go. But never a failure.'

He smiled and glanced at her.

'I've never felt any expectations on me, I suppose. Or if I have I just ignored them.' He paused. 'I can't believe you're a total failure.'

She could feel the gentle pressure of his questions. She knew where they were going, padding towards what he had registered last time they'd met. And then, confusingly, he stopped short. He ordered a sweet, tiramisu, while she had a cappuccino, and then he sat back after finishing his dessert, looking out to the river. She could see the lines around his eyes and forehead. Is that what having kids does to you? she wondered.

'Ian kept talking about marriage and kids,' she said, unable to stand the suspense any longer. 'I can't stay with him any more.' Her heart was beating into her voice. 'And I've met someone else, John D.'

He frowned slightly and looked at her. 'I think last time we met,' he said, 'you didn't sound happy then.'

'I never mentioned Ian then,' she said, knowing she was wrong, but David conceded and drained his glass. 'I'll be happier with John D,' she went on. 'He's the opposite of Ian.'

Again he was committing that sin. He wasn't reacting enough for her. Men always reacted to her.

'I am doing the right thing, aren't I?' she asked abruptly. 'And don't give me the party line about, well, if you're happier then that's what matters because I'm sick of hearing it.' She took another tissue. 'Do you know Ian punched me once when I told him I'd snogged someone else at a party? He forgave me, of course. I didn't know he had it in him.'

His response was gentle. 'Is that why you've dyed your hair?' he wanted to know. 'New man, new hairstyle?' She could've told him that John D hadn't noticed.

They tried to order a taxi to take her back to the train station, but the earliest booking was half an hour away. He took her in his car. She noticed the children's car seats and the story-time tapes. He drove carefully to the short-stay car park, and didn't hesitate to get out and follow her before she could say, it's OK, you don't have to wait. The train was delayed and they sat in the coffee bar; him swigging his bottle of water while she sipped hot, tasteless tea.

'What are you thinking?' she asked.

'I don't know,' he sighed. 'I'm trying to phrase something in my head to make sure it doesn't come out wrong.'

The train was approaching. They stood on the platform

and then faced each other as the train stopped. She closed her eyes and went to lean into him but stopped and got on the train without saying anything more. She looked to see if he'd waited on the platform but he'd gone.

'Have a good Christmas,' she murmured to herself.

John D was in crisis. He stared out of his window at the takeaway across the road, its rippling bank of lights hypnotizing him. Julia's attention slid from *EastEnders* to check his shape for movement and back again. She quoted one of David's comments to see if John D would bite, particularly the one about soaps levelling everything to its lowest common denominator, but John D didn't stir, not even to put the left-wing intellectual's position on the credibility and validity of popular culture over high culture's counterparts.

So why was he in crisis? She tried to think. It couldn't be sex; she knew she was good at shagging and didn't have to reassure John D about his early performances as she'd had to with some of her other boyfriends (Ian being one of them). She gave him space. She let him talk for hours about ideas for his films. She had refused his spliffs but she didn't imagine that had caused the crisis. No: it had to be the wedding invite, and the idea of going to a wedding as a couple, an item, that had probably freaked him out. Maybe she should go on her own, but the thought of being single at a wedding full of couples depressed her.

Idly, she wondered how David would react in such a situation. She could imagine him at weddings. Maybe alcohol would melt his initial stand-offishness, make his tongue freer. She imagined that maybe his wife would tut at some of his wilder remarks or the liberties he might take when commenting on someone's hat. His façade occasionally allowed flashes of something else to break through, leaving her to wonder what was underneath. What he was really like. What might she have to do to get him to react properly?

But John D was a more pressing concern. She'd have to get him to snap out of his fixed state somehow. Her lexicon of phrases, gestures, poses, expressions, positions was broad enough to head off any panic she might have felt at seeing him standing like someone who hadn't taken their medication. So when he sat down she put her arm through his and pecked his stubbly cheek, offering soothing remarks like, you haven't yet decompressed properly from the editing suite. She felt quite pleased at this remark, at its perceptiveness and metaphor, and he turned to smile at her.

What then followed puzzled her at first. He had a list of questions about Sarah and Richard who were getting married. How long she'd known them, what they did, which university they'd been to and so on. She joked about getting him a copy of *Tatler* so he could check them out for himself. He didn't find that funny and she let go of his arm, looking up at the ceiling and thinking, well, it's a trip across London back to my place. Maybe he smoked more hash than she realized, stronger stuff than he admitted to, and he was turning slowly paranoid. The first apple had fallen off her perfect tree to bruise on the ground. And then he asked her why she hadn't yet got married. She stood up and went to get her coat and told him to have a para-cetamol, he'd probably feel better in the morning.

He jumped up and blocked her way. His eyes looked black, shiny, like two orbs set in a face that frightened her.

'I'll call you in the morning,' she said, slowly, quietly, unwavering. He let her through. Outside she ran to her car and slammed the door and locked herself in and drove away, just missing an oncoming car.

She made David promise to look after her at the conference. To make sure she didn't drink too much or say the wrong things. His emailed reply told her that a conference at the University of Sheffield was enough to make anyone drink.

She hadn't seen him since going up to Leicester. And she'd had to break their email silence. She didn't like having to chase men.

At first, David was perfect at the conference. In the coffee breaks and at lunch he always had someone to talk to, seemed to know so many people. He made one slip, though, when they were alone momentarily in the foyer, cold February air blowing in through the doors. He said he wished he could talk to people as easily as her. When she wondered out loud what the hell he was talking about he whispered that it had taken him five conferences to act as he was doing.

He asked her about John D. 'Oh, that was a rebound relationship,' she said dismissively, and avoided his eyes.

At dinner she found herself being steered away from him by a man who had tried to talk to her all day. Bob Gilworth insisted that she sat next to him and told him all about her work. He kept filling her glass with wine and leaning forward, his eyes widening still further, his odd face reddening. Eventually they peeled away to the bar. David was nowhere. She couldn't seem to resist Bob's invitation to join him and his mates for a drink, despite her skin crawling each time he touched her. By the time she escaped to the brightly lit toilets her ears were ringing and she felt sick. And her escape route back to her room was blocked by Bob, who appeared in the foyer and cajoled her into one more drink. Going along with the drinking, the innuendo, the constant nudges from him, simply going along, her resolve confused by the supply of gin and tonics that didn't taste right.

On her second escape to the toilet she saw David's distorted shape coming towards her.

'Where the fuck have you been?' she demanded, grabbing

his shirt and swaying against him. He mumbled something about being whisked off to the pub by someone important, someone he had to network with. She told him she didn't care. How dare he abandon her to Bob fucking Gilworth? David's words were coming down a tunnel. He put his arm round her and steered her to the door.

'Can you remember your room number?' he asked.

'Fuck knows,' she slobbered, 'and I'm not climbing fucking stairs.' Her legs gave way with the slap of fresh air. 'Why did you leave me when you promised you wouldn't?' She'd lost control of her mouth and when she tried to kiss him she missed by the same margin as her attempts at forming words. And then they were in a corridor, and it all began breaking up, until she heard, *Julia, Julia, can you hear me?*

Was she puking?

A separation had occurred between her and her body. A clear, lucid voice in the centre of her being recognized the distress signals from her senses but could do nothing to help. 'Look at me, Julia,' came the command. Her eyes couldn't focus on him.

It was all his fault, anyway. What did he expect? He'd wrecked her plans. She'd imagined what he'd be like in bed. Just being in bed with someone who didn't make her feel like a failure. What he would smell like. She wanted his reaction. And now he was walloping her on the back to stop her choking. It was all his fault.

Weeks later, and much to her annoyance, she had no choice but to revert to more involved contingency plans. Sipping coffee while the dregs of another all-day hangover settled in her stomach, she drew her legs up and looked out of her office window as rain swept the Bloomsbury squares. This would be the scenario: she wanted David's professional expertise on a contract she'd just won. She'd invite him down again to London to talk about the work and the role he could play. This wasn't idle daydreaming. She had won a contract to work with Jubilee Charity on transition management, and each time she contemplated it her stomach reminded her of the number of all-too recent occasions when she'd spent the night and the morning retching into various toilets. What role David would play she hadn't a clue.

She fretted at the state of the trains, terrified that he would phone her at the last minute to say he wasn't coming. But he arrived on time, his hair looking as if it had been thickly gelled, his face running with raindrops. 'It was like walking in a cold shower,' he said, dabbing his cheeks. She thought he looked thinner, his face more boyish. As they walked up the stairs she promised to try and find him a towel but he smiled and waved away the offer. In the narrow corridor and the confusion of doors she bumped into him, not always accidentally, but he seemed not to notice.

How can you just sit there? she thought. How can you sit there as if nothing happened in Sheffield? All his subsequent email had said was, Bob's notorious, you should complain about him spiking your drinks. Nothing about how he'd tried to sleep in a chair between bouts of holding her head as she heaved and heaved, sick to the pit of her stomach. Nothing about how he'd cuddled her as she howled. Nothing about calling the doctor the following day. Maybe he was embarrassed. Her friends had simply raised their eyebrows when she'd told them what he'd done.

Discussions about the work came and went. Of course he was interested, she knew he would be. She leaned closer to him and said he looked tired, reaching out to touch the heaviness under his eyes. It hadn't been a good fortnight for him but he declined to say more. The rain was still heavy when they went out for lunch to the same restaurant as before. She handed him a long corporate umbrella and linked her arm through his as they walked. That his manner didn't change, his voice remained friendly, neutral, threw her but she held on as they walked in step. As the rain thickened she couldn't help wittering on about John D and the rebound effect.

'You know,' he said, 'I've only ever had one relationship and that's with my wife.'

She looked at him quickly, stung by the rebuke she'd interpreted in his words, but he smiled at her and didn't break his stride.

As they ate he seemed to grow more tired and she asked him what was wrong. He drew his hand across his face and looked down into his plate and shook his head. His mother hadn't been well, a heart attack scare, he said matter-of-factly. For the past fortnight he'd been up and down to Liverpool where she lived and that was tiring, dealing with all the relatives, dealing with all his mixed emotions. It was all probably her indigestion, he laughed, but she noticed how the laughter died on his face.

'Did it remind you of your father, and all the mixed feelings you said you had for Liverpool?' she asked. He continued looking down into the table and so she took his hand. It was warm, surprisingly small and soft.

'Have I told you about that?' he asked, frowning.

And then he continued quickly, saying that to cap it all, his wife, who was never ill, had had the flu in the past week and so that just made life a bit more interesting.

He cupped his chin in a way that was now familiar. 'It's funny,' he said, 'this friend of mine once said that you never give it all in a marriage. You just never do, you have to keep something back for yourself almost as an insurance policy. And I saw it with my mum, you know, she gave it all, she never got remarried after my dad, it was like, that's it, the love of my life has gone and nobody else will ever come close.'

He withdrew his hand and she watched as he rubbed his face before resting his chin in his clasped hands. His smile was always ready, but not like a politician's.

'I don't really know what I'm trying to say,' he said and before she could start breathing properly again he asked her if she'd seen a particular film. They swapped opinions and he reminded her of how he could jump from idea to idea in pursuit of the example that would really clinch what he was trying to say. After paying the bill, and back outside, all she could do was kiss his cheek and hold his arm. He thanked her for listening with a politeness that could have been held up in a documentary as being typically British. The rain had eased but being under the umbrella she felt safe with him, safe in a way she'd nearly forgotten how to recognize. She wondered at the reaction she'd wanted from him. He'd just explained and measured his feelings with an accuracy more suited to report writing.

He turned to her before they got back to her office. 'I'll have to go,' he said. 'I've a train to catch.'

She followed him to her office where he collected his briefcase, less dark now that it had dried out, and he smiled quickly, saying that he knew his way out. He offered bland exit statements like, if you want anything more from me then don't hesitate to give me a call, and I look forward to working with you. As he opened the door she managed to call him back and he turned, eyebrows raised, nothing more.

She put her arms around him and held him, his slim frame, the press of his cheeks sweet and sour with softness and bristles. He held her, too, in a way that she'd wanted for months and now she had it finally.

She stepped back and squeezed his arms and blinked.

'Get out,' she said.

Holding My Breath Underwater
Sidura Ludwig

When I was eight, I wanted to be Esther Williams. Esther could hold her breath underwater for ever. And she never got water up her nose, so she never came out of the water spitting and snorting and generally looking piggish. Esther always looked like a swan, or a dolphin floating along, making ballet, her toes pointed and her bathing suit sparkling. Somehow, she could smile and keep her eyes open underwater without using goggles. Now that's classy.

But next to Esther, I wanted to be my Auntie Sarah. I wanted Sarah's rose lips, her white, straight teeth. She was eighteen with the longest legs – and I really wanted those legs. My mother called them dancer's legs, the kind that men couldn't stay away from. Not that I was interested in having men around my legs, but Mum always said she got the brains and Sarah got the beauty. And I did want to be beautiful.

Every day that summer, Sarah took me to the swimming pool in Kildonan Park. She wore a white straw hat with a floppy brim and dark oval sunglasses. I couldn't see her eyes but I knew she was watching everyone watching her. She walked slowly except that her legs were so long it took me three steps to keep up with her one. She swung her hips carefully like a grandfather clock pendulum, back and forth in time with her steps. Sometimes I copied her and for the first few steps I felt eighteen, not eight. I had her long legs, her strappy high-heeled sandals and a wrap-around skirt to cover my curvy bathing suit. And then someone would catch sight of me, little Beth Levy, wiggling and tripping beside her grown-up aunt. They'd start giggling. I'd have to stop and watch all of my beauty melting away.

Sarah had lots of friends, women who'd crowd around her in the changing room and tell her what a beautiful figure she had. I'd change into my bathing suit and be flat as a sandwich board. Once, I saw Sarah in the changing-room mirror. She was putting on her bra, adjusting her breasts into the cups. She saw me watching and told me that one day I'd have breasts and hips too.

'Will they make me beautiful?' I asked.

'Hmm,' she said, 'sometimes.'

That summer it was very hot in Winnipeg. Too hot. Every day we listened to the radio to find out it was going to be 30°C again. My mother said things like, 'It's another Great Depression,' and she walked around the house slowly as if she carried the heat itself on her back. The heat made you feel like you were choking all the time. It was like being under a hair dryer all day. And it was even worse in the house, especially upstairs. I slept in the living room with the windows open on all sides so that the wind could pass through. But it had been so hot there wasn't any wind, only mosquitoes, one or two buzzing and tickling in my ear as I slept on the couch. So, in the middle of the night, I woke up swatting.

Even though God hit us with such heat, at least we could thank Him for the pool. When the mayor found out that it was going to be hot and dry, he announced, 'The summer of 1960 will be a summer of clean, wet fun.'

He made all the park pools open seven days a week and

he brought us lifeguards. That's how we got Jonathan. Jonathan was from Toronto. He was very tall and never wore a shirt in case he had to jump into the pool and rescue someone. He had blond hair but it was really the colour of sand, which I figured made sense because he was a lifeguard. When he sat up in his lifeguard chair, the sun made his hair sparkle like he was wearing a crown.

But Jonathan was not a king or a prince. He was a lifeguard and my swimming instructor, which meant he made me swim when I was tired and he wouldn't let me come out of the pool for even a minute, even when I was cold. In the changing room, Sarah and her friends said things like, 'He's just a dream,' and 'I'd be in heaven if he'd just smile at me.' He smiled at me plenty and I never did enter heaven.

But always after my lesson he'd bend down and ask me to call my auntie over, like it was a secret. And when she did her walk to his side of the pool, wearing her shiny black bathing suit, the one that glimmered in the sun when wet, he stood up by the wall, leaning on his elbow. She walked right up to him, so close they could whisper by the noisy pool and still hear each other. That's when she gave him one of her white smiles and he looked like he was ready to go run a marathon.

My mother once said to me: 'Your Auntie Sarah is very powerful. But sometimes that can be dangerous.'

Sarah moved in with us that year after my grandmother died. Her room was across from mine. One night, while she was out with her friends, I got into her closet and tried on her strappy sandals. My body was wet from the heat and my nightgown stuck to my stomach. My feet slid into them on an angle and already I felt like I was going to fall over. My toes hung over the edge and the red leather straps rubbed against the middle of my foot. I walked out of the

47

closet and across the room to the full-length mirror. The shoes reminded me of tin-can stilts. The bottoms of my feet were sweaty and sticky. With each step my foot unstuck and then rose off the sole, slapping back against it when I raised the next one. I held my arms out wide to keep from falling and I glanced up to see myself in the mirror. I looked nothing like Sarah. In my head I was tall, leggy, glamorous behind dark glasses. But really, I was just a little girl struggling to stay balanced in her auntie's shoes. I sucked in my tummy thinking maybe the pudge would rise to my chest and give me breasts. It didn't work.

'I will be beautiful,' I whispered, letting my tummy sink back down to normal.

It took Sarah a while, at first, to convince my mum to let her take me to the pool. Mum was still nervous about public swimming pools, even though we'd had the polio vaccine for six years. She didn't want me to end up like her friend Sonia's daughter – paralysed in her legs and never able to walk again.

'Lighten up, Goldie!' I heard Sarah say to my mum one night, at the beginning of the summer. They were in the kitchen and they thought I was asleep on the couch. I lay with my eyes open and listened to their voices as if they circled above my head.

'She's a little girl. Let her have a bit of fun,' Sarah continued. 'You can't keep her cooped up in this house all summer.'

Mum put down the pot she'd been drying and it banged against the counter, which made me gasp.

'What I don't need,' she said, like scissors cutting paper, 'is for my daughter to be learning tricks from you.'

She said the word tricks as if spitting it as far as possible onto the floor. It made Sarah go quiet and I heard my mum turn the tap back on. I wondered about those tricks, which Sarah knew and maybe my mother never learned.

'I won't be like that,' Sarah said, in a different voice than before, a quieter one. 'I'll look after her.'

Mum kept washing dishes and, after a moment, Sarah left the kitchen.

The next morning, at breakfast, I pretended I hadn't heard them the night before and I asked Mum if Sarah and I could see the pool today.

'If you'd like,' she said, sipping her coffee. I smiled but watched her watching Sarah without blinking.

Sarah and Jonathan spent a lot of time together. She would rush me to get ready and we walked quickly to the pool. That is, Sarah walked – I ran. After I tried on her shoes, I was amazed at how she moved in them. They clicked beneath her in perfect time. My shoes pounded like a two-year-old's toy drum. Also, she never sweat. Not even on her upper lip.

Then, when we got to the pool, Sarah stretched her neck to spot Jonathan and usually he was doing the same. She smiled once she caught his eye and took a deep breath.

'Go and get changed,' she told me, never breaking his gaze.

'Aren't you coming?'

'Soon,' she said.

By then, Jonathan was coming towards us and I saw enough of him during our half-hour lesson so I ran into the changing room. But when I turned round from the doorway, he had his hands on her waist and she was looking up at him with her head tilted, as if he were crooked.

During my lesson, Jonathan said he was going to teach me how to tread water. He sat on the edge of the pool while I held onto the wall.

'You know how an egg beater works?' he asked.

I nodded.

'So that's what I want you to do with your legs. Make like you're an egg beater.'

He moved his legs in little circles in the water and I tried it holding onto the ledge. When we tried it in the water together, he held my hands so that I didn't sink under. I swung my legs around and around and tried to keep my chin above water.

'Hey,' he said. 'No drowning. You have to keep your head up.'

'It's hard.'

'I know,' he said, but he stayed up no problem. 'So talk to me. That will make it easier.'

'Can I show you how I hold my breath underwater?' I asked.

'Later,' he said. 'Right now I need you to show me how you stay above water. If you do that, I'll get your auntie over here and we'll both watch you hold your breath.'

And before I knew what I was saying, I asked, 'Are you going to marry my aunt?'

He stared at me a bit and then laughed. 'We're a little young for that, you think?'

My chin sank under so I pushed myself harder with my legs. 'But you like her.'

'Sure I like her. But that doesn't mean we'll get married.'

'She'd marry you if you wanted,' I said. I didn't know this for sure, but I said it anyway. 'I bet she'd marry you any day.'

He laughed again. 'That's certainly good for me to know.'

Later, once Sarah came over to our side of the pool, I stayed underwater for ten seconds. They clapped for me when I came up and Jonathan said, 'You're just like Esther Williams.'

I went under again to keep my cheeks from burning. I did a somersault and the water swirled by my ears like I was floating. I wondered if that's what heaven felt like.

*

In the middle of August, the pool hosted a late night swim because we'd had two weeks without any rain. Sarah asked me if I wanted to go. I had never swum in the evening before. And the poster promised a bonfire on the grass with marshmallows and hotdogs to roast once it got dark. I wanted to roast my marshmallows until they were crispy on the outside and the inside could dribble down my chin.

Across from my room, I saw Sarah sitting at her dresser, putting on make-up. She had her hair pinned up and she looked like a movie star. She wore her bathing suit under her blouse and blue pleated skirt. She had a blue cashmere sweater to match, which hung on the back of her chair.

I knocked on her door.

'Hi, sweetheart,' she said. My stomach jumped. There was nothing like being Sarah's sweetheart. She had mascara on so her eyelashes curled up and made her eyes wide. When she smiled at me the skin at the corners of her eyes folded up and looked like stars. I knew I was getting too big for this, but I crawled onto her lap anyway.

'Hey, big girl. What can I do for you?' she asked.

I watched her hair in the mirror all piled up on her head like a pillow of soft curls. I wished I could grow mine longer.

'Can I have some lipstick?' I asked.

'Your mum would kill me,' she whispered.

'I won't tell! I won't even look at her when we leave. Please?'

She picked up a round pink container and rubbed her finger in the paint. 'As long as you don't say a word!' she said, as she put her finger to my lips and spread the colour over my mouth. It felt smooth, like honey, only it wasn't sticky. I watched in the mirror as my lips seemed to jump off my face. I made kisses into the mirror and this made Sarah laugh.

'You look very glamorous,' she told me, lifting me off her lap. 'The pool won't know what hit it.'

On the way to the pool, Sarah held my hand and walked with a very straight back. I talked a lot, asking things like, how big would the bonfire be? Would it be very hot? How many marshmallows would I be allowed? Every time I moved my mouth, I felt the lipstick like clothing on my lips.

'Do you think Jonathan will be there?' I asked.

'Umhmm,' she answered.

'Will I have to take a swimming lesson, then?' This made her laugh.

'No, silly. It's a free swim. You don't need to worry about him at all.'

'I'm not worried, I was just wondering,' I said, then I took a breath, 'I don't like him.'

This made her stop. She turned to me. 'What makes you say that?'

I shrugged my shoulders. I don't know what made me say it. I just did. I wanted to grab my words back and swallow them.

She bent down so that her eyes were the same level as mine. She smelled like vanilla and cocoa butter.

'We're just getting to know each other. I like him a lot and that's all. When two people like each other, they like to spend a lot of time together.'

'I didn't mean it,' I said, quickly. 'I really like him. Really.'

Sarah smiled. 'You just don't like it when he makes you swim too much.'

I smiled back and we began walking again.

'Yeah,' I said. 'That's it.'

At the pool Sarah and I changed quickly in the changing room. Jonathan sat in his lifeguard chair, slouched with his chin in his hand. When we walked out of the room, he sat up fast, as if there was some emergency. Only it was just Sarah wearing her new green bikini. She looked like a model and everyone was looking at her. They couldn't believe someone like her was at the pool in Kildonan Park. The bikini was like satin, shiny and the colour of grass after a rainy day. Sarah's friends oohed over her and she said lots of thank yous. One friend sighed, 'If only I had a body like yours.'

None of them did. It's true. Sarah's friends either had fat legs or really skinny arms. She was the only one who was perfect.

Jonathan came over to us and stared at Sarah as if he'd never seen her before.

'Look, Jonathan,' I said, hopping on the spot, pretending I was tap dancing. 'Look at my lipstick.'

He looked over at me and raised his eyebrows. 'Very sexy,' he said, and all of Sarah's friends laughed. I blew kisses in the air and this made them laugh even more until Sarah told me to stop because it was inappropriate.

I went to play in the shallow end and did some Esther Williams handstands. Underwater, I breathed out of my nose to keep the water from rushing up my head. I was practising how long I could hold my breath. I also wanted to keep my eyes open, but the chlorine stung, so I closed them.

One banana, two banana . . .

I got as far as ten and then I rushed to the surface to grab more air. Sarah sat on the side of the pool with Jonathan behind her, his arms around her neck.

'Auntie Sarah, count how long I can hold my breath!' I called to her.

'All right,' she said and I heard them laugh as I dove back under.

One banana, two banana . . .

This time I counted up to twelve.

'That was ten,' Sarah said when I came up for more air. Jonathan made little kisses on her shoulder.

'Was not! I counted twelve,' I argued. 'You weren't paying attention.'

'Try it again,' Jonathan said. 'This time we'll watch more carefully.'

So I went under again. I was going to hold my breath for at least fifteen. *One banana, two banana.* I liked playing this game with Sarah and Jonathan. I could pretend, if I tried, that Jonathan was my uncle and they were taking me out for the evening. *Five banana, six banana.* And after the bonfire, they would take me in their car for a milk shake. *Nine banana, ten banana.* If they really did get married, I would be a flower girl. I could wear a shiny white dress that came to my ankles and swung around my legs like a bell when I walked down the aisle. And I would be allowed to wear lipstick. *Fourteen banana, fifteen banana.*

I burst through the top of the water.

'Did you see?' I yelled, my eyes still closed to squeeze out the chlorine.

Only they weren't at the ledge. I turned around in the water and they weren't anywhere. One of Sarah's friends saw me and said, 'Beth, honey, they went that way,' pointing to the changing rooms.

I wouldn't leave them if they had asked me not to. I wouldn't leave anyone in the middle of a game. I took my towel from off the lounger and wrapped it around my shoulders. The terrycloth was rough, not soft, and the water from the pool stuck to my skin. I couldn't find my sandals, but I walked to the changing room anyway. I was crying, but not hard, and I hoped that my face wasn't red and just looked wet from the pool. I had stayed under for fifteen seconds and they would never believe me if they didn't see.

I almost went into the changing rooms but I couldn't decide which they would be in, the men's or the women's. And then I heard some shuffling and whispering from around the building. The sound of feet sliding over gravel, the sound of someone catching her breath, like coming out of water.

I peeked my head round the corner and that's where they were. But they didn't see me. Jonathan had Sarah up with her back against the wall, her chin on his shoulder, and he pushed into her with his hips. He had one hand under her bum and the other on her back and she squeezed her eyes shut, her face tight and red. He rocked against her and her bikini strap fell loose off her shoulder.

I turned to run away, because suddenly I knew I shouldn't be there. But the ground was slippery and I fell hard against the palms of my hands and my knees. I cried out and sat on the ground crying and crying so that they'd stop and know I was there and remember where they were.

'Dammit,' I heard Jonathan say and then the sound of them scrambling away from the wall.

'She was spying,' he said.

Sarah was beside me, all of a sudden. She held me close to her chest and rocked me on her lap.

'Leave her alone, Jon,' she said to him, like spitting. 'She's just a little girl.'

I looked up at him while wrapped in my auntie. I thought, that's what I look like when I'm in trouble – big eyes, white skin, mouth partly open. Then Jonathan took off, away from us, and I watched his back as he disappeared.

Sarah's hair was down and messy around her face.

'Do you want to go home?' she asked. I did, but her asking made me cry harder.

'But what about the bonfire?' I managed, in between sobs.

She kissed my hand, which stung. 'You'll have plenty of bonfires,' she said, softly.

We walked back home slowly. Halfway there, I told Sarah that my knees hurt and she carried me on her back. We didn't talk at all about the pool. I looked up at the sky and counted the stars beginning to peek out.

When we got to the house, Sarah put me down to unlock the door.

'I won't tell,' I said, while she struggled with the key that always stuck a little anyway. She took it out of the lock and sat on the steps, taking off her sandals.

'Thank you,' she said, looking at her feet. She moved some of her hair behind her ear. I was afraid she would start crying so I wrapped my arms around her waist and lay my head on her lap.

'But I'm quitting swimming,' I said.

She laughed a little and rested her chin on my head. 'I'll tell your parents he left to go back home,' she offered.

We sat like that for a while and I danced my fingers over her knee. It was nice – just me and Sarah on the steps with our shoes off. I held my breath to see how long it would last.

And Weel No Wot to Do
Godfrey Featherstone

Dere Marleen,

Well ~~Oi~~, Im ere, Marleen. And your ~~ther~~ there, Marleen. Ope you ~~har~~ harwell an in the pinke – luveley pinke ?!"! Orlroite? Im ~~sur~~ sir - viving. Djuste about. But thinking ov ~~yow~~ you meks me appi.

Wee dint mene it. Did we? Eh?

I dint mene it You dint mene it. No!? You neent be so ~~unappi~~ unhappi, Marleen.

Abowte er. Wee djuste dint no wot to do. She woz ~~bewtiful~~, ~~bute~~, ~~butifule~~, a bueifule litel thing. Wee luved er.

She woz the reeley nice thing in mi live, Marleen. Alonga you, Marleen. Alonga you, mi litel chuckie.

Won tit luvely wen you woz ~~grower~~ growing bigge and bigge and we luved and luved still!?"! We ~~felet~~ felte more and more like luving orle the time. And we saw ~~yow~~ you growing and we sed the babbies cuming and we smilede a lot! Sumthing to live fore. Eh?

She woz luveli wen she kem out – like a ~~brid~~, like a berd. She ~~fli~~, ~~flu~~, ~~flue~~, floo out. And she woz so quite – djust the wun smack and the wun cri to get er ~~bref~~, breth going. It woz nice and warm in that ospitle. Cumfi.

She fed offa yore tittie and I felet like ~~fee~~, feding offa the othere wun! Mi ~~mothe~~, mi mowthe din tarf watere?"!"

And they were evere so kinede and showed uz. Ow to pin er nappie on. And give er er botel. – If yore titties went dri – and luke after er, but it woz ~~difficlut~~, difficult to unnerstand.

Ever-i-thing.

And we dint ~~loike~~ like arsking um coz they wer nice. Wee thort weed lerene, well I leren't to rite din'nt I, even if you cunt quite manidge it, swete-art. Will sumbodi rite wot you saye wen you rite back. Or I s'll never ear anyhting agen. Djuste sende these out?!

Pleeze. Pleeze sumbodi reding this, pleeze rite back for Marleen. ~~Oi~~ Im evere so loneli I sumtoimes don ~~thi~~, ~~think~~, thinke Im ere. And if I ent got Marleen. Ent got a litel traice ov Marleen, Is'll djust van - ish. I wunt be ere at orl. (Pleeze don rede that bit to er, pleeze don't.)

It woz ~~diffe~~ diffrent wen we got ere to ower noo ome. Up ther in that towre ~~baloc~~, bloc wernit luvvie?

So colde. And Frite - ning.

We lerent tho! A bit. And litel Tina she ~~choke~~, she ~~chookled~~, chuckeled and she ~~gar~~ glurguled.

Wee thort a ~~live~~, a loife on ower owne and a babbi – on ower owne. We woz appi them first fewe daze. Appi more than before.

~~Oi~~ I dint mene it. We dint. Did we? No. NO!?!

Things startid to go rong a bit. She dinarf smelle, ower Tina. And we cunt remembre wot to do muche. We wipide er bumme, but it dinarf get redde and urt er – a lot!?"!

Well, she startid ~~eroi~~ cri-ing, and, well, she dint stop for owers. Til she fel aslepe. It felt like daze. Sune it woz daze. Sumtoimes. And you cride. You dint stope mutche, even wen I ~~kist~~, kissed you. I cunt cri. Im a man and mene dont cri, but I felet like cri-ing. Mi ed woz urting orl the toime.

We orl got so ~~tried~~ tired. Orl in a daze. Tina dint unnerstand. Nun ov uz reeley did unnerstand.

The ~~loite~~ lite dint elp, cos it woz so i up and if we went offa slepe for a minit ore toow, it woak us up. It woak us up erli and kep us awaik late agen. Ore the rane, the noize ov it. Anna winde! Ratteling and the windoes. Djuste wen a bitta peece kem.

I got ANGRI withe the lite. And the winde anna rane?!!!

Then it woz getting summere and liter still. Otter. If you opined the windoes to ~~kule~~ kool uz, well the winde kem in strongge and the noize from the citi and the brum, brum ov the kars orl the ~~toime~~, time, brum, Brum, BRUMMM, djust like that. Orl the time.

Them pepul startid cuming, cos silli olde bagge Missis Perkins tolde um, nozi, bludi olde bat! They smilede, but I dint like um.

It woz orlrite them smileing. It woz orlrite them showing uz wot to do. But it woznt wen e sed and she sed – otherwoize they mite av to tek babbi away. NOT orlrite – at ALL?!

I dint like um then. Tekking ower babbi. And frite-ning you! Well, uz. And we forgot wot they sed.

Then yore poor olde titties got sore – I tried kissing um betere and they wernt anni betere and you stoped me kissing um betere. I dint like that. You dint like that. You dint like fedeing babbie no more. Well a bit. Then a litel bit, then nun.

The botel woz no ~~goo~~ gud. The ~~ma, mi,~~ milke woz orlrite, but babbie wunt suck it. Mebbe we shud ave given it er colde. But it got ot too quicke and then she scremed and screemed wen we triede. It woz no use cos she scremed and screemed wen we dint.

That woz wen I erd the thuddes wen I woz aslepe a bit. You were bagnin yore ed agenst the worl a lot, remembre? You sed you cud see stars wen you dint bagn yore ed and you cud see stars we you did bagn yore ed, so you mite as well bludi bagn yore ed!

And dint we larf! We larfed til we cried. And we cried til

we cud see the stars owt the windoes aniway.

Wen babbie woz quite, it woz funni. There woz the um ov the citi, but the quite sort ov sang.

It sang in my ed and med me fele dizi. I dint no weathere I cud stan dup ore not, but I did stan dup. And wun ~~noat,~~ note kep whining and mi brane throbed. Yore brane throbbed too. I cud fele it throbeing for a long toime. I urt a lot and I woried a lot. You worried a lot.

Wen babbie cried and wen she screemed, them upstares and downstares use to bagn as well and showte narsti things at us. You startid feleing like bagning the babbies ed. You kep feleing like that.

Wen you bagned yore ed it was cos otherewise yud bagn the babbies ed. Bagning er ed. Picking er up and thro - ing er. Agenst the worl?

I got to say I felt like that. I got to fele a lot like that and wen you tole me that I felt like thro - ing you agenst the wol and the more you tole me, the more I felet it and wen them peepul kem, I felet like thro - ing THEM against the worl. I got so ANGRI. Ever-i-thing was begging, begin - ning to mek me angri. Even mi toothebrushe was mekking me angri wen it urt mi gummes.

Well, wot with them pepul cuming and them peepul upstares and downstares. Wot withe the babbies cri-ing, we cunt go owt mutche and we got veri angri sumtoimes. And you fel down sumtoimes cos we got weaker. But babbie got quiter for a bit.

Then wen we went owt for a bit and brung ~~mlike,~~ milke and food for uz (fags fore me and them frute gummes for you) the babbie got louder agen.

Evere so shrille?!"

I felet mi brane woz going to burste outta me ed veri soone. But it dint. Thinking ov it knowe, it wudda bein betere if it ad. Insoide mi brane felet loike a prison – hah! – But I dint fli owt. No!

Babbi SCREEMED lowdwer, longer. I eld mi ears. I cud ardly stan dup. So dizi. I eld on the worls and they sway - ed, the ~~baloe~~, bloc swayed. Babbie smiled, gave a litel larf. Mi brane bled red smoake. In mi eyes. In mi ed.

I toke its litel ankels and eld it upsaide downe over the railings. And I felet sutch a releve. I kep doing that. It woz a secrete release. Well, more than a bit.

Eache toime the babbie dint utta a sounde.

Babbie adda turnede ower wurld upsaide down and I turned ers upsaide downe. I no I shunna, but it elped. It did!

The last time I dun it woz a longe time. I felet mi grippe weaken-ing and er ankels slipping. Orl the citi soundes went. It got veri quite. I auled er up and brung er in and sat er downe and ran to the railings and jumped up and did a andstand on the railings and mi eyes blurred and the winde blew at me and I sway-ed and I woz wirling rounde and rounde faster and faster and the sunne woz a plugole suck-ing me up and I fel face-downe KRASH on the ~~blac~~, ~~bale~~ balconi.

The KRASH eckoed throo a sort ov WOOOO-shing wirling tunnel in mi ed and I woz swoo-ping downe it towardes a litel boy sat in the sofa corner, ugging Tedi, shiver-ing and cri-ing with orl weerd shadoes leeping from the fire. Dad woz cuming in.

Mum killed erself Krissmas Eve and Dad cried and then e went out and got pist. I woz alone all night and e kem in, walking throo torn-up bits ov presents. Not cri-ing. Angri. And I sed Mummi, mummi. E sed shes ded, boy, gone. And I sed Daddi and cried agen. Then I woz on the flore and dad ad bludie nuckels and mi noze woz wet with blud and snot.

E sed Don't Dad me, oi ent yore fuck-in dad. And you can fuck-in stop cri-ing NOW??!!

So I dint Dad im. I dint cri. Agen, til Tina.

The second time I tooke the nive offa you nere babbie, I djuste new we ad to tawke. Seeryuslie. And we put babbie downe. And I eld you and we eld and kist each othere.

And we sed we luvved babbie. Evere so mutch. And we ad a gud cri. They adnt let me luv anithing befor. But I luved babbie and I luved you, Marleen. We cunt giv babbie up. Ower litel Tina, ow cud we?

They sed it ud be for the beste, but it wunt. Ow cud we? We felet evere so lone-li ther in that towre. An we eld on to eache othere. Above the wurlde that dint like uz. That dint unnerstand.

We cunt urt ower litel Tina – I luved er beste ov orl the wurlde! More than Tedi wen I woz a babbie and you more than Cindi wen you woz a babbie. But they dint cri and screme and shit theirselves.

They dint sing with no words – so buteiful – neithere. But more screme and cri. We cunt urt er. We ad felet loike it a lot – djust to stop er. Djust for a bit ov peece and quite sumtoimes. But we nevere it er, the irone woz a ~~hac~~, ~~ack~~, ~~aksi,~~ acksident and the bruzes kem wen she woz thin. Wen we eld er tite they djust kem. Then.

So we cunt urt er ower butie, ower loveli litel buteiful, cud we, mi litel luve? And we cunt urt owerselves enuff reeley to kill uz, ow cud we? We luved eache othere. And we thorte a longe toime and we ugged. We thorte abowte jumping, but it woz so Hi. And frite-ning. And wot wudve appened if wun ov us staid alive. Eh?

So we med ower mindes up, din we, mi shugare. It ud be natchrul, We'd die ~~nat,~~ ~~natch,~~ natchural. We djust wunt eat. And Babbie. She djust wunt eat. Babbie wud die natchrul. Withe uz.

She got so luvely the babbie wen she got thinne. Er skinne shone pail silvere in the moonelite. Then it got like ivori and blu and sumtoimes you cud see throo it, well halve throo it. And the mussells and veins wer wurking away ther. A bit like a wippit orl bunched and graceful. A live and nuth - ing wasted. Too spair if you see wot I

Nere the toime, er eyes got bigger. Even more bute-iful. You cud see the reel er. She cud see the reel me. In ower eyes.

Then they orl kem and sheed died befor we ad.

And they dun orl them things to uz and callt uz them names. They lied and they lied, they DID!?!"

And no wun wud lissen wen we tried to tell wi it appen?ed, the trouthe. They wernt intrestid. In the trouthe. They red me from the paperes in ere. Did they rede you from the paperes in there?

They called uz monstres like them Nartzis and ole Adlof Hitel. We woz nevere monstres. Weer not monstres nowe

I feele a bit bad about wot we dun, Marleen. I carnt elp it. They med me. Dont you feel bad. Not even a bit bad, orlrite, mi duck. Cos your NOT bad. And I'm not. Weer not. Are we? Eh?

Well, I'm ere nowe and your ther, Marleen. Well I spose I'm gladde I'm ere. Inne a way. But I'm not gladde your there. But in ere its like the orfinage after they founde dad ded. And the borstle. I no wot to do ere. No more Tina, no more Marleen, no more ome, but I'm at ome if you see wot I mene.

I no wot to do.

If I do rong they it me.

If I do rite they it me (sumtoimes)

I no rite from rong (sumtoimes)

Ther rite from rong

So sumtoimes I no wot to do.

You neene so unappi abowte er, abowte Tina. We djust cunt unnerstand.

That's orl

I rote this so wel cos I ad the toime. And you'll ave the time too the gard sed if sumone'll rite wot you say. I'll ave the time to do sum more I ex-spect. O yes an

xxxxxxxxxxxxxxxx
x APPI KRISMASS x
xxxxxxxxxxxxxxxx

Marleen. That's wi
I've got the time. I'm bagned up in mi sel on me owne.
Ther downe stares aving a parti. And getting a bit pist on
the quite. Ther getting lowder. I dint get no Krismass
present, but they've promist me wun wen they cum up. I
no wot that ll be, but I ennafraide. At leest wen they it me I
no Im a live.

Aniway, I'm not nobodis nuthing. I'm yores, ent I? Eh?
But I miss mi Tina and mi Marleen – and even mi litel Tedi
sumtoimes – So quite and no bothere to nobodi. Dont cri
abowte Tina. Its so ard in this loife wen you dunno wot to
do. She dint no. We dint no, so mebbe she's bettere ov were
she is now. I orlways luv you, mi treasure so you tek care.
If I dunt see you in this loife, in the next. mebbe. – And
Tina.

And mebbe weel no wot to do. (Sumtoimes).

A Walk Across the Rooftops
Jackie Gay

Gloria works in a strip club, fetching drinks for the punters. From seven at night until three or four in the morning she hauls crates up from the basement, washes glasses, weaves her way between the shuddering tables with trays of drinks. She wears a miniskirt, halter-neck; it's a uniform. The men leave their hands too long on hers when they pay, slide them round her hips when she's bending. Surreptitiously; they know she's out of bounds.

– That's men for you, says Gloria. – Always want what they can't have. I mean, there's a girl on the table in front of him shaking her bits in his face and he wants to grab *my* arse.

– You're the best one in here, say the punters.

Gloria arches her eyebrows. She can't believe they use this line. – Honestly, Fay, she says to me, as we stand in her top-floor flat overlooking the city. – You'd think they'd get bored of the sound of it coming out of their mouths.

– It's a code, I say. – Like shaking hands or something. If *they* do this you'll do *that*.

– Yeah, well, says Gloria, smoothing gel through her cropped hair. – Who makes this stuff up anyway?

She's been made redundant four times, from office jobs, shyster companies. She worked in Marks & Spencer's one

Christmas, but got the sack for pulling a shopper's leg about his overflowing basket of lingerie. – Someone's gonna be having a festive season, said Gloria, winking as she flashed through the labels. His face twitched and glared; he complained, she got sacked. Everyone else thinks that was funny; would have laughed if the po-faced assistants at M&S said it to them.

– Just my luck, says Gloria, to get the miserable git.

I work in the garage opposite the strip club, just about the same hours as Gloria. Dispensing petrol, cigarettes, chewing gum; solace to a few, who whisper into my capsule.

– There's a curse on this place, did you know that? The gypsies cursed it when they left.

– I'm going to kill that cunt. I'm going to *kill* that cunt.

– Fay, phone an ambulance, quick.

– You're the only person in the world I can talk to.

– Wotcha Fay, long time no see. I don't s'pose you can lend me a tenner?

Disembodied neon legs flash and twitch outside the strip club. Rain sluices down the garage windows; blurring neon, car headlights, traffic signals, streetlamps. Pink, orange, red. A flash of blue as a police car screams down the underpass. Strands of light loop around the city, tyres roar and fade on sloshy roads. Inside my glass box it is quiet, I can read. Three to four a.m., the graveyard watch.

Inside the club it's the end of the night. The girls are tired, they dance awkwardly, resentfully. They want to sit down, have a fag, count their tips. Gloria is trying to shift people. She has a broom, a cloth. The men don't like it, this reminder of domesticity, and they complain to the boss.

– Hey, he says to Gloria, his brandied breath blasts her face. – Watch what you're doing.

– Do you want this place cleaned or what? says Gloria, hand on hip. They're all looking.

– Wait a bit, will you?

– I'm only paid till four.

She comes over for a smoke. Her hands are raw from washing up, her legs bruised from slipping on the cellar steps. – Fucking job, she says. – They should give me fucking wellies to wear behind that bar.

– Oh I don't know, I say. – Some of them probably go for rubber. You'd never get any peace.

– Fucking job.

A punter comes in the garage, tries to cadge a B&H off Gloria. I'm smoking roll-ups, my wages don't stretch to real fags.

– I don't know how you stand it, says Gloria. – Sitting there all night with every cig in the universe behind you and smoking rollies.

– You must be joking, I say. – Herrington'd feel it in his bones if I took anything. They'd sort of creak and he'd be out of his bed and through that door before I'd even lit the thing. I had a can out of the fridge once and he gave me a written warning.

– I don't think my boss can even *write*.

– How does he run a business if he can't write?

– Has mugs like me do it for him.

We sit and smoke, me in my capsule, Gloria on a garden chair we gave up trying to sell, horticultural interest being nil around here unless you count hydroponics. I warned Herrington, but hey, what do I know? She takes off her shoes, puts her feet up on the magazine rack. The soft skin under her eyes has gone grey, but she won't be able to sleep for hours yet. You get like that on the night shift, wired. Outside it is black, wild; like a tin of pitch has been flung around the glass. I can't even see the pumps.

– There's a shift going here, I say. – If you want it. Crap money, though.

– Oh no, says Gloria from behind closed lids. – I couldn't be on my own like you all night, Fay. I don't know how you do it. Have to have someone to talk to, me, even if it's more than likely a complete moron. D'you remember that job I had counting traffic – on the ring road, you know, where there's not even a frigging pavement to walk on – I tell you, by the end of the shift I was ready to jump in the road and drag someone out of their car just for a wee chat.

– Did you manage to count them?

– Nah.

– Everyone knows there's too many, anyway.

– Course.

People drift in and out. Subway Sam to cadge fag ends and a bit of shelter. He's wearing a black bin bag over his string-tied coat and berates me for not selling beer. – They do in America. Garages, he says. – I saw it in a film once.

– Sam, you can't even afford any baccy, says Gloria, and this is fucking Birmingham. She's reading a magazine with the headline WOMEN AND THE NEW WORKING WORLD.

Cab drivers dart in and out – it's a busy night for them; wet, bleak.

– Yo, Glo, they say.

– Hey, Fay.

One tosses us some fags he found on his back seat.

– Nice one, Amit.

– Give you cancer, he says.

– Look at this, says Gloria. – *Female Executive Stress: the nineties timebomb.*

– Oh yeah? I stare at the clock, trying mind-power on the sluggish second hand.

– Yeah. Listen: *How my dream job turned into a nightmare.* Gloria's eyes are darting across the page, sucking up the story. – Oh. Seems her kid got sick. That was when the trouble started.

– Did she lose her job, then?

– Yeah.

– Must have got fifty quid for selling her story, though.

– Is that all you get? I'll end up robbing a fucking bank at this rate, says Gloria.

The wind stalls, the darkness shrinks around us. There's some rustling, pitter-pattering outside – stray dogs? Rats? At this time of night people aren't in charge. I know for a fact that I could close the garage for an hour or so, get a bit of kip, but Herrington's bones would start to clack, and I never sleep till daylight anyway. Gloria is stretching, getting ready to go.

– See you tomorrow, she says, I'm going to get my bath.

– Have a soak for me, I say.

– You working this weekend?

– I'm off Sunday.

– Fancy going out?

– Yeah, but where?

The door creaks open. Gloria is thinking. – Dunno, but there'll be something, I'll find out.

It's a young kid, no one I've seen before.

– Might be an all-dayer somewhere, says Gloria. – They're fun. Everyone else wiped from the night before and you go in and stir it all up again.

The idea appeals to her, she wiggles her arms in front of her, dances a few steps round the slippery floor.

The door is still open, a draught ruffles Gloria's skirt.

– Hey, she says, spinning round. – Shut that door, will you?

The kid has a syringe. The blood in it swirls, prehensile. Gloria screams. The door snaps shut.

Gloria is in the General. Cars roll off Spaghetti Junction and land at the hospital. They're good at car wrecks; Friday night is gunshot night. Gloria has a bandage on her head and a drip in her arm but still smiles weakly.

– Did you bring my lippy? she says. – I must look a sight.

– Better than yesterday, I say. – More colour in you.

– I cadged some blusher off that Sister Marion. She's all right, she is. Do you know the stuff they have to *do* in here?

– I can imagine.

Gloria's legs are in traction, something's happened to her back. Her hands are chalky white with blue veins, like cheese. They tremble.

– How're you feeling? I say.

– Shite, says Gloria.

I go for a ciggie. Gloria's not allowed, although they said we can wheel her bed out in a day or two. Into the corridor. There're people there now, though; ill people. The hospital is old, red-brick, due for closure, but the wards are overflowing. The corridors are peeling and yellowish; I pace them. Lights flicker and give out when you reach dead ends, lifts creak and judder. Auxiliaries lurk in corners like me, smoking. Trollies rattle and groan. It's not like *ER* – the soundtrack is hushed whispers, the staff tired and workaday – but they save lives. They saved Gloria's.

Gloria's mum is here. She has tight white curls and wears her overall from the bakery.

– Come home, Glo, she says, sniffing back tears. – I'll look after you.

– Mum, I'm thirty-five. I can't come *home*. There's still a room for Gloria at her mum's house, with a too-small bed and a stuffed bear.

Her ex-husband comes too.

– What are you doing here? says Gloria. He shifts from foot to foot, glances at her sideways. He is shocked that he's shocked, I saw him start when he realized which body in a bed was Gloria. Last time he saw her she was letting him have it. All the tellings-off no one dared give him over his whole life, in one go. She can breathe fire, Gloria, scorch you at fifty yards.

– Come on, says Gloria, pushing herself up onto an elbow. – Out with it.

– I just came to see you, Glo.

– Liar.

Both of us are out of a job. Gloria's boss said he was going to have to let her go anyway. Mine has closed the garage for repairs. The glass cracked and fell away – glinting shards crumpled, they melted into the darkness as if they were ice – and all the stock was exposed to the night. I just left it, took Gloria in. I'm sure Herrington thinks I had some of the fags.

– Oh yeah, I said to him, while my mate was lying there spurting blood I stuffed my pockets full of Marlboro, B&H, all the pricey ones. I left the cheap fags, though; did someone else get to them after me?

– You've got a mouth on you.

Silence.

– I think I'm going to have to let you go.

– You should get compensation, says Gloria's ex.

– Piss off, Kenny, says Gloria.

– Especially if you're . . . you know.

– What?

– You know . . . if you've got it. He is scraping his shoe on the lino, staring at it.

– *Got what, Kenny?* says Gloria.

– Nothing.

– I'm alive, Kenny, says Gloria, suddenly luminous. She holds out her wrist. – Feel that pulse.

We go out clubbing. Gloria is hobbling, but upright.

– What happened to you? people say.

– I was a lollipop lady, says Gloria. – The bus's brakes failed.

– I fell off my ladder cleaning windows, she says.

It's twilight. The city is changing one set of colours for another. Night is sliding in, but we're not working, we stretch our legs, shift into relaxation. It's warm enough to prop the bar doors ajar and music leaks out in blasts, beer wafts are pumped from underground pubs, snatches of chat escape.

– Get that smell, says Gloria. – Reminds me of the strip club.

– The strip club smelled stickier, I say. – Saltier.

Gloria laughs, pulls her mouth down as if she's tasted something bad. The last of the sun angles down Corporation Street, casting long shadows; we look at ours, stretching out behind us.

– You know, says Gloria, I never want to work in a place like that again.

– You won't, I say.

Gloria looks sideways at me, goes to ask me something and then stops. – Ah fuck it, she says. – Let's go.

So we're off. In and out of the pubs, me nudging paths through the crowds for Gloria, who follows regally, bestowing smiles and thank yous to anyone who shifts. Into the clubs, where the music throbs in our throats and we seat-dance, laughing, and splutter into our drinks. At dawn we emerge, blinking, to a sky like the inside of a shell, lacily delicate and new. We take the lift to the top of our block and watch the city awake; it starts with a distant buzz and hum, cranks and judders like a reluctant engine. Flares into life.

– Wicked, says Gloria, looking out over the flats and factories and tower blocks to the distant blurred green of the Lickeys. – I feel like I could walk right out over the rooftops.

– You can't even walk down the fucking road at the moment, I say.

– Oh you, says Gloria. – Where's your imagination? Go on, then. You'll have to tell me some time.

The sky is brightening, hardening. The shell is opening out. Cars rumble in and out of the underpass, looking cute and brightly coloured from this distance. We could pick them up, rearrange them, send them off in a different direction.

– Tell you what? I say.

– Where you got the money.

– What money?

Gloria clicks her cheek. – The money for *this*, she says, peeling back the sky as she sweeps her hand across it. Up here you can smell the fresh air blowing in from Wales, the city is at your feet, you can step out of it, like a dress. – For bars and clubs and going out on the town.

– Good, isn't it? I say.

– Bloody great, says Gloria.

Gloria works in the market, selling flowers. I got us a pitch with the money I stole off Herrington. The garage money. The money the boy with the syringe was after. When Gloria was in Theatre being stitched, I slipped back, a smudge in the rain, moving from doorway to alley, down into the tunnels which run, miasmic, under the city. Slide up the steps, a slight crunch of glass, a hand in the till. Around the money. Mine; ours, actually. A spray of rain from a car slung sideways in the road, a figure lunging out. Quick, but not quick enough. I'm gone. Gloria was still under when I got back to the General.

– Go for a ciggie? said the nurse.

– Yeah. I needed one, I said.

– She'll be OK. She patted my hand. – We see a lot worse in here.

– I bet you do.

– I knew it'd be there, I say to Gloria. – The money. She is sorting out bunches; carnations, gypsophila, lilies with lush green ferns to set off their colour. She's quite an artist. People come back every day to buy flowers from Gloria.

– *Lovely, these are*, she sings, trimming off leaves, rolling and wrapping. Her voice is clear, cuts through the market hubbub. – *Pound a bunch. Buy some for your wife, your girlfriend.*

– *Or boyfriend,* I add. – *Why not buy* him *some flowers?*
Some boys walk past and cast us coy glances. We pose at our cheekiest. Are they really allowed to like flowers?

– You did great, girl, says Gloria. She picks out some sweet peas from the tin buckets behind us, twists a few together. The smell – vanilla-ish, heady – hangs around the stall, catching people as they scurry past.

– Better than petrol fumes, I say.

– Or sweat and spunk, says Gloria. We are laughing.

– Better use of Herrington's money, that's for sure, I say.
– Poppies are for flowering.

– I'm surprised he didn't catch you, says Gloria.

– They don't call me fleet feet for nothing.

The needle didn't go in, Gloria thinks. She told me in one of the clubs, in a dark corner. She whispered it smokily into my ear, and then vanished off to the loo. A breath, a whisper; something too important to be said solidly. She's not sure. You have to wait six months to be sure. I'm not sure either. A lunge and a crash was what I saw, Gloria dive-bombing the plate glass to avoid the needle. The boy vanished, dematerialized, the noise and screaming shattering him out of existence. A lunge and a crash, it was. But it could have been a lunge and a crash and a prick.

– Who calls you fleet feet anyway? says Gloria. We're going for lunch, linked arms, scrabbling up the ramp along with a couple of hundred others, funnelled through the arcade. – You're full of shit sometimes.

– *You* would have, mate, if you'd have seen me.

– All right, says Gloria. She opens the café door, waves at the working girls behind the counter. – Do me a favour and keep them on the ground *occasionally.*

– Sure thing, boss, I say.

The Country of Glass
Joel Lane

At the age of forty-seven, Matthew Lang stopped being an alcoholic. It had to do with a bottle of mescal that his friend Jake had brought back from a trip to Mexico. They shared the bottle one evening in Lang's flat, over a meal of spaghetti and wood mushrooms. A calm Latin silence, underscored by the chirping of distant cicadas, drowned out the mechanical fugue of traffic along the Alcester Road. They were more than halfway through the bottle when Lang noticed the worm: a pale, dragon-like creature drifting inside the glass. Jake explained that the worm flavoured the mescal, and was meant to be eaten. An hour later, they finished the bottle by sharing the worm. As he bit into the soft drugged flesh, Lang realized something.

He floated it in his mind that night, letting the insight flavour the murky dregs of his consciousness. Being an alcoholic was like refusing to eat the worm. It was a denial of the essence. Just as a fetishist created false challenges through his inability to deal with sex, so an alcoholic created his *drink problem* through fear of alcohol. The truth would admit no compromise. Whatever conflicted with drinking had to be set aside. Lang stared at his thin curtain, seeing the contents of his bedroom by sodium light and by the liquid-crystal lucidity of distilled alcohol. He didn't know it, but that night had brought him to the ragged border of Vitraea.

It had been coming for a while, of course; or rather, he'd been travelling unconsciously towards it. The social pub and party drinking of his thirties had given way to lonelier practices. Regular drinking sessions with a group of friends had fizzled out after he'd thrown up in a friend's car twice. For a long time, he'd felt trapped in a vicious circle: loneliness drove him out to pubs, where the presence of young and possibly available women awoke in him a mixture of desire and fear that he had to drink to overcome, until he was too drunk to do anything except go home. His only affairs were with women who drank, and their self-hatred tended to evolve into resentment of him. Lang refused to be tragic about alcohol. In retrospect, the taste of the worm had always been in his mouth.

Solitary drinking means never having to say you're sorry. For Lang, rearranging his life around alcohol had given him a measure of control and even of artistic vision. The way last night's vodka remained as a slowly melting icon in his gut through the afternoon at work; the way sweat crawled lazily over his skin in the first light of morning; the way ice chilled the flame of malt whisky without putting it out; these were at once reliable and startling, the painful treasures of his life. Sometimes he'd go to an unfamiliar district and comb the off-licences for exotic bargains or obscure links to the drinking lives of other cultures. Wine was an occasional delight, liqueurs a sentimental journey, strong cider a dose of cold realism. Spirits were the truth: cynical vodka, melancholic gin, turbulent whisky, furious rum, erotic tequila, devout cognac. He'd gone to great trouble to obtain a regular supply of the Dutch spirit jenever, which was like gin with more juniper berries and less essence of razor blade. On special occasions, Lang would go into a quiet bar in Digbeth and drink his way along the row of optics, including doubles of his favourites. He was a connoisseur of jukeboxes, able to define a pub's clientele and district from a glance at the list of selections; but he disliked pub-rock bands, and hated karaoke almost as passionately as he hated fascism.

Just as a brilliant summer creates deep shadows and pockets of decay, Lang's drinking had its unpredictable dark moments. He tended to glimpse a kind of wavering or rippling in buildings, like the effect of a heat-haze. It included, but wasn't caused by, the crawling of beetles or ants. Sometimes he'd see them on bus windows or people's shirts, though he managed to control his reaction. He shaved thoroughly, though he often cut himself, because stubble was a perfect hiding-place for them. Worse, sometimes he'd look along a tree-lined avenue or a sunlit canal and see images from his own past clotted with dust and dead leaves, abandoned: his junior school, his parents, his first girlfriend, the black ornamental railings of the tenement house where she'd stayed with him that summer. All of it blurred and corroded, but still there. The past was not biodegradable.

One still evening in August, Lang decided to go to the Triangle Cinema in Aston. He'd not seen a programme in months, but there was usually something good on. And if not, they had a quiet café with film magazines and old posters. He caught the bus into town and walked up through Corporation Street, past the red sandstone buildings of the Law Courts and through the disinfected subway to the University. He found the cinema from memory, but it had recently closed down. Through the tinted windows, he could see tarpaulins over shapeless furniture. Angrily, he walked past the back entrance into the sloping terraced streets of the student quarter. The sky ahead of him was marked with dark bruises of pre-rain. He chose the smaller and older-looking of the two pubs within sight.

The interior was desiccated and smoky, dark wood hung with old photographs of railway bridges in the Black Country. The husk of Shane MacGowan's voice was drifting over the tense piano chords of 'Rainy Night in Soho'. It was still too early for the main evening crowd; but a handful of after-work drinkers on their way home, students preparing for a night out and soberly dressed couples on adulterous dates were scattered around the heavy, unvarnished tables. Lang was into his third glass of Smirnoff Blue with fragmented ice when a voice spoke in his ear.

'Matt, how are you? Haven't seen you for months.'

It was Jake. He looked greyer, more angular than before, unevenly shaved; but there was a youthful fire in his dark eyes that Lang didn't remember.

'Good to see you.' They sat down at one of the smallest tables, by the railings above the cellar steps. Lang realized they hadn't met, only spoken on the phone, since the mescal evening in April. 'How have you been?'

Jake didn't immediately answer. He was drinking malt whisky, neat, no ice. 'I've been looking for something,' he said. 'I think we both have. But I know its name.' He lifted the glass to the light, watched a star dying in a twist of smoke. 'Do you remember what you said about the worm in the mescal bottle?'

Lang didn't recall telling him about it, but then he'd been a little drunk. He nodded.

'Well, that's only the start. Have you ever heard some of the old farts in places like this talking about Vitraea?'

Lang stared. The name didn't so much ring a bell as strike a bass chord somewhere underground, causing reverberations in parts of his memory he didn't know were there. He was sure people had been talking about it when he'd thought they were talking about something else. But what did it mean? 'The country of glass,' he said without thinking.

'Have you been there?'

Lang shook his head, blushing. He felt foolish.

'Don't worry, not many people have.' Jake sipped his malt whisky thoughtfully. 'It's a region, but not necessarily a country. The wine district. The house of spirits. Its location has to do with some kind of secret geography. Lines and borders created by alcohol. There's only one thing that's widely known about it. Lager louts and beer monsters have no key to its gates. Vitraea is definitely Latin rather than German, Sephardi rather than Ashkenazi. It's the place where the bottle is never empty, and the drinks are so pure that hangovers are unknown. Imagine drinking rough blended whisky all your life and then discovering single malt. In Vitraea, the whisky is to single malt what Isle of Jura malt is to the Claymore.'

Lang shuddered, recalling low-budget trips to Moseley off-licences in recent years.

They finished their drinks; Jake bought another round while the pub filled up with students and Brett Anderson's voice crept uneasily through 'The Wild Ones', yearning for the celluloid kisses of ghosts. When Jake returned from the bar, he was in a sombre frame of mind. Lang was used to his mood shifts, and waited a while before asking him: 'You said you've been looking?'

Jake nodded wearily. 'It started in Mexico. Then Amsterdam. Lately, Glasgow and the west coast of Scotland. Maybe it's within myself. The distillation of the soul. When I started to think of it as a religion, I realized that I already had one. It was buried, but still there. The skullcap under the skull. You were brought up an atheist; maybe you've got a better chance of finding it.' He lifted his glass and stared at the pale liquid. 'Tell you something, though. It's a quest you don't come back from. Whether you find it or not, there's no way back.' His troubled eyes met Lang's as he tilted the glass back to his mouth. 'Cheers.'

Waiting at the bus shelter in Dale End, Lang marvelled at the things people came out with when drunk. Especially when friends drank together, building a card-house of delusion on the table between them. Jake had walked on through Aston to his home in Gravelly Hill, near the concrete forest of Spaghetti Junction. Up here in the city centre, the dense air was curdled with traffic fumes; the threatened rain had failed to materialize. Lang could hear the faint muttering of people in the shelter: drunks asking for cigarettes, lovers saying goodbye. The sound intensified into a consistent rhythm, a chant. He turned around. They were all staring past him at the approaching bus. All their faces were deformed by madness. When the bus stopped, Lang threw himself onto it. Nobody followed him. All the way to Moseley, he sat on the top deck and watched his hands shake.

His flat was warmer than the street outside. He could smell the remnants of food in the kitchen, the used plates and the full bin liner. Swaying slightly, he walked through into the bedroom. He'd not changed the sheets in a month. Behind his alarm clock, an unfinished nightcap of vodka was cloudy with mould. He'd never known that spirit could decay, let alone that it could decay so fast.

In September, Lang was offered voluntary redundancy. He'd been with the same company for nine years, and they knew they weren't going to get any more out of him. What kind of person would put their heart into computer systems analysis, Lang didn't like to think. Alcohol was a factor in his lack of ambition, if not in his actual performance. He never drank before work or even at lunchtime, because he didn't want his drinking to be tainted by the unwholesome vibes of the office. The redundancy would allow him to take an extended holiday, maybe until Christmas, before drying out and looking for freelance work. If he was ever going to find the country of glass, it had to be now.

His new life started awkwardly. Years of suppressed fatigue dropped their black leaves inside him. He lost the will to go out of doors for anything but essential supplies, and even then waited until it was dark. By day he kept the curtains shut, sometimes pulling the duvet over his head, as he listened to records and drank neat Scotch. The stillness frightened him, but he was afraid to break it. Without vision, light could only bring pain.

When he began to go out again, the nights were longer and colder. Instead of going to pubs, Lang started hanging around with the older drunks in Moseley's graveyards and car parks. Some of them were homeless, but most lived in bedsits on the cheap side of the district and came out for company. Lang was quite happy drinking alone. What he needed was some kind of information about Vitraea, however distorted or speculative. Most of the piss-artists he approached seemed to know nothing. A few said they'd heard the name long ago, but didn't know what it meant.

One very old man said to him: 'It'll find you while you're looking for it. You won't have any way out.' Lang tried to make him explain, but he was barely conscious and just muttered again and again: 'I swear to God, I once fucked a woman with three tits.'

Desire was never far from these conversations. Prostitutes also hung around these places, and drunken couples hid in the shadows. Lang would store the occasional glimpse of an exposed breast or buttock in his memory, for use on those occasions when he woke up with an erection. Like the sentimental songs that people wept over in pubs, the sexual desire evoked by alcohol had no real substance or depth. The permanent light of Vitraea dispelled the need for sex, just as it dispelled the need for tears.

One night in October, Lang was walking past a row of derelict houses on the edge of Balsall Heath. Lamplight glittered from the teeth of broken windows. Rain was beginning to fall, smearing the rear lights of passing cars. Lang had bought some fish and chips and been unable to eat them. He felt choked with emptiness, as if he might throw up a void. The Old Moseley Arms was still open; but instead of going in, he stood gazing down at the city centre. All you could see were the lights: blue and gold and white, a mass of buildings reduced to points in a man-made constellation. As he watched, the rain made the city's lights blur and waver. The pattern rose towards him and began to spin gradually, like a Catherine wheel starting up. What did it represent: a flower, a symbol, a face? It trailed a pale fire below itself, reducing the buildings to meaning-less rubble.

'Got a light, mate?'

It was someone who'd just come out of the pub, his white face luminous with sweat. Lang shook his head. When he looked back at the city centre, all he saw was the familiar view. He stared at it for several minutes, but it refused to change. The rain was soaking into his collar. Moving slowly, as if underwater, Lang walked back towards the off-licence on the corner of Mary Street. He passed the children's playground behind the pub; nobody was there, but the metal roundabout was revolving slowly. The cold air wavered and shimmered around him as he walked on.

Autumn ended in a feverish cluster of bright days and frozen nights. By then, Lang had given up dreaming of Vitraea. He was too drunk. The honeymoon was over. Too many nights spent out of doors had given him backache and severe rheumatic pains, but he felt nothing. His breathing had grown thick and deliberate, a monologue silenced only by complete inaction. His laundry basket resembled a compost heap. What he would do when the money ran out didn't concern him: he couldn't imagine living that long. For now, as long as his fridge and coat pockets were full of cheap vodka, it was OK. He could manage without the ice. It was cold enough inside him.

On the last day of October, drawn by a nervous energy that felt more like sleepwalking than conscious action, Lang revisited the district where he'd grown up. It seemed appropriate: a way of saying goodbye, of making the ghosts unreal. His parents had long since moved on. The High Street was very different; but much of the suburb had hardly changed in thirty years. It was part of Edgbaston, neither wealthy enough nor run-down enough for redevelopment. As the afternoon light flickered through trees like a distant candle, Lang walked through the park where he and his brother had played cricket with a tennis ball. Clouds of midges hovered over the pond like a belated heat-haze. He pulled his coat tight around his shoulders; every few minutes, he took a quiet sip of brandy from his metal flask.

His primary school was still there, its flaking red-brick mass surrounded by paler new buildings. It had a different name. Further downhill, the second-hand bookshop had gone but the fire station was unchanged. Here was the railway bridge where two eleven-year-old girls, twins, had exposed themselves to him one summer evening; he'd not been aroused, though the memory seemed erotic in retrospect. The house Lang's parents had owned was still there, but painted red over the black; recognizing the porch and the leaded windows, he felt a wave of disorientation pass through him. As if he were a tunnel with a train running through.

It was getting dark; the streetlamps pulled curtains down between the tall houses. Around the corner was a cross-roads where one road came over a hill and another came out from under a bridge. Apparently it was still an accident black spot, since a crashed car had been dumped on the pavement. The whole of this block had been demolished in the late fifties; it was still waste-ground. A few apple trees were scattered at the lower end, close to a ruined brick wall; their fruits were blackened, mostly unfallen. Across the road, an off-licence shone its message of promised glory. Lang went to investigate.

Later, clutching a discounted four-pack of Special Brew, he sat in the shadow of the wall and drifted between sleep and waking. In his experience, being inconspicuous was the best way to evade trouble. It worked so well that when, later on, a group of children in luminous Halloween masks started playing some complicated game of tag involving passing on a broken doll, none of them noticed him.

Fibres of rain twitched in the yellow light, tangling the air. He felt as unreal as a charcoal drawing on stone. Some more children had come from behind the wall, carrying something. Through the acidic ferment of Special Brew, he could smell petrol. A beetle or an earwig crawled over his hand.

As Lang watched, the children formed a ring around the wrecked car. Its front end had been torn back and side-ways; the windscreen had a hole the size of a fist punched through it, sheathed in white. One of the children, wearing an expressionless ghost mask, threw the doll inside. Another spilled petrol over the roof and tyres, as if pouring brandy over a Christmas pudding. The children backed off, masks glowing faintly with the reflection of a secret light. One of them lit the end of a rolled-up newspaper and threw it. Lang shut his eyes; the wave of heat touched his face like an angry wound. When he looked, the waste-ground was on fire.

All around him, the smell of burning leaves was mingled with the smell of alcohol. Small knots of fire were pressing up through the soil; above them, insects were streaming through the grainy air. The car was still burning with a soft blue-white flame. The children, their pale masks sweaty with rain, were dancing. The waste-ground was a forest of drowned lights. The rain tasted faintly bitter. Lang put his tongue out to catch a drop. Juniper. He picked up a handful of dead leaves, crushed them and tasted the damp fibres. Then he stood, trembling as his lungs filled with the charcoal-tinged air. Patches of frost drifted in the reddish light, looking for a surface to crust on. The rain was gin, the dead leaves were soaked in brandy, the air itself was vodka. He looked up at the stars; they drifted, hard and bright, making new patterns and symbols across the fluid sky. Then one of the floating scars of frost bound itself across his face, and all the lights blurred into the dark fire of underground.

Much later, he was vaguely aware of being picked up and shaken; of daylight; of something sharp being inserted into his arm. But he didn't want to know. As long as he didn't wake up, he was still there. Eventually he was forced to return by a tense hand on his shoulder and a voice repeating: 'Matthew, Matthew.' He opened his eyes to the half-light of early morning indoors. A young woman with short dark hair was leaning over him. She was wearing a nurse's uniform; the name-badge on her lapel read *Virginia*.

They didn't keep him long. Apart from some bruising and a painful cough, his exposure to the night had done no real harm. That morning, he was encouraged to eat breakfast and drink a lot of water. The need for a real drink hit him almost at once; but he kept quiet, aware that the next time it could well be a police cell. The ward seemed full of glass: bottles, tumblers, vases, drips, syringes, windows. Outside, trees were swimming in the drowned light. Insects swarmed on the ceiling, where the mercury tubes wept silent trails of moisture. Lang fantasized about breaking into the hospital's medical store and finding bottle after bottle of pure ethyl alcohol. For all he knew, they kept it for scrubbing down the operating theatre.

In the twilight of late afternoon, he fell asleep and dreamed of walking through a forest. The path was buried under layers of dead leaves that were slowly turning to soil. As he walked, the drifts of leaves grew deeper. They absorbed the sound of his feet into a gentle, unbroken whisper. The topmost layer was red and gold. They were letters and photographs, sketches and certificates. The magazines in the garage; the furniture in the canal. They were memories waiting to be recovered, held up and loved in the grainy auburn light of Vitraea.

He was released that evening. Pressure on available beds made rapid patient turnover a necessity. The doctor gave him an appointment card to see a clinical psychiatrist later in the week. Lang stopped at the off-licence on his way home. By midnight he was blind drunk; but the visions didn't come. Only the black specks, the insects crawling between areas of shadow, less phantoms of Vitraea than reminders of the polluted world. Days passed in a drizzle of vodka, washed down with dry Martini. He didn't keep the appointment. As the nights grew longer, he felt their darkness settle inside him. Outside, frost whitewashed the city.

The build-up to Christmas is usually enough to get even sober people drinking. By opting out of the festive mania, Lang gained a certain measure of control. Violent, destructive boozing was unlikely to help him find Vitraea. But he didn't know how to keep his spirit pure, untainted by the world. After months of redemptive drinking, visionary drinking, he'd gone back to merely being an alcoholic. Maybe Jake could have told him what to do; but Jake had moved on, his phone disconnected, his flat occupied by a new tenant. Maybe he'd found what he was looking for; more likely, he was still searching.

On Christmas Eve, the centre of Moseley was snarled up with traffic. The cluster of antique and craft shops had drawn a mass of shoppers, while the off-licences were shifting enough good-quality stock to make the liver of God feel queasy. At the other end of the district's economic spectrum, a restless community of the homeless and destitute were scattered along the Alcester Road: in bus shelters, around the church, in the doorways of boarded-up shops. Lang had already stocked up with enough Smirnoff and Johnnie Walker to see him through to the New Year, and had already bought the few gifts he intended to give. It was loneliness that drove him to wander around the so-called village, coughing quietly from deep in his chest. Loneliness, and a hope spread as thin as frost.

Just off the Alcester Road was another, older church whose graveyard looked frosty even in midsummer. The entrance from the road had a little wooden porch where local drunks often sat and solved the world's problems. This afternoon, as darkness closed in around the ribbon of shops and pubs, two men were staring from the low benches. Lang recognized one of them: an ageing tramp who was an expert on the Biblical Apocrypha. Lang had tried, and failed, to pump him for rumours of Vitraea. The other man was younger, his beard slightly flecked with white. They waved at Lang.

'Hey, pilgrim! Come and join us. Did you remember the myrrh?'

The older man passed Lang a half-bottle of sweet sherry. Lang drank from it, though the honey-petroleum odour made him gag. The tramp looked at him warily, as if deciding whether to trust him. Finally he muttered: 'You remember that place you used to go on about? The country of glass?' Lang gazed steadily at him. His eyes were china-blue, cracked and smoked. 'I found something from it. Want to come and see? It's not far from here. Me and Barry, we hid it. Too precious to carry around.'

Lang glanced at the younger man; he nodded. 'OK.' He had nothing to lose. They walked, in no great hurry, down the steep hill of Salisbury Road. To their left, giant trees curtained off an area of parkland. To their right, further down, the lights of a submerged housing estate floated like phantoms of a drowned city. At the bottom, two adjacent roads ended in derelict houses. One house was little more than a façade, moonlight shining down through the roof-timbers and edging the smashed windows with silver. The other house was shorter and more enclosed, its windows boarded up. Lang's two companions walked silently towards it.

One of the side windows, concealed by a low brick wall, was unboarded and shattered. 'In here.'

The younger man went in first, Lang second. When they were all inside, the younger man opened his rucksack and took out a torch. Lang had a glimpse of stained walls, damp like a giant spider, a few rotting kitchen cupboards. Then, suddenly, his arms were gripped behind his back. The rucksack was opened again, and something small and dark was taken out: a cosh. He was struck three times, hard enough to drain the strength from his arms and legs. Darkness streamed around the torchlight, spilling over his face like water.

They'd lit candles in the four corners of the room. When Lang surfaced, his arms had been spread across a table and tied down with rope. He was lying face up. The other two men were sitting on rotten fabric-covered chairs, one to either side of him. Damp had painted a forest in the walls. Lang craned his neck, trying to see what was going on. The two silhouettes in the chairs didn't seem to notice his awakening. Around their feet, and wherever he could see that far down, the bare floorboards were littered with bottles. Some full and unopened, some empty. Wine and sherry, he thought. Belatedly, he realized that the room stank of alcohol. Had he failed to notice because he was used to waking up in a similar atmosphere? One of the seated figures bent down, lifted a glass and drank. It took Lang several minutes to find the courage to ask: 'What the fuck's going on?'

Candlelight played on the surfaces of green and brown light. As if explaining the obvious, the older man said: 'It's the only way. We can't get to Vitraea, but it will come to us if we give it an offering.'

They're mad, Lang realized. He needed a drink. After a while, he asked for one. There was no response. The presence of booze, in such quantity and of what appeared to be fair quality, was having an effect on him. His eyes and mouth felt painfully dry. Despite the cold, he was sweating. In a corner of the room, he glimpsed the movement of dark insects. If there was a window, it was behind him; no light came through it.

Hours passed. His two captors were almost insensible from drinking. They wove unsteadily across the floor, choosing bottles, struggling to open them. A glass broke; kicked over, a bottle spilled red wine across the thirsty floor. Lang's mouth was so dry he found it difficult to breathe. He'd tried arguing, begging, cursing. His lips were cracked, and the chafing of his tied wrists was like a Chinese burn. The branches of damp in the walls were beginning to waver and swim. The eyes of flame were crying. Little black crabs were scuttling furiously across the dim ceiling, as if it were an intertidal zone.

Silence flooded the room. A faint green light, from no window that he could see, made the bottles invisible. Lang felt a cool wind strip the last traces of sweat from his drying face. The two men were on their feet and stumbling. Or rather, they'd been lifted and their bodies were shimmering, like candle flames about to go out. Waves of soft light crushed all the bottles, and the shattered glass dragged back and forth across the floorboards like sand. And then his two captors were floating, twisted, pulled into vortices of light. The smell of alcohol was so intense Lang could taste it. But he'd never been more sober in his life. The cold air thickened, turning momentarily to glass. Then all the lights went out at once.

The police found Lang the next morning. Someone had heard him crying for help, provoked by the faint shafts of daylight through the boarded window. Two officers forced an entry through the front door. They found him fully conscious, but unable to loosen the ropes from around his wrists and ankles. The room was empty apart from Lang, the table he'd been tied to and a couple of badly deteriorated chairs. And a layer of finely ground glass that crunched quietly under their feet. Lang described his kidnappers, said they were after a ransom. He and the two police officers had a laugh about that, back at the station. They even offered him a glass of Scotch, but he declined. He didn't tell them that he hadn't really been calling for help so much as crying out in despair. And he never touched alcohol again. There was no need for any pledge or twelve-step cure: he simply couldn't drink. It would have been like screwing a prostitute after losing the great love of your life.

Flowers for Doña Alicia

Penny Rendall

I'd been to the new season's preview at Federico's. It was sparsely attended. The poor man positively fawned over me.

'The new ladies don't appreciate the best of Milan and Paris,' he confided. 'Soon, I fear, there will be no one left with your sense of style.'

And when he follows his old customers to Madrid or Rome, as he undoubtedly will before long, there'll be nowhere for us to satisfy it. 'It's worse than that,' I told him. 'They're going to Miami now for their flashy tat. Day trips in their husbands' planes. Really, I can't think why they bother. It doesn't impress me, for one.'

Such barbarians. We thought the cartel was just one more irritant, of no importance in the long-term scheme of things. To be endured, like mosquitoes in the rainy season. They couldn't touch people like us, people who made this city – this country – what it was: civilized, democratic, literate, with universities the envy of half the continent and a rich, proud culture. But they've destroyed everything. They splatter the city with their coke and Coca-Cola philistinism and the people sniff and slurp and worship them as national heroes simply because they're standing up to the 'Yankee imperialists' and their pointless demands for extradition.

Rodrigo wasn't with the other bodyguards at the entrance so I assumed he was waiting at the car. But when I reached the parking place neither it nor he was there. And Manolo, the old man who's supposed to guard the cars, was nowhere in sight either.

I called him. His straw hat emerged from behind a pickup and he limped over, all smiles and cringing apology.

'Where's my car?'

'Your car, Doña Alicia?'

'My car, yes. It's gone.'

'Gone?'

'Stop repeating everything I say, for God's sake. The car's been stolen, as you very well know. I hope they made it worth your while.'

'I didn't see anyone, señora, I promise. It may have been . . . well, I had to answer a call of nature . . .'

'You can't play the innocent with me, Manolo. Waste of breath.'

'Shall I get you a taxi, Doña Alicia?'

'Don't be absurd,' I said. 'Do you want to see me kidnapped? Go and find my bodyguard, would you? I suppose they paid him off too. He'll be in the bar.'

Behind me I heard that swish a Cadillac window makes and felt a wash of refrigerated air on my back. Of all people, it had to be Consuelo. Not my day.

'Alicia, darling,' she said. 'Is something the matter?'

I explained about the car. She offered to drive me home and of course I had to accept. 'As long as you're not rushing to catch the dregs of the preview champagne,' I said. 'Oh, obviously not. Were you going to the gym?' She blushed, almost to match her clothes: a sort of tracksuit in Puerto Rican-pink silk.

The front passenger seat was occupied. I sat in the back. The young man who had failed to offer me his seat was a stranger.

'Aren't you going to introduce us, Consuelo?' I said, eventually. She tries hard, but she's a lot to learn.

'You've met José's English colleague, Jeremy Ashbury, on one of his visits, haven't you? This is his son, Oliver. Oliver, my good friend Alicia Rivera y Montalba.' Close connections I can no longer deny, but friendship . . .

'It's a great honour,' I said. The ambiguity seemed lost on the boy.

'How do you do?' he replied civilly enough, in English.

Perhaps Consuelo *had* picked it up. She was quick to intervene. 'He only arrived yesterday. I'm afraid his Spanish is rather rudimentary,' she told me. What fascinating conversations they must be having, I thought, if her English is, as one has to assume, even less accomplished. To Oliver she said, more slowly: 'Alicia's car has just been stolen.'

'We go to the police?' he asked.

We couldn't help laughing at that, but I could see in the mirror that the boy was hurt. 'Welcome to Colombia,' I said in my gentlest voice.

'We're taking Alicia home,' Consuelo said. 'The people who stole the car will telephone her there. She will have to give them some money and they will give her car back.'

'The police, they do nothing?'

'It depends who's paying,' I said. 'In this case they'll have looked up the registration for my name and phone number.'

'The famous cartel, I suppose,' Oliver said.

'Of course it's the bloody cartel,' I said. 'Who else?' It's all any foreigner knows now about our beautiful city. It makes you want to weep. When I think of what we've lost – the opera, the arts festivals; showing the world that South America doesn't have to be synonymous with brutal dictators and wild-eyed revolutionaries; distinguished visitors from all the great capitals complimenting us on our atmosphere, revelling in our eternal spring.

Consuelo explained that the car racket had been far worse in the days before the cartel because there were so many different gangs. 'It's very efficient now,' she went on. 'It works rather like a car tax or an insurance policy. We don't have those here. And they're careful not to push their luck – they don't take the same car too often or demand outrageous ransoms.'

I thought that was a bit rich, and said so: they'd taken my car only a couple of months before. Her vulgar monster, it occurred to me, hadn't been stolen for at least a year. And here she was, praising the cartel for their restraint. Further evidence to support my suspicions about her slimy husband José's new connections. Accountant? Don't make me laugh – dirty laundryman, more like. She's dispensed with her bodyguard, too – what's the point, when they don't kidnap their own?

We were getting close to my house by then. Consuelo was having to concentrate on getting the Cadillac round the mountain bends.

I left them on the veranda while I phoned Eduardo to ask him to be prepared to come home early with whatever they considered a fair ransom this time.

When I came back out I found my new girl had served them coffee in the kitchen cups. I know it's an age-old refrain, but it really is impossible to get decent servants these days. We have the cartel boss, the so-called people's champion, to thank for that as well, since he turned 'philanthropist'. No sooner have I trained a new cook or maid than she's off to snap up the illusory good life of one of the houses he keeps building them. Where she'll find no work to pay her rent, tumble into prostitution, get pregnant, become a mule and spend the next ten years in some European prison as likely as not, her children on the streets.

Consuelo was quick to seize her chance. She's certainly coming on: she managed to achieve just the right balance of graciousness and condescension when she said, 'Don't worry, darling. It doesn't matter if you don't use the best china for friends.'

Dear God. Again. There's only a handful of people I can call friends who haven't already sold up and fled. If it wasn't for Eduardo's sweet notions about loyalty and tradition and honour we would have done the same long ago. There's no problem getting a good price for the land: these people are all desperate to buy themselves landed respectability. It's not as if we can enjoy the estates, it's far too dangerous in the countryside. I've even lost the children. After the nightmare of the Vasconcelos case, I had to agree to send them away to school in Spain.

Now I know the meaning of the old insult, 'idle rich'. I never had time to be idle before, with all the committees, the receptions to arrange, doing my lady bountiful bit in the country, visiting the health centres and so on. Not to mention my lovely children. Managing a single, childless household is hardly a full-time occupation. To think people are *jealous* of my life of luxury. If they only knew. I'm stuck here on my own all day, bored out of my mind. Except that I'm never completely alone, because of the armed thugs we're all surrounded by. I can't even throw my energies into giving a decent party – there simply aren't the people. The tedious round of dinners is our only entertainment, an ever-shrinking circle of faces, meaning we're reduced to inviting the Josés and Consuelos of this world to make up the numbers. I get some pleasure from showing them how it should be done, I admit, but even that's beginning to pall. Especially since Consuelo has taken to reminding me with every gesture, every expression on her overpainted face that Eduardo's found himself a new diversion.

She insisted on staying to keep me company while I waited for the phone call and seemed to think she was doing me a favour. One thing I was grateful for: with Oliver there, I wasn't subjected to the usual catalogues of her latest purchases and social conquests.

The boy was badly dressed, as you'd expect. Too long, too baggy trousers and a hooded shirt advertising some US baseball or football team, which was no advertisement for himself. Northern European men have no style. Still, he was rather good looking, in a pale, gangly sort of way, and had a certain gauche charm.

He tried in his stumbling Spanish to be complimentary about the house and the view, without being overawed – a good sign. I decided to give him a break and switched to English. What had possessed him, I asked, to come to Colombia, if he just wanted to improve his Spanish? 'Surely your father must have contacts in some nice part of Spain?'

The boy laughed. 'His point of view exactly. But I told him I wanted to see the real world.'

He planned to travel all round South America, by bus and train. Not so long ago I would have thought he was mad. Now I can understand something of the appeal; I'd put up with a fair amount of discomfort myself for a mere taste of adventure. Consuelo had been trying to dissuade him apparently, but he was determined. He said Colombia wasn't turning out to be nearly as dangerous as he'd been led to expect.

'But you've only just arrived,' I said. 'If you stay for a while, I'm sure we can provide all the excitement a young man could possibly want. And you couldn't ask for a more accomplished and experienced hostess than Consuelo, though you may find her rather *occupied* at the moment.'

It was right over the boy's head, but Consuelo's English must be better than I'd imagined. Her mask slipped for a moment and she flashed me a look of pure hatred, which went a long way towards improving my mood.

The phone rang at last. The voice was smarmy. 'Please accept my most sincere apologies for taking your car again so soon, Doña Alicia. One of the new lads was a little too keen. You'll find it in the usual place. There'll be no charge.' Then he hung up on me before I could think of a suitable retort.

When I told her what he'd said, Consuelo's response was typical. 'There you are,' she said. 'It proves my point about the cartel. You must admit, darling, it's very decent of them to waive payment.' As if it was the money that mattered. 'I can take you down,' she went on.

'Oh no, thank you. You've already done more than enough. One of the men can drive me.'

'No, I insist. It won't even be out of my way. Oliver wants to explore the city centre, don't you?' He was leaning over the balustrade, gazing down at the city. He turned and nodded. 'I'm expected at the club,' she explained with a little smirk to me. 'You know, all the arrangements for the disco.'

I managed to repress my shudder at her nicely aimed double reminder: that our elegant club has sunk to holding discos – discos! – and what she would really be up to. It seemed best not to rise. The afternoon held distinct possibilities, if I cared to exploit them. And why not?

I phoned Eduardo. He was delighted. Naturally. 'That is a relief, my love,' he said. 'I've got an important meeting this afternoon. I had hoped to take my client for a drink at the club afterwards. Would you mind terribly?'

Sometimes you have to give a little if you're going to gain anything in the way of a reward for yourself. 'We've nothing else on this evening,' I pointed out, unnecessarily. 'Why don't you make it dinner?'

'If you're sure you don't mind.'

'You go ahead. Especially as it's such an important client.'

I had what was left of the afternoon and the whole evening to play with: plenty of time for what I had in mind. In the car we discussed the most interesting sights Oliver should see.

'La Casona,' I said suddenly, all innocence. 'Of course. You really must see Don Rigoberto's birthplace. Don't you agree, Consuelo?' I don't make a habit of bringing up my illustrious forebears in conversation, but sometimes, with Consuelo, I can't resist the temptation to watch her being torn between envy and the chance of reflected glory.

'You've heard of our founding father, Don Rigoberto, Oliver?' she said.

'Yes.'

'Alicia's a direct descendant, you know.' Aha!

Oliver fumbled for a suitable response in Spanish. 'I am honoured, therefore,' was what he came up with. Perfect.

'Bravo!' I said.

Consuelo was not amused. 'Don Rigoberto's house is open to the public. It's been restored and has a little museum. But you can't get there on your own. It's quite a way out of town. I might be able to take you tomorrow – no, the day after perhaps, if you're really interested.'

'Why don't I, Consuelo?' I said. 'You're always so busy.'

She managed to paste on a smile. 'That would be too much to ask.'

'But Eduardo's tied up this evening, as you know. So I'm at a loose end. Let me take the boy off your hands. It would be a pleasure, really.'

I read a *touché* in her expression. She talked through the mirror to Oliver, who was in the back this time. 'What do you think?'

He clearly wasn't sure how to reply. Now was the time

for my trump card: 'What day is it? Isn't it Thursday?'

'Yes, why?' she said.

'Oh, good. The house isn't open on Thursdays, but I can go when I like. I could give you a private view, Oliver, with no risk of interruption by any of the few remaining tourists. We could buy some things before we set out and have a picnic supper there. Take some candles. Very romantic. Consuelo would probably be pleased to be able to stay on late at the club, with all those arrangements to make, wouldn't you, dear?' My turn for the knowing smile.

'What about your bodyguard?' she said slyly.

I was ready for that, too. 'I seem to have mislaid him. I'm sure I'll be safe with Oliver, though. Can you handle a weapon?'

He looked shocked. 'No, I'm afraid –' he stuttered.

'Never mind. I can,' I said quickly. 'That's settled then. What fun. It'll be like Rigoberto's assignation with Eugenia.'

Oliver didn't seem to know the legend.

'You tell him, Consuelo. I've had to tell the story so often, and you're the expert when it comes to passionate encounters,' I said. I was enjoying my advantage.

We were in the industrial part of town now, block after block of run-down or abandoned textile factories, on which the city once thrived. Who'd want to bother with all that when you can make easy millions turning green paste into white powder for export?

My car was in the factory car park as expected. It gleamed black and sleek in the centre of a desert of cracked concrete, hard white under the afternoon's overcast glare.

From a distance nothing was visible through the tinted windows, but as we drew up I could see the flowers. The car was stuffed with them, gaudy bouquets of gladiolis and tiger lilies squashing delicate sprays of freesias, common pink carnations and scarlet canna lilies jostling rare orchids from the west coast. It was as if someone had bundled in the entire contents of a flower shop, quite without discrimination.

Consuelo's glee was disgusting: 'Darling, how wonderful! What a perfectly charming gesture.'

It's hard to keep cool faced with such provocation. I gave up the leather-scented chill of the Cadillac for the dead heat outside, wrenched open the door of my car and started chucking out the flowers, reeling from the stench, while the telltale prickling at the back of my nose announced the onset of my hayfever.

Consuelo made great play with pretended concern about my well-being and suggested I call off the trip, thereby forcing me to go ahead. The road was a quagmire after the rains, my eyes and nose streamed and Oliver, solicitous and on his best behaviour, treated me like some rich maiden aunt from whom he hoped to inherit. A complete washout. All the skill it had required to set up, ruined by a few bunches of flowers. How could I have anticipated that?

And I handed it to her on a silver salver: the gift of hours of freedom with Eduardo in their love nest at the club. A trivial incident but symptomatic. The cartel has ripped up the barriers and let anyone into the game. Consuelo won, on the day. The barbarians always win in the end.

There's a serious test of my talents ahead, convincing Eduardo that the time has come: this is no longer a place for people like us. And in Madrid, even London – Stockholm for all I care – at least we could have the children home.

The Glumbo Glisae
Leon Blades

Ivan, who was born and grew up in Buenos Ayres, was quite familiar with the traditions and conventions of village life. He heard numerous stories about haunted houses, soucoyants – those evil women who flew at night and illuminated the skies with balls of fire; they sucked the blood from their victims' veins. Many mornings a depressed neighbour lifted her dress and Ivan's mother saw the blue mark on her leg. His mother then shook her head, disgusted by what she had seen, and distressed by the plight of her unfortunate neighbour, made the sign of the cross to keep the evil powers away from her.

It was on everybody's lips in Buenos Ayres about those horrible nocturnal visitors, the glumbo glisaes. Young men whose affiliation was with the devil forced their way into people's homes and corrupted their young daughters. As you walked the only main road, you saw dried cactus stems made into crosses suspended at windows. Ivan knew some stories about ghosts, witches and witchcraft which he believed; others he dismissed as pure fantasy, the beliefs of superstitious people whose fear of the dark tropical nights allowed their imagination to play tricks upon them. He remembered the night when he was a boy, ten years old. He and his brother were returning home from a visit to their grandmother and a black cat followed them. It walked behind and mewed; they tried to drive the animal away but the cat refused to run into the bushes. They concluded that it wasn't a real animal, it was a ghost. They began reciting the Magnificat Prayer, for they had heard the elders say there was no stronger prayer to keep away evil spirits.

Every morning, old women with their heads wrapped with cloth, sad-faced, spoke to their neighbours about what had taken place the previous night. One morning Ivan's mother said to her neighbour, 'Ma Jones, how you look worried this morning.'

She said to Ivan's mother, 'You eh know it ha ah glumbo glisae does come and worry the young girls at night. Last night ah went to sleep worried, ah get up and take me Sharplay and say me prayers, then ah take me prayer book and ah read the Magnificat. Ah went to sleep, ah dream a man tell me to get up and go in Ruby's room now. Ah get up and tiptoe in Ruby's room. Ah see a brown skin man naked as he was born sleeping in Ruby's bed.'

'Way you do, Ma Jones?' Ivan's mother asked.

'Ah bawl hard, you eh hear? Doh tell me all you does sleep so hard. If you see people come in de house they say they think Mr Jones dead.'

'You mean de young man and dem eh ha notten to do but to read bad book and go round interfering with people's daughters in de night.'

'Ma Johnson, you doh know how dem young boys in Buenos Ayres worthless, they won't look for work, dress nice. That young girl could see them and like them, they could come and court and get married. They only thiefing and reading de Lawrence book. Ah hear dey does read one dat does make dem turn all kind of beast, they call the *Seven Keys to Power*.'

Ivan's mother said, 'Yes, Ma Jones, ah hear bout dat book. Me frien' Tommy start reading that book, 'e frien' lend 'im it. He read one night until 'e reach a place way dey say stop, 'e still reading, 'e hear ah noise, 'e see ah skeleton in broad white sheet come before him. 'E drop de book and bawl. Dat night 'e mother and dem hear chain pulling round the house, nobody could sleep. The next morning she get up and make tea, the tea turn molasses. The woman one Sunday cook she nice crab and calaboo with beef and stew, pigeon peas. When it was twelve o'clock de whole pot ah food smell ah idoform. She ha to throw way de food.

'As for she son, every day twelve o'clock the boy would run and scream running to the pond to drown 'e self. Big strong man used to ha hold down the boy.'

Ma Jones said, 'She ha time to worry she self. Ah would ha ley 'im drown, any ah me child go and deal with de devil, ah throw dem out boy or girl.'

Ivan's mother continued, 'She dream one night ah tall red man tell she 'e want ah soul. She get up dat morning worried, she husband take in sick, de next week de man dead. The man always strong and healthy. The boy turn stupid, always walking the road, gazing the sky.'

'It good for him,' Ma Jones said. 'Dem so they must talk the wicked things they do before they dead.'

All the stories about glumbo glisaes on the rampage at nights – but Ivan, now twenty-two years old, always boasted to his friends about his romance. As far as Ivan was concerned, whether those stories were true or not, he'd had experiences in the night that few young men in Buenos Ayres could speak about. He would sit on the bridge with his friends until it was twelve p.m. Then he would bid his friends goodbye and make his way to Mr Nevenson's house where he threw pebbles at the window. Mr Nevenson's pretty daughter Norma opened the window, then switched on a flashlight. In the illumination she saw Ivan's brown face, smiling. She fetched a rope and let it down. He climbed into the house and slept with her.

The Nevensons and the Johnsons did not agree. The Nevensons, who were landowners in Buenos Ayres, ordered their employees to kill the villagers, goats and fowl that strayed onto their estate. Most of the villagers rented small plots of land from the Nevensons. On these plots they built their thatched-roof houses and planted vegetables in their kitchen gardens. Most people in Buenos Ayres did not like the attitude of the Nevensons but they feared them. They were powerful and tyrannical landowners.

Whenever Ivan's mother's pigs, goats or fowl strayed on Mr Nevenson's estate, if his employees killed any of the animals, she would rush down the road, her tattered clothes and apron flying in the breeze, perspiration running down her ebony face. As she rushed to Mr Nevenson's house, she swore every abusive word known in the Trinidad dialect. The women would leave their washing and ironing to witness the scene. Men doing road repairs seemed happy; they smiled as they witnessed the quarrel between an aggressive Mrs Johnson and the Nevensons. The Nevensons considered themselves respectable people and did not like the idea of Mrs Johnson, who was known to be a vulgar woman, quarrelling with them. The villagers enjoyed this spectacle for they liked the courage of Mrs Johnson who opposed the Nevensons' tyranny. Whenever she was cursing the Nevensons, she'd lift up her clothes, exposing her underwear to an embarrassed Mr and Mrs Nevenson. The crowd of people gathered at the roadside would then give a loud outburst of laughter.

Mrs Nevenson, a tall brown woman, was very proud. The villagers accused her of behaving like a white woman. When Norma Nevenson was a child her parents forbade her to play with the villagers' children. They told her these stray-away children had nothing good to tell her. Her playmates were children who lived in other villages, whose parents were civil servants in the county or clerical workers with the oil company.

Mr Nevenson was the president of the village friendly society and Mrs Nevenson the secretary treasurer. Almost all the residents of Buenos Ayres belonged to the society. Most of them were peasant farmers; others were employed in the local quarry. They considered it their duty to pay their dues. If they kept up to date with their subscriptions, they received benefits whenever they were ill, and as the people became ill regularly in Buenos Ayres because of the poor diet, the sacrifice was worth it. When any member died, their relations received money and then they purchased a decent coffin from a funeral agency in the town of San Fernando and also a hired hearse which transported the corpse to the village cemetery.

On Sunday evenings, Ivan and his friends stood by the roadside. They talked and laughed as they amused themselves with local jokes. Old women in long white dresses, beads strung around their necks, talked solemnly to each other. 'Ah ha to pay me society card because when ah dead, ah doh want dem bury me like a pauper.' They would say, 'Respect the old ladies,' if the young men told any smutty jokes.

Mr and Mrs Nevenson seemed to be officials in the friendly society for life. Most villagers, especially the young people, never knew anyone else who held these offices. They behaved as if they owned the friendly society. There were annual elections but only the old people, the majority of them women, would attend on that date. Those people were loyal to the Nevensons and voted them back into office. The young people scarcely attended any meetings; they paid their dues every Thursday to Mrs Nevenson who entered and initialled the sums on the printed columns on their society cards. She recorded the subscriptions in her book.

Whenever Ivan's mother visited, Mrs Nevenson, with a frown upon her face, looked at her over her tortoiseshell glasses and muttered in a barely audible voice: 'You owe thirty cents for twelve weeks, that would bring the total to $3.60, which would make you financial.' She had contempt for her, but was careful how she spoke to Mrs Johnson who would take offence at any sign of arrogance, shouting loudly, 'Listen, woman, listen,' and pointing her right middle finger as if to stick out her eyes.

The fear of glumbo glisaes continued in Buenos Ayres. Parents of teenage daughters took every precaution that these evil men did not enter their homes. The scene most mornings: neighbours sharing experiences, worried parents inspecting their young daughters. They shuddered with the thought that prospective husbands would refuse to ask for their daughters' hands in marriage when they found the girls were not virgins. For, simple as life was in Buenos Ayres, these things mattered a lot to the villagers. There were no cinemas, no public sports ground. Teenage boys and young men stood by the roadside, made jokes and admired the shapes of young women. Girls were forbidden by their parents to stand and speak with the boys at the roadside. They believed earnestly that such behaviour was bad, that people would question the girls' morals.

Friends of the families who visited the various homes, when shown around the houses, noticed in the girls' rooms small madonnas, prayer books opened to the Magnificat Prayer, tiny strips of palm leaves made into crosses on the pages of the books. Every morning anxious parents looked at their daughters carefully to see if anything was wrong. The Nevensons, although they belonged to the Roman Catholic Church, as did most residents in Buenos Ayres, never spoke to anyone about glumbo glisaes. There was never a hint in their conversation that they believed in witchcraft. Their daughter Norma was a student at St Joseph's Convent in San Fernando and it was their desire to send her abroad to study medicine. It was their aim that in future she would be the first woman medical practitioner from Buenos Ayres. On bright sunny Friday evenings, she walked the main road; her neat white bodice, blue tie and skirt flew in the breeze. The other girls who were primary-school dropouts looked at her with envy. On Norma's sixteenth birthday her parents gave a debutante party for her. Their guests were various civil servants in the county and clerical staff from the oil company.

A few of Ivan's close friends knew about his affair with Norma. On moonlit nights, when they sat on the bridge where they amused themselves with jokes, he discussed his romantic experiences with her. He explained everything in detail. His friends were thrilled to hear these stories. Many times he went into motion, demonstrating his sexual prowess. He was a hero: they saw him as defiling the arrogant Nevensons' daughter. To them, his mother was a heroine: she did not fear the Nevensons as other villagers, she opposed them, and the young men saw her as a courageous woman.

Whenever Ivan passed any of his close friends during the course of the day, some stood immediately to attention and saluted him. Others bowed in mock obeisance. These acts were gestures of respect to the great man. They made Ivan feel happy and he only desired to carry on his affair with Norma.

The Cambridge school certificate results were published. Norma received a grade one pass. Her parents were thrilled when they heard the news. The dream they cherished that their only daughter would pursue her studies became real. Two more years at the Convent, with a higher certificate, and she would have the entrance requirements for most British and Commonwealth universities.

During the course of that week, curious villagers noticed cars and bicycles parked outside the Nevensons' home. Their friends visited and congratulated them on their daughter's success. Friday and Saturday nights, the Nevensons celebrated; there was music and dancing. The villagers stood at the roadside; they envied the men they saw in well-fitted, tailored suits and ladies dressed in fine silks, their jewellery glittering in the dark night as they made their way into the Nevensons' home. That Sunday, relations and friends had dinner with the Nevensons, it was a small feast. They seemed to be generous that week, although the villagers often thought of them as wicked people. The Nevensons thought providence was in their favour. They were landlords; they were also the two principal officers in the friendly society. Their only daughter was successful in her exams.

Ivan heard about Norma's examination success. He desired to sleep with her at the earliest opportunity to increase his prestige among the boys. Norma wrote on a slip of paper that he should not attempt any visit that week. She dropped the crumpled paper at his feet as she walked past him one evening with a friend. He stood relaxed at the roadside, grazing his goat. She desired to keep their affair a secret; her parents would have gone berserk if they knew she had a relationship with any young man in Buenos Ayres, especially the vulgar Mrs Johnson's son. He read the note, he thought it was cowardice on her part – their stunt had worked successfully in the past. He thought there was nothing that she should be afraid of. He hadn't slept with her for a week, and he should have a new experience to tell his friends.

That night he sat on the bridge with them. They talked about cinema films. The light of the full moon appeared above the trees. His friends left and went to their homes. Ivan sat alone on the bridge. He looked in the distance and saw a car parked in the entrance of the Nevensons' house. He knew they had visitors, but thought maybe Norma was in bed reading her novels or romance magazines. He went to the house and threw a pebble on the window. There was no response. He went to the gate and peeped inside. He saw Norma and her parents with their friends talking and laughing. He thought about going home but, to him, that was accepting defeat. He looked at the house once more and saw a ladder by Norma's bedroom window. He entered the yard quietly; he climbed the ladder. He shook as he heard the sound of a vehicle approaching. He hurriedly stepped on the bed in Norma's room and was happy that he had made no noise. Then he crouched under the bed to await Norma's entry. The visitors said goodbye and goodnight; a voice said: 'Keep up the good work at the Convent, you eh know how your mother and father want to see you go away and come back a doctor.'

He heard footsteps coming in the direction of the room. To him, all was well: Norma was on her way to bed. Norma entered the room. Ivan touched her left foot as a signal that he was there. She screamed hysterically and her parents rushed into the room. Norma pointed under the bed, she was trembling with fright. Mr Nevenson looked, he saw Ivan trembling too. He flew into a rage, screaming: 'Way you doing here, man?' Mrs Nevenson picked up a broom, hit Ivan and screamed loudly for help. Norma stood there, shocked by it all.

A crowd of people gathered on the roadside – a glumbo glisae was caught. People fought each other to get a glimpse of the culprit. They recognized Ivan. Old women said: 'Oh, God, it eh Ivan, Ma Johnson's son.' His mother heard the noise; someone shouted: 'Ma Johnson, get up, they catch ah glumbo glisae in Nevenson and dem house.' Mrs Johnson hurriedly rushed out of bed and ran down the street. She saw her son being beaten and spat upon. An old woman said: 'Ah good-looking boy like dat doing this thing.'

Mrs Johnson broke down, she cried loudly. The people ignored her; her son was an evil young man who had committed an atrocious crime against a young woman. The rest of them did not like the Nevensons, but they reasoned it could have happened to one of their own daughters.

The Nevensons saw a subdued Mrs Johnson as she wept bitterly. Her son was caught in their daughter's room and the police were called. The police sergeant fabricated a charge – breaking and entering with intent to steal – for there was no law in the British colony of Trinidad and Tobago that recognized the existence of a glumbo glisae. Ivan was arrested and taken to the police station.

Next morning, men on their way to work in the oil company spread the news: 'Ah glumbo glisae was caught in the night in Buenos Ayres.'

On Ivan's way to court in the police van, old women stood at the roadside and shouted abuse: inside the moving vehicle, battered and bruised, his head slumped between his shoulders, this simple thought plagued him. He was known to the people of Buenos Ayres and neighbouring villages as a glumbo glisae, a culprit who deserved no sympathy.

Heart Trouble
Gaynor Arnold

My mother's collar had rain on it. Perfectly circular beads of rain. On the black coat she always hated wearing. 'It reminds me of death,' she'd said when she brought it home on appro. But Dad and I had said it looked nice, with its swagger back, its stylish yoke, so she gave in, and hung it up in the wardrobe. But she pulled a face every time she put it on: 'Dull old thing.'

She liked bright colours. She had an appetite for life – singing, dancing, acting the fool. Everyone said she looked young for her age.

But not now. She looked a hundred years old, now. And black *didn't* suit her. She stood at the front door, her eyes small, screwed up, staring inward. 'Sorry to ring the bell, love. I've forgotten my key.'

She'd just come back from the hospital, seeing Dad again. Everything was supposed to be all right. The oper-ation had been a success, and she'd told me I needn't bother to visit any more. But I didn't like what her face was saying to me, now.

'How is he, then?'

The calls came from behind me. The family had the kitchen door open. I could hear the sound of frying, Uncle Ron's radio, the *Light Programme*.

She kissed me, wet collar rubbing my cheek: 'Has she had her tea?'

I turned to see Gran wiping her hands on her apron, patting her secret Woodbines in the pocket, her thin old wedding ring loose on her bony finger. 'I gave her a bit of bread and butter, but she wanted to wait for you.'

Mam took off her coat. It looked heavy and dull as she hung it over the banister. 'I think I've got some soup. Something, anyway.' She slumped; her hands still in the folds of the coat.

'Come on! How is he?' Uncle Ron shouted down the passage, sports page in hand.

'I've got to ring them later. They said to come home. There was nothing I could do.'

'I knew there'd be something. It was like this with my Frank.' Auntie May's head was in the kitchen doorway now, curlers under chiffon scarf. Gran pushed past her: 'My legs. I've got to sit down if it kills me. And your Frank was years ago. Things have come on since then.'

'Bloody women,' said Uncle Ron, and disappeared out the back, seeing to his sausages.

'You won't have to go back, will you?' I didn't like it when Mam went out in the evening – although Gran would let me watch what I liked on television. I wanted to go with her, but the hospital was two long bus rides away and I knew I'd feel sick. Sometimes I *was* sick, throwing up the minute I got off the bus. Mam said it wasn't worth it.

'I don't know, love. It depends what they say. Dad's not so good just now.'

I wanted her to stay home. After all, the operation had been a success. The doctors would look after him. Why did she need to go? I didn't think about Dad. It was Mam I needed to be there with me; Mam who kept a watch on my whole life – plaited my hair, took me shopping, sent me out to play when the weather was nice, worried about me being warm enough without my cardigan, made sure I had my mac when it looked like rain. Without her, there was a hole in my life.

Dad was more distant. He'd spend his evenings sitting in the armchair reading the *South Wales Echo*, or tinkering with the innards of a watch, his black eyepiece monocled fiercely in his right eye, tweezers in hand. He was irritable if disturbed. On Sundays he'd fiddle about in the only bit of our garden that got any sun, tying up zinnias and asters, checking for slugs. On his days off he'd spend the afternoon in the cellar developing and printing our summer snaps: Ilfracombe, the bandstand talent competition, the harbour full of boats – until my mother told him to come up before he froze to death. When he came up his fingers would be white, and my mother would start on him: 'Why do you keep on doing it? That damp old place? You know it does you no good.' And she'd chafe his fingers and make him sit down and hold a cup of tea bowled in his large hands. 'Stubborn as hell, you are.'

And quiet, too. My dad was known for being quiet. Conversation was my mother's domain; she had words enough for two. But he'd hug me and give me a kiss, and sometimes he'd show things to me, explain them, like the piston engines on the Campbell's paddle steamers, and how to build a proper three-tier sandcastle. I loved him, of course – because loving him was unquestionable, best in the world, next to Mam. But his being away made little difference to my days. Except making playground talk more interesting: 'My dad's got a bad heart. He's having a New Operation.' I felt pleased to have something new to tell them. We kids loved everything new, everything bright and clean and modern. As we dawdled home along Albany Road, we took excited detours around the new British Home Stores with its pastel flooring, plastic fittings and enormous plate glass windows – and turned up our noses at Woolworth's dark wooden counters and splintery floors. We watched with joy as our houses grew brighter with jazzy curtains, mix-and-match wallpaper and (if we could afford it) the picture of a Chinese woman all done in green. We adored television and *Quatermass* and the progress of science. We hated anything old-fashioned.

The hospital at Llandough was new. At least it seemed new, compared with the tall, church-like Infirmary where I'd gone to have the stitches in my forehead just the year before. The first few visits there had been exciting. I felt important, going all that way, walking along the drive with the grown-ups, my mother hissing quietly at me, 'Remember to say you're twelve!' But I hated the journey, juddering along in the smelly *Western Welsh* diesel, trying to gulp fresh air from the window as the bus twisted and turned up the hill away from Cardiff.

And the visit itself started to be less interesting – me sitting night after night by the bedside with the stiff white coverlet at eye-level, and the whispering of hushed voices all around the ward. I'd listen to my mother talking – her raconteur style, imitating voices, the arguments of Uncle Ron and Auntie May, the quirks of the customers at the shop, all the people who sent good wishes. I would smile, not knowing what to say. He'd make an effort: 'How's school?' and I'd tell him we were doing a puppet play Mr Williams had written about the women of Fishguard. And that Andrea Jenkins had the main part because she had a loud voice, and other kids had parts because they had good puppets. But that I'd helped to paint the scenery. He'd pat my hand: 'Good girl.' Then we'd pause, no hooks of small talk between us. Sometimes I'd read a book. (He'd taken a photo of me reading like that, sitting on my own on the deck of the *Bristol Queen*, absorbed in Enid Blyton while the sea washed over the rail.) But really I was hoping to be in time for a bit of television when we got back. I'd kiss him goodbye as soon as the bell rang, anxious to get the bus.

And now something was wrong. I couldn't understand it. After the operation he'd been fine. 'He'll be all right, you'll see,' Gran kept saying to Mam. Saying it over and over again as she laid the cloth and put out the plates: 'He'll be all right. He'll be all right.'

Tea was quick; devilled ham sandwiches. Mam cut herself on the tin and cried all over the plaster. When we'd cleared away, she crossed the road to ring from the phone box on the corner, came back not looking at me and mouthing over my head: 'They think I'd better go back.' She asked Uncle Ron to go with her. As a rule she'd never go anywhere with him. He was a bit touched, she said, and liable to make a scene. It was all right for him to pick rows at home, but you kept away from him outside because he'd shout and show you up. But now she was asking him, and he was saying, 'All right, love,' and looking serious like a normal person. Mam said she'd already rung for Glamtax, not to waste time.

We only ever had taxis to get to the Pier Head to catch the boat for holidays. I had this feeling in my stomach like before a ballet exam, or going back to school. Horrible, but exciting too. 'Can I come?' I said, following Mam around as she put things in her bag. Mam kept hugging me and saying, no, it would be all right, I'd be better staying with Gran, Dad would understand. She put on her coat. It made her look suddenly grey.

The taxi arrived – a man in dark red uniform and cap – and I saw Mrs Marks next door holding back the curtain to see what was going on. We stood on the front step, waved them off, Auntie May going on about Frank that last time, and Gran whispering, 'Quiet, you. Think about the child.'

I stayed up late, watching a film about a tap dancer with

a ribbon in her hair and a tiny cupid-bow mouth. And a blonde friend who talked fast and smoked, and wore a fox fur round her shoulders. And then hundreds of smiling dancers marching out of nowhere on a vast shiny stage with a boom of co-ordinated feet.

'Stay home tomorrow,' said Gran, which was another treat. She let me sleep in her feather bed, which dipped in the middle.

When I woke up, Mam hadn't come home. Gran said no news was good news, and gave me toast and Marmite. Then Uncle Ivor (not my real uncle, just a friend of Auntie May's) came knocking on the door with a message from Mrs Rice across the road who had a phone and was always willing to take a call. 'Sticking her nose in, mind you,' said Uncle Ivor, heading for the kitchen. 'But you can't complain.' They shut the kitchen door, shut me out, but I hung over the banister, trying to catch the words. No words, only the sudden wail. I galloped up the stairs two at a time, heading away from them. I knew they'd have to come and tell me. Sit me down like David Copperfield to give me the news. I waited in my bedroom, in the little armchair Dad had made, drawing doctors and nurses, patients in bed. And coffins and crosses and graves. Plenty of shading, thick 2B pencil. I listened for the rattle of the kitchen door as I built up the shadows.

It was Auntie May who came, knocking on my door like a servant in a play – but not knowing her lines, and crying all the time. She said she'd come to say my daddy was in heaven. She was holding her best white prayer book with the shiny cover. I'd been asking her for weeks if I could have it, and she'd said no, not until you're grown up. She handed it to me now.

She tried to say something more, but I told her to leave me alone. That's what people said in plays and films. *Leave me alone!* I threw myself down on the bed as she closed the door, and writhed around in grief on the shiny green eiderdown. The prayer book slid sideways and fell open onto the rug. The bookmark fell out so I could see the picture of the Infant Jesus, swaddled like a rolled-up parcel, halo curling round his head like a giant turban. I looked at it covertly through my tears. The halo was interesting. I thought of copying it in my new drawing book, shaded to look more shiny round the edge.

At dinnertime, Pat and Jenny came from school, wondering where I'd been. Laughing up the path, expecting influenza or a cold. Standing on the front tiles, ringing the bell.

I told Gran I'd answer the door. I felt important, and wished I had a black dress with a veil like a Victorian orphan, not a tartan skirt with straps and a Fair Isle cardigan with a button off. But, opening the door and seeing their smiles, their questioning faces, finding I couldn't say a word, and starting to cry. Uncle Ivor, temporary man of the house, took over, said the necessary words in a whisper, and: 'Tell the school, will you, girls? Save us going down.' They ran off, sad and gleeful, hoods up against the rain.

Not much for dinner. Bread, and Gran's sugary butter from the still-laid table. A bit of paste, some jam. I sat and drew whole funerals, paying special attention to shoes. (I'd just learned how to draw high heels and feet from the front.) I sat in the front window and watched for my mother. But she didn't come. 'She'll have a lot of things to sort out,' said Gran. Other people came, though. Relatives we only saw at Christmas. The neighbours. Friends who'd heard. Someone's daughter who was a nurse. Gran made tea and smoked in the back kitchen with the door open: 'I wish to God they'd all go. Fly their kites.'

Time dragged. I drew clocks. Uncle Ben and Auntie Flora came in see-through macs, she very jolly, discussing the sales and the new black wallpaper they were having in the bathroom: 'Well, you got to keep going.' He kept telling funny stories, glancing round for an audience, noticing my half-smile: 'Liked that one, did you, love? That's the way.'

The curate came in a wet cloak, had a cup of tea and went again. 'Hoping for something stronger,' said Gran. 'Well, he won't get it from me.' She swept up sugar from the tablecloth, threw it in the fire. It crackled and burned briefly blue. She stood, hand on the high mantelpiece, staring down.

Half past four. Still no Mam. No food for tea either. Nobody'd been shopping. Uncle Ivor fancied chitterlings and sent me off: 'Something for her to do.'

I stood in line on the sawdust floor at the pork butcher's, an orphaned child out in the Wide, Wide World, blinking back tears. The man behind the counter paused as he swung the bag closed by its corners. He looked in my face, kind for a minute: 'All right are you, love?'

The kindness was the worst thing. The tears rose but I nodded, brave. He gave me the bag. 'Two and six, then.'

I walked home slowly, head down. I splashed through the rainbow puddles on the pavements. I didn't care if I got my shoes wet. I wanted wet shoes. And wet hair. And a wet face. I trudged in a funeral procession, holding the wrapped chitterlings in front of me like a wreath. I went down the lane to the back of the house. And in through the back gate – wood swollen and needing a push. And past Dad's roses hanging their heads. And up the high kitchen step and into the house. With the parcel of meat in one hand and sixpence change in the other. Expecting Gran and Auntie May and Uncle Ivor round the kitchen table. But not expecting Mam. In a black coat that didn't suit her. With pale face and red eyes and rain on her collar. And the hot tears bursting from me as I leapt across the room.

Crosstown Traffic
Steve Bishop

Late out to the bus stop this morning, Mum's practically chasing me out of the house waving swimming gear at me, and when I get out onto the village high street, guess who's there? Yeah, *her*. Joanne Fox. Standing against the bus stop all moody, staring at the traffic drizzle by, her hair up in a ponytail, like the girls in the American mags Nigel brought back from Florida called *Cheerleaders' Beavers*. There's a big silver skull thing been graffitied on the shelter behind her.

I've seen her out with Terry Marsh, which is a bit scary. I've never seen her snog him or anything, but sometimes he comes to the bus stop and lights her fags for her. Maybe he's not her boyfriend. I hope not, the guy's a nutter.

The bus comes up behind us. She's trying to light a fag, but her lighter's broken. I hold mine out for her. Ta, she goes, looking at me with this sort of smile, like she knows a secret. I ask her if she's on her way to school, sounding like a total sad case. She just shrugs. She's wearing an Adidas tracksuit and trainers with a grey skirt. Maybe the skirt is just her way of saying she's wearing school uniform. I'm going to stop wearing uniform soon too. Part of my campaign under article 19 of the universal declaration of human rights. All her mates are like that too. They've got

119

faces that look like they're already grown up, and voices that are hard and gravelly. But not her, she's gorgeous. Baby skin and naturally curly hair. Her mates have all got acne and poodle perms. I think her mum's a prozzie. Her mate Karen's already got a kid. It's hard getting the lighter going in the breeze and I have to stand really close. I can hear her breathing.

The driver goes, D'you want this one or not? And she sort of looks at me in a way that makes me feel all weird, so I say, No, s'all right, and the bus wheezes off. I tell her we're going to be late, in a 'like I really give a shit' kind of way. She smiles again. I think I'm winning her over. Nick's bro says you've got to say things like 'come on baby light my fire' or 'if I said you had a beautiful body would you hold it against me?' if you want a girl to like you. He was taking the piss, like, but I'm feeling desperate for something clever or funny to say. The only jokes I can think of are the child molester ones Uncle Pete told me at Christmas, and girls think you're sick if you tell those. In the end I ask her if she likes George Michael, but she laughs and says, No, he's shite. I'm thinking I've fucked it completely when she goes, Do us a favour? So I go, Yeah. Dead cool, without even asking what.

– Get us ten B&H?
– They're lung bleeders . . . why don't you try Marlboro?
– OK then.

The school tie comes off. They know my face in the newsagent's and they think I'm sixteen cos I've been buying fags in there for a while. I'm getting quite a bit of stubble on my lip now, and even some on my chin. I was thinking of trying the offy in a few weeks. It's still quite a buzz buying fags when you're underage, even though no one really gives a shit. There're kids at our school dealing smack. I come back with the fags feeling quite good cos I've thought of something to tell her.

– You know the Marlboro ads with the guy on the horse, the Marlboro man?

– Yeah.

– You know he only started smoking because they gave him all these free fags for being on the adverts?

– Yeah?

– Yeah, then he died of lung cancer.

Her eyes open wide and she laughs. – That's fucking *great*. Poor bastard. Imagine that. Poetic justice or *what*?

I can't help grinning as I light her another fag. – Should've got you some matches while I was in there.

– Never mind, we've got your lighter.

Another bus turns up. It can't have been ten minutes since the last one; they must be making them more regular just to be annoying. We get on and she goes straight to the top at the back; me thinking, shit, I'm in trouble if anyone hard gets on, but fuck it, it's worth the risk. I'm trying to think of ways to get her back to my house without Mum and Dad knowing and without looking too obvious about everything.

– D'you know . . .

– Yeah?

– D'you all hang out round the park, like?

– Sometimes, just for a smoke and a drink. You should come along, it's a laugh.

– Aren't there loadsa fights and stuff?

– Not really, depends.

By the time the bus gets into town, it's already sort of assumed between us that we're not going to school today. I can always catch up some other time. Now she's looking bored again, so I tell her we should try and have an adventure.

– Yeah, she goes, have you got any money?

I explain about having to get my mum a birthday present. I was going to get her a cookery book. I've got

121

£20, she's got just over a fiver that was supposed to be for her school dinners but, she tells me, she never eats anyway.

In Smith's she's looking at *Cosmo* and the *Face*, features on prostitution, the porn industry, how to be a dirty thirty. I've got the book in my hands. It's £20 near enough. She tells me to go and ask if they've got *American Psycho* by Bret Easton Ellis.

– Why?

– Just do it.

– But I don't want . . .

– Don't worry, they haven't got it, I checked.

– Then why . . .

She rolls her eyes to the heavens so I go to the desk and ask for the book, wondering what she's up to. The cashier's not sure if the book's in stock or not and goes to have a look. The beeper goes off as Joanne rushes out of the shop clutching a book to her chest like an American high-school girl in a fifties movie. The security guard is old and a long way behind her. The cashier gives me a stern look over her glasses and then sees that I'm just as surprised as she is. Outside, Joanne is nowhere to be seen, so I wander over to the park to find her sitting on the roundabout smoking a fag.

– Da-daa! she says, holding the cookery book up like a trophy. I think that's probably a once-only type of stunt – the staff would recognize her a second time – but I don't want to kill the moment by telling her right now.

– Now we've got £25 to have a laugh with.

– We could go to a restaurant for lunch.

– Ha ha! Yeah, good one . . . I was thinking an offy.

– Oh . . . yeah, why not.

They don't know my face, especially not here in town. I look at least as old as some of the YTS lads painting the bus stops. They're all kids who got kicked out last year for failing their mock GCSEs or generally just being a pain in the butt. Some of them are Terry Marsh's pals. I'm surprised he got to stay. Must've got a C in CDT or something like that.

It's her idea to swap clothes.

– Can't exactly buy booze in a school uniform, can you? she says.

The shelter at the back of the park stinks of stale fags and piss and there's a piece of cucumber stuck on the wall from someone's sarnies – I fucking hate cucumber. But I put off the urge to retch and feel rewarded when Joanne starts taking her clothes off.

I think Mum would call her a brazen hussy. And then she'd remember about political correctness and say, but of course being brazen isn't really wrong as long as it doesn't demean anyone. I wonder how Joanne feels about what her mum does. It's one of those things. Everyone knows about it but no one says anything, except when girls want to slag her off behind her back. I wonder if Mum would like Joanne despite the brazen hussy bit. And then if she did, if she'd still like her if she knew what her mum does.

I'm out of my uniform, standing on the concrete at the back of the park in my underpants feeling like a complete twat and hoping no one's going to walk past and notice me when I glance over and get a look at her in her bra. She's got full-on woman's cleavage. I have to tear my eyes away before she catches me staring at her and decides that all men are scum and goes off in a huff or something.

The next time I look, I've got her trackie on. It's two sizes too small, but hopefully it'll make me look like a young scally not a schoolboy. She's wearing my school shirt and trousers, the shirt half open and billowing because my clothes are big and baggy on her and you can see bits of skin through the gaps in the buttons. She looks like a centrefold.

– All right, Foxy, ye slag! some scally shouts from over

the hedge. My chest tightens and I feel like I'm about to shit my load. It sounds just like Terry Marsh, but it's just one of his junior scallies. – Gives great fuckin' blow jobs, her, y'know, he shouts to me. I pretend to laugh so he won't start anything. Luckily, Joanne doesn't notice. She's gone all red and shouts, Fough off, Megsy, y'pervert! But he just laughs and walks off all cocky like he knows something.

– I never gave him a blow job, she says.

I tell her he's a sad pervert who obviously makes stuff up about girls because he's so plug ugly himself he can't get any.

I sort of feel dead sorry for her. It must be tough having a reputation that you've inherited from someone without necessarily deserving it yourself. We laugh a bit about what Megsy must get up to in the toilet. Then I ask if she wants beer or cider.

– Er, cider. Get some Merrydown. An' maybe some Martini as well.

She probably thinks Martini's sophisticated or something.

Going into the shop, I'm really nervous. My hands are all clammy and they slip on the metal door. I must look ridiculous; red-faced and sweaty, wearing a trackie two sizes too small for me. With a bit of luck they'll think I'm on my way back from a jog. Either that or a teenage alcoholic. I try the cider first and grab a bottle of Merrydown from the fridge.

– One fifty-nine, love.

She doesn't even look at me. You have to ask for anything stronger than wine from behind the counter.

– And a bottle of dry Martini as well, please, I say, trying not to let my voice crack and go all reedy. The old woman stumps up the goods, no questions asked.

I get back and she's still at the shelter. Her face lights up with a big smile when she sees me.

– You got it. You star! Give us a swig.

– Here . . . Can I have my clothes back now? This trackie's too small and it's chafing me nads.

She laughs and tells me how comfortable the shirt is. I tell her it's an old one. I'd be embarrassed to tell her how much it cost so I start unbuttoning it from the top. Then, when she puts her hands up in mock protest, from the bottom. Then she gives me this look that makes my dick turn to stone. She goes red and laughs and says, Coum on then.

We kiss. She's hot and smooth and tastes of cider. I put my hands in her curly hair and we lick each other's tongues gently, but not too gently. Her tits push into my chest and her hands are all over my back. I go to take her top off so I can get my hands inside her bra and she pushes them away.

– I'm norra slag y'know, she says.

I put my hands around her back and we kiss some more. After a while she pushes me off to swig at the cider again. We've drunk a load of it already. I haven't got too bad a capacity for booze, but I'm starting to feel a bit light-headed. I need to know more about her.

– D'you like Terry Marsh? I ask her.

– The fough 'as he got to do with anythin'?

– I dunno . . . I've seen you with him.

– Well, just so you know, I think he's the biggest pile of shite on the planet, but I didn't say that.

I can't resist a broad grin. She thinks he's a wanker, she likes me. Now I've just got to get her to come round to my house some time and we're in business.

– Are you a virgin? I ask her. Sometimes girls get all arsey when you ask them that, but she just laughs.

– Mind your own business, she says. – I told you I'm norra slag, that should be good enough.

I tell her I was just curious. She knocks back a load more cider. – You'll end up an alky, I say.

– Yeah well, better'n a bag'ead innit?

People she knows must say that to each other and actually mean it. – Can I ask you something dead personal?

– Yeah, I s'pose.

– Do you get a lot of hassle for what your mum does?

– Like that dick'ead just before?

– Yeah.

– Not too much. She takes a huge gulp of cider. – It's usually when someone's gorra problem with ya for some other reason, they might try an' use that against ya then. Mum keeps work totally separate from home, y'know.

– Good idea.

– She's norra slag either, she's just got problems. She's cool really. This one time there was some dirty old bloke came round the flat an' was tryin' te gerroff with me. Offered me a grand fer me arse.

– Cheeky fucker.

– Mum chased 'im down the road with a carving knife, sayin' she was gonna chop it off.

– Cool.

– She'd a done it as well.

I was going to say I'd like to meet her but the more I know, the more I don't want to. It's good to hear, but I don't think I want to be around that stuff. Fucking hard-core. I still want to see Joanne, though. Couple of years, she can get away. No reason why she should end up like that. But no wonder she acts so grown up. I used to think she was a snotty bitch and it was just a front to make people leave her alone. I lean over and we kiss again. She asks me what my mum is like.

– Dunno, just a mum really, I tell her, not wanting to talk about my mum while I'm snogging someone.

A colder breeze rustles over the park sending sand and crisp packets up into litter-whirlwinds. It's starting to get late. I can hear little kids out in the playground so they must either be going home or be outside for a break. The cider is all gone and the Martini gets opened as soon as she's sent the cider bottle sailing over the hedge. I wonder if I'll have to face any consequences for any of this. I usually get away with pretty well everything. We chat and snog and drink some more. She sends me to the shop for more fags and we talk about stuff like what's on TV and what clothes we like. I'm still in her trackie, which is way too small and I suddenly realize how uncomfortable I am.

– I'd really like my clothes back now, please, I tell her.

She gives me this funny look and says, All right then, like I've said something wrong or something. She pulls off the shirt, looking a bit peeved, but I can't help staring blatantly into her cleavage.

– Coum on, you as well, she goes. – I'm not sittin' here with nothin' on while you gerran eyeful.

I get up to take the trackie bottoms off, but I'm so dizzy from the Martini I can't stand up properly and I fall over with them still around my ankles. She stands up and goes, Coum on, I'll help ya.

We're both laughing. All I can see is her feet in those trainers, our laughter ringing off the shelter wall. She falls on top of me and we're kissing on the concrete, totally oblivious to the rest of the world. Over the other side of the park are the voices of kids just out of school. Three o'clock already. I get the trackie bottoms off dead quick, wrestling them over my shoes. It's like getting changed for gym when you're a kid and you're in a hurry and you get everything round the wrong way.

– Coum on, hurry up, she goes.

I tell her the last thing I want is to go stumbling out of the bushes with my trousers round my ankles and fall under the wheels of a pushchair.

– Yeah, that might take a bit of explaining.

– I don't think there's a universal human right to get you out of that one.

After a bit, I'm sat in my own clothes again. I've got to go home at some point, Mum will be expecting me. Joanne wants to hang out some more but I just can't take any more booze. I don't want to be so pissed I can't handle my parents. I tell her it's been a great day and we really must do this again some time. She laughs and tells me to come and find her later if I want. I give her a big grin, a final big snog and we're stumbling back to the bus stop to go back to the village.

I get back around five after lying on my back in one of the sand traps on the golf course for an hour. Mum looks round as I come in through the veranda; she's cooking, rushing around with steaming pots and rinsing things under the taps. Her friends will be here soon.

– Your face is very red, she says.

– I had to run for the bus.

– Nice of you to wash up your breakfast things this morning.

– I was in a hurry.

– For school? You did actually get there at some point, I take it?

– Yeah. Anyway, happy birthday.

I give her the book. It's looking slightly the worse for wear, but she smiles and says, Thanks, it's lovely, why don't you have a glass of champagne? I help myself to a glass and pretend to drink it so as not to raise any suspicion that I'm already pissed.

– Where've you been?

– Oh, just out and about really.

– I bet he's got himself a girlfriend, says Dad, being all 'I'm being cheeky'. Now my red face will be put down to embarrassment. – Ah, I knew it! he goes.

– So when do we get to meet her?

– Don't rush him, Cass, he'll bring her to meet us when he's ready, won't you?

– Am I really supposed to answer that?

They both think this is incredibly funny. I guess they've been at the booze too. Then they look at each other and give me this 'now we're going to talk about something serious' face.

– We want to have a word with you, Mum says and hands me a letter.

It's from school, addressed to them. It says I'm being excluded for repeated poorly explained absences and continued impudence to staff. Mum wants to know what I've got to say about it, so I tell her I think it's an amusing irony they're kicking me out of school for not going to school. Probably a bit flippant, but then I'm not really paying attention to what I say. My head's all swimmy and I feel like nothing matters and nothing can really touch me. But Mum's worried and Dad's cross.

– I thought we'd discussed all this, she says.

– *You* discussed it. *You* decided I wasn't having *my* intellect stimulated.

If I'd been less drunk I'd have told her that I'm sick of being told that school is a place of learning and education when anyone can see it's a prison that young people get sent to for the crime of being young.

I can see that Mum's about to well up and Dad's ready to start going on about how I have to do something with my life, so I make my excuses and get the fuck out the house. Joanne said she'd be around.

She's sitting on a bench with her mate Karen, the one with the baby. They're cooing over it and making stupid noises at it to make it do things. I sort of half wave, then make as if to go on past. I don't know if she'll want to acknowledge me or not in front of her friend, but then she gives me this big wave.

– I've still got half a bottle of Martini, she says, holding it up with a grin.

We leave Karen and her baby, and wander slowly across the village, the traffic muzzling through the smog and mist. After a bit we come to the bridleway that goes along by the side of the railway track, earth churned up with horses' hooves and bike wheels. The sky's all yellow and grey as the sun sets behind the clouds. It's not cold, but the warm drizzle and half-light make everything seem like a weird French film or something. We walk for ages. She steps round the piles of horse shit. Her Nike trainers must have cost £100. Maybe I should've been honest about the shirt.

Over a level crossing and across the lines there's a load of wagons in a siding. She rummages in her bag for a bit then comes out with this big silver spray can.

– Fucking hell! I try to make my surprise sound like enthusiasm as it comes out, all unexpected.

– Good innit? She beams. – I've done loadsa bus shelters and stuff. I thought trains'd be a laugh.

We go over the crossing and down the line past a sign that says: TRESPASSERS WILL BE PROSECUTED MAXIMUM FINE £200. She shakes up the can expertly and sprays a big silver swirl on the sign.

– Wonder what the penalty for that is? I say. She laughs again. I'm glad she likes my sense of humour. She seems to be having a good time. Another shake from the can and a mad squiggle goes down the side of one of the wagons.

– That's my tag, 'ere y'are, let's see yours.

I'm shaking a bit but don't let it show as I do a rough approximation of my name in squiggly, space-age writing. It's a bit dribbly where I've got too close to the wood, but it still looks pretty cool.

– Cool. Never seen that one before, she goes, ignoring the dribbles.

– Well, I don't do much, just a bit here and there. I'm gonna do some at school though.

– Hey, good idea. Do a classroom.

I go over to the next wagon and put a huge love heart. She looks at me as if to say, I don't believe you're that soft. Then I put an arrow through it and underneath:

MEGSY 4 JENNY TAYLOR 4 EVA

Jenny Taylor is sixteen and weighs sixteen stone. We're both laughing as she takes the can and puts:

TERRY MARSH IS A SHEEPSHAGGER

right next to it. She cracks open the bottle and we each take a big swig and kiss again. She's sexier than ever. I unzip her top and can feel her tits pressing into me. I feel my shirt getting unbuttoned and her hands all over my chest.

Then she points at the rails and goes, Let's go over there.

I'm not sure what to do for a second, it feels all wrong somehow. Everything's happening too fast. My head is swimming from the booze and she starts to pull her tracksuit off. She steps out of her trousers and pulls me over to the steel girders and bites my neck. You aren't supposed to do this. Any of it. I give her a love bite. The ground feels all slippery as we stand half-naked between the rails. Our ribs rattle together like train wheels over points.

She rests her neck on the inside rail, while her bum bumps up against the outer one. We hold and touch each other pushing against the hard cold metal, the oily stink of the stones. I push a finger into her and she gasps. Feeling inside her is so warm the rest of my hand feels cold. She pulls me on top of her and starts feeling for my cock. I can't quite believe we're actually going to do it on a railway track.

– Coum on, she says.

This is mad. I nearly come right away as I push it into her. She's so warm. I keep it together and relax a bit. We keep moving together, oil and dirt on my hands and all over her arms where I was stroking her. Her limbs are cold and wet; it's raining again. We grab each other's hair and kiss faces. I start to move deeper and faster; she rolls her hips and scrapes her nails gently up and down my back. She puts her legs up and starts moaning.

Underneath us there's a vibration. Slight but getting bigger. Then a sound. It's like electricity pylons walking the earth as giant robots. A train is coming. We both look down the tracks. They're dead straight here, you can see for miles and miles, and right on the horizon there's a tiny light moving slowly towards us.

She goes, It's a freight train, it won't be here for ages. Coum on, first one to move's a chicken.

There's no way I can finish now. Several hundred tons of metal are bearing down on me at God knows what speed. So I keep going, hoping that this means we can do it in a bedroom at the earliest opportunity. My brain is racing. Is this some mad initiation ritual? Has she done it before? Does she know it will make me frozen with fear? I don't know how near I'm supposed to let the train get before I move. I want to stop. The giants are stamping up and down next to us now, the twanging so loud you can hardly hear over it.

I shout, Come on, let's get off.

– Stay here and finish, don't be a fough'n mummy's boy.

I feel her tense up under me, hold me really tight, look down the track. The light's so bright it's dazzling. Images of our bloodstained clothes ripped and snagged down the line and scattered bits of meat. The clanging metal sound is replaced by rushing wind as the train blasts the air apart. I put my arms under her back and grip the nape of her neck. I pull myself over backwards with her still against my chest. The air explodes next to our heads in light and grinding metal as I slide down the stony bank on my back with her on top of me, stones ripping into my body. We land in brambles as wagon after wagon full of oil, gas, coal, grain, whatever, go lumbering past.

She stands up, exposed and skinny; she tries to pull bits of her clothes around her, shivering and blue. She gives me a hand up out of the brambles, not seeming to notice the stones under her feet. I feel some water on my arm and then some on my leg. I brush it off, but it comes back again. I look at my hand and it's all red. I've been badly scratched in the brambles. The stones have ripped my back apart and I must've pulled every muscle in my stomach.

Dumbly, we pick up our clothes. My soft, cream-coloured shirt now has mud and oil stains on it. As I put it on, the blood starts soaking through. The cloth fuses with broken skin, taking the edge off the horrible stinging of the scratches. It hurts to bend my knees as I put my oil-stained trousers on. She's way ahead of me, already dressed. She doesn't say anything, just sits looking vacantly down the tracks. Maybe I've done something wrong. I pull on my jacket over my shirt, which is ripped at the elbows and bloodstained down the arms and back. I go over and put my arms around her and she softens into me, squeezing my sides.

– Chicken, she says.

We walk back arm in arm in an easy silence. We're both wasted. My back is killing me. But she's bound to want to go out with me now.

We wander back up to the road and I watch her disappear into the alley where the door to her mum's flat is. I look down at my clothes. They're completely ruined. People are staring at me. I look a total state. Mum's going to freak as soon as she sees me.

I look up and my heart misses a beat in terror. Terry Marsh and Megsy are strolling up the street towards me, drinking Special Brew. My legs hurt so much I can't run, so

I just keep on walking and hope they won't notice me. About ten yards off and they're staring right at me. I'm thinking, oh shit here we go, whatever they do can't be much more painful than falling down the embankment, and fortunately they see it my way cos they just laugh at me. Terry goes, I 'eard she goes like a train.

And they both walk off, falling over each other in hysterics. I don't give a shit, at least I didn't get punched. Thinking about Joanne again, I want to kiss her. I went to kiss her good night as she went home, but she just said, I'll see you some time, and walked over towards the alley without looking back. I suppose that's the way people like her do things.

Sinners

Barbara Holland

'What an idiot! Where does he think he is?'

'That water's so cold, it'll turn him to ice.'

The mocking continued as Rashid struggled to drag the hosepipe out into the small backyard, but he was determined to do it. It was July 1969, and the sun was pouring its heat over the web of back streets by the docks, dominating the usual Saturday bustle and making it unusually quiet for early afternoon. To the Pakistani men sitting on kitchen chairs in the yard it felt like a warm spring morning in the village, when people would be up early to take a walk along the narrow paths separating the fields, to see how high the wheat was growing and to chat to neighbours about the prospects for the crop.

Rashid had suddenly wanted to wash himself down in the open air, as he used to at least once a day under the hand pump in the mosque. And so, dressed only in his underpants, he ignored the jeers of his friends as he got the hosepipe set up and finally turned it on himself, shuddering as the cold streams of water sparkled round his head, washed the heat from his back and soothed his body like a massage.

He called to Bashir to turn off the tap in the kitchen and while he was gone he swiftly sat down on his chair to dry off. When Bashir returned he didn't mind, he was feeling restless. He lit a cigarette and after a moment's thought suggested to no one in particular, 'Let's go to Barry Island. That's where all the whites have gone. Why shouldn't we?'

'Pah! I know your game. You're only going to look at the women, God help you!'

Fazal, who had a small beard like a mullah, was always the one to bring God or the Prophet into everything. The others joked that he only grew his beard to save money on razor blades, but his reminders of the old rules could still make most of them feel uneasy. Bashir, though, was harder to disturb. He had worked as a sailor on oil tankers before settling in Britain in the mid-sixties, a few years back, and he had left his Islamic sense of sin behind in a fair number of ports.

'What do you know?' he challenged Fazal. 'You sit here talking, but you've seen nothing. It was God who made women nice, so why shouldn't we look?'

He turned to Afsar, who was rocking his chair and pretending not to listen.

'Afsar, you've not seen much yet, have you? You know, down on the beach it's not just their legs they uncover. You come! What else have you got to do?'

Afsar's chair stopped rocking. He was too embarrassed to show any interest in front of Fazal. Since his infancy, nineteen years ago, he had never seen a woman who was not covered from shoulder to ankle in a shalwar kameez suit. He remembered odd glimpses he'd had of his mother and aunts washing clothes, when sometimes their suits would get splashed and cling to the shape of their bodies. Before he'd left for Britain the men had whispered to him about what he would see there, about the bare legs and the shameless women. If you were lucky one might even go with you, for free. It seemed his chance had come, and he was too shy to take it.

He looked at his closest friend, Rashid, hoping for help. Rashid jumped up and shook the last drops of water off his legs.

'All right, we'll go. You come too, Afsar. We won't go too near. We'll keep to the other side of the road.'

Afsar was relieved, but as they left the yard the 'mullah' had to have the final word.

'Go then, you sinners. But God is nearer to you than your jugular, and God will be angry.'

It was all true about the shameless women, Afsar discovered, after a hot, sticky bus ride. The beach at Barry Island was full of them; you couldn't help but look. He was excited but afraid that someone would notice his excitement. His feet slipped awkwardly on the dry sand as he followed the others round the reddening sunbathers to the water's edge, where they stood and watched the near-naked swimmers splashing and jumping over the incoming ripples. None of them could swim. In any case, they felt far too inhibited to strip off themselves, to get wet or even to stretch out on the sand. Back home, they used to laugh at stories of white people lying in the sun like cattle.

They had come to enjoy themselves, though, so they left the cool of the sea and went back up to the road behind the beach, where the shops and arcades leading to the funfair were gaudily painted, gypsy-style, like the trucks and buses that sped up and down the Grand Trunk Road from Peshawar to Lahore. After they'd spent more money on the fruit machines and the big rides than they usually parted with in a week, Bashir bought some cans of beer to share and they wandered back towards the beach, looking for a place to rest.

Afsar wanted to place his arms round the shoulders of his friends and saunter along, as the young men did in the village, but he sensed that it would attract unwelcome attention. The eyes that turned hurriedly away to avoid their presence, and the occasional pointed stare, had already made him feel uncomfortable. And then, Bashir and Rashid would keep on making startlingly loud comments about this or that woman's shape, which would surely have got them into fights if they'd been in English. Afsar stuck his hands into the pockets of the thick nylon trousers that clung to him, especially round the embarrassing bulge near his zip, and kept a pace behind the others.

Eventually they found a patch of grass away from the crowds and sat down cross-legged. They ripped open the cans and the warm, fizzy liquid eased their thirst, allowing them to relax at last. When he had emptied his can, Bashir wiped his mouth with the back of his hand and leaned back.

'So you see what life is like in England, eh, Afsar? See how different it is. People are free, not like back home.'

Afsar looked down at the limp grass, not knowing what to say. People here were free, more free even than the actresses in the Indian films, so free they seemed to have no morals at all. He remembered what the men returning home used to say, that in England there are three things you can't trust – your work, the weather and the women. He was beginning to see why.

'I know what you're thinking,' Bashir said. 'You're thinking about that fat one – everything wobbled when she turned over! We saw you looking, didn't we, Rashid?'

'Yes, that was the one for you. Shall we go and ask her out, Afsar, see what she says? You know, it doesn't matter if she has a husband. They don't mind here.'

As he wondered if this just might be true, if they did have some chance with the woman, the other two started laughing. They were worse than his uncles going on about the failure of his beard to sprout.

When Bashir calmed down he said, 'Well, Rashid, shall

we go to Top Rank tonight? What do you think? I've an itch on my palm. We could be in luck.'

Afsar looked at them, hoping they would explain. Rashid helped him out.

'It's where the whites go, to meet women. Decent women too. No paying.'

Rashid had only been to Top Rank once before, and though he'd been impressed by the way strangers could go right up to the women and even touch them while they danced, he'd not found the courage to approach any women himself. But the idea interested him. Perhaps it would be different with Bashir there too. 'All right, I'll come,' he said.

They started to discuss how to get Afsar back to the house. They both knew they stood the best chance of success if they went as a pair, like most of the women did. To be trailing an extra man, and such a new arrival as Afsar, could spoil everything. Afsar didn't protest. The spectacle of the beach and the unaccustomed effect of the beer had made him feel even more lonely and out of place. Placidly he let himself be put on the right bus, and directed home.

The house was empty. The warm evening had made it impossible for the men to sit at home and Afsar found them all, even Fazal, in the King's Head at the corner of the street. The door of the lounge bar was propped open with a brick, so the dusty air could give some relief to the drinkers sweltering inside.

They were the largest group in the pub and their frequent, loud laughter drew resentful glances from the other customers, particularly the single men standing up at the bar. Most of the other tables were occupied by middle-aged or older couples, busy with the week's gossip. The exception was the small table in the centre of the room, which was second home to Carol, well known in the pub for selling her sexual favours. Usually she came alone, but tonight she had with her a much younger woman, almost a girl, who had been carefully made up and dressed in a tight leather miniskirt for her first appearance in the pub.

Carol was anxious to make a good deal on her. When the barman called over, 'Who's yer friend then, Carol? Been here long?' she answered, 'Just arrived, love. From the valleys. Bit of a row at home. She's very, er . . . new. Untouched, like.'

'What's her name?'

'Julie. Give the man a smile, Julie.'

Julie looked up shyly, but seemed unable to think of a suitable throwaway remark. Carol was annoyed: she'd told the girl you had to chat to the punters, be nice – it was all part of the game. Sighing, she glanced around the room. She knew that the men at the bar would be a dead loss. Most of them were Saturday nighters, who spent the evening checking over their local area, just a pint in each pub then on to the next. Of the two regulars, Doug was a nancy boy and old Taff didn't approve of her, was rude sometimes. No, it seemed the best bet tonight was going to be the Pakis – she'd been with one or two of them before. At least Julie wouldn't have to talk. They'd sipped to the bottom of their glasses by now, so Carol got up and told Julie to wait: she'd soon get them filled up.

Afsar was warmly welcomed by his friends, and after he had shaken hands and explained knowingly that Bashir and Rashid were at Top Rank, he was sent to help Ali fetch a new round of drinks. Ali loudly ordered six pints bitter, two mild and one Coke, then leaned over the counter to whisper to the barman, 'Do like before – rum and Coke.' He grinned at Afsar as he said, 'Fazal's not being a good Moslem tonight.'

He sent Afsar off with the first four brimming glasses and was about to pay when Carol slid along the bar towards him.

'Hello there.'

'Hello,' he replied reluctantly. He could feel the eyes of the others on him. He had nothing against Carol – he knew Bashir had been with her and had said she was all right, wouldn't cheat you – but he thought she was a bit old for him.

'We're both having rum and Cokes, too – me and Julie.' Carol managed to get Ali to look in the direction of her friend, and noticed that she'd made an impression. Encouraged, she flapped the top of her low-cut T-shirt. 'Suppose your lot like it hot, like this?'

Ali didn't understand, but smiled politely and bought her the drinks, as a sign that he might be interested in Julie later on.

As he left her at the bar, Taff came up and spoke angrily. 'What d'you wanna be so friendly with them for? Filthy lot. All stink of curry.'

'You can fuck off, Taffy. You never buy me a rum and Coke.'

Taff ignored this. He was looking at Julie, his face showing not lust but sudden smugness, as if some penny had finally dropped. 'Where d'you say your new friend's from, then?'

'The valleys. What's it to you?'

'Nothin'.' He emptied his glass and hurried out.

As Afsar settled down in the shelter of his friends, he started to feel more like himself. It was on just such warm evenings in the village that they would gather by the well, to play cards and joke and pass round a tobacco-filled hookah. When the others started to make comments about his fruitless trip to the beach, he only smiled.

'So you didn't find anything, then? We could have told

141

you that it was a waste of time. No one will go with us.'

'You'll learn.'

'We were all new once,' Ali reassured him. 'Why, when I first came I was as thick as a young buffalo. When I was coming here, just off the aeroplane, I went to the railway station and asked for a ticket to Newport. "Which Newport?" asks the man. Says England has five Newports. A long queue behind me and all I knew was Newport!'

'That's nothing. You ask Karim about his first time. He got in the taxi at Heathrow, and the driver drove him straight here – thirty pounds it cost. Three weeks' wages. And you try asking him for a pint or a cigarette.'

They all joined in the raucous laughter, except Fazal. For some time, his small pointed beard had been rising and falling on his chest in time with his slow breathing. The loud noise made his eyes jerk open. With an effort he pushed himself up. 'I'm going back, to bed. I . . . I can't seem to stay awake.'

'No, don't go yet. Stay and have another Coke.'

'Stay till we all go. We won't be long. Those two women there might be coming too.'

Fazal managed to grasp the meaning of this and, offended, walked as steadily as he could towards the open door. They called after him:

'You can start making the chapattis.'

'Make a few more for them!'

As he reached the street he was almost pushed over by two men hurrying into the bar. Taff, wheezing with excitement, was leading a small but stocky man, whose tense anger was making the muscles of his upper arm bulge menacingly under his Aertex shirt.

'So there you are, my girl. What the hell are you doing here? I've been asking for you in every pub around. Get up, you're coming home.'

Julie burst into tears but did as she was told. Wisely

Carol didn't attempt to cling onto her, but the whole pub fell silent to enjoy the scene as she turned her anger onto Taff.

'That's just like you, you bastard. Can't you mind your own business for once? Fucking bastard!'

'Serves you right, you fuckin' whore,' he rejoined, and followed Julie and her father out the door.

The silence lasted another moment before a murmur of voices rose up. The scene, which Afsar and his friends had followed easily, gave them a sense of reassurance that for once things were as they should be.

'At least there are some real men in this country, some who care about their family's honour,' said Ali, and the rest agreed.

Carol did her best to settle down again, adjusting her T-shirt and smoothing her skirt. Feeling uncomfortable on her own, she went over to the bar and stood by Doug. As potential rivals they normally kept their distance from each other, but given her recent humiliation Doug was prepared to be generous.

'Never mind, love. You can't win 'em all.'

Carol sighed. 'Pretty though, weren't she? Not that you'd care much, you old faggot.'

Doug could accept this from Carol. He shook his head cheerfully and said, 'No . . . but we've another pretty new'un in tonight, over in the corner. Think I might just stroll over and be friendly, like.'

Leaving Carol with a double Bacardi, Doug went over to the corner table and managed to squeeze in next to Afsar. Most of the men already knew Doug and tolerated him as one of the few whites in the pub who would chat to them and buy them drinks. Doug, in his turn, liked the feeling of being included, of being part of their all-male group.

'Hello, sit down. You all right?'

'Hello, Doug. Got a drink? Got any friends tonight?'

'No, I'm free for the taking – open to offers.' He leaned towards Afsar. 'Well hello, darling. I haven't seen you before. Are you new here?' As Afsar looked blank and the others laughed, Doug turned away saying, 'He does look smashing, doesn't he? Such smooth cheeks.'

Afsar slowly realized what was going on. He was puzzled. Doug was so unlike those boys in the frontier area who, he'd been told, would spend the last years of their childhood as the close companion of an older, established man. No well-off Pathan would be without one, but back home such things were always talked of in whispers.

Afsar was saved from further compliments by the arrival of Bashir and Rashid. They pretended they'd had a great time, were all fixed up with two women for next week, but no one believed them. At the bar ordering drinks, Bashir was soon approached by Carol. Instead of rejoining the others he stayed there with her, whispering and laughing. Before long they left, his arm around her waist. He wasn't at all bothered about the remarks that followed them out the door, about how cheap she was and how he spent all his money on prostitutes, never sent any back home.

'She'll do it for pennies. And he'd go with anyone, a donkey even,' said Rashid, made sullen by his friend's desertion. 'She doesn't even like him. None of the whites do, they never wanted us here.'

He realized he was sitting next to Doug, who smiled at him amiably, not having understood a word. A crazy idea crept into him. When the barman called time he found himself saying, 'Doug, number seventeen, you come. Our house. Five minutes.'

'Number seventeen. OK, mate.'

Doug did not turn up in five minutes. Afsar, who was still learning, helped Rashid make the chapattis for all the men, while a large saucepan of spicy mutton was warming on the stove. When they'd made a big pile of chapattis, wrapped in a tea towel to keep them hot, they took the food through to the small back room. Settees and chairs were pulled into a rough circle and they ate companionably, laughing as they recalled Fazal's drunken departure and Carol's big disappointment. They'd forgotten about their invited guest and were rinsing their dishes at the sink when the doorbell rang.

'Oh no, it's him. Tell him to go away.'

'No, let him in. We'll have some fun.'

With fewer of them about, Rashid might well have invited Doug to his bed. He'd felt desperate enough earlier on, but now he didn't dare go about it openly. Too fed up to take part in their teasing, he decided to slip upstairs, to avoid seeing Doug. But when he reached his room he saw an opportunity too good to miss. He went back to the top of the stairs and called down, 'Doug, come up here. Somebody for you here.'

He showed him to the bed where Fazal was gently snoring. The rum had sent him into a deep sleep, but Doug's action in lifting the blanket and inserting a leg was enough to wake him. He jumped up as if bitten by a snake and ran to the light switch. When he saw the strange man sitting on his bed, he started moaning and cursing.

'Who has done this? Who could play such a trick? You sinners, all of you! Oh, my head, it's spinning.'

Hurt and angry, Doug fled down the stairs and out. Open-mouthed, Afsar watched as one by one his friends succumbed to a wave of shrill, anguished laughter.

Dance With Me

Michael Coverson

In those days, before Christmas 1979, when I was twenty-eight years old, most of my spare time was spent searching for Eddie, finding him, only to lose him again.

The night a woman I didn't know came to my door and invited me to a party that never took place, I'd just returned from trawling those half-dozen pubs in Sparkhill that I knew he occasionally used, not finding him, but then not really expecting to. After three days of looking, there was no sign of him anywhere. Not even the two pissheads crouched in a shop doorway out of the drizzle, a pair I'd known him to share his drink with, could remember the last time they'd seen him. Instead they just shook their heads, passed his name back and forward between them, an echo whispering.

By the time I decided to try his bedsit, the rain was coming down hard and the side streets were empty except for the odd passing car. Fairy lights flashed out the shape of artificial Christmas trees in bow windows. Once there, as I always did, I hammered on Eddie's door, shouted his name through the keyhole. If he was there, he didn't answer.

I gave up and went home.

I was running the comb through my hair, feeling the wet run down my neck, and trying to ignore the old man in the next room shouting at himself, when the knock came.

I can see her now: black dress, black top, black tights, black shoes, looking at me slightly disappointed as if I wasn't the person she'd expected to open the door.

'You look wet.' She moved her head slightly as if to get a better look at me and I remember the bare light bulb above her head made her cropped black hair shine that blue of a magpie's wing, lighting up one side of her face, allowing me to see lines around the eye. 'You look very wet.'

What's she come to complain about? was my first thought. They were like that, the other tenants: always moaning about each other, poking their noses where they weren't wanted. There was an Irishman, Willy, had the back room, overlooking the overgrown garden. His gripe was people leaving their washing on the line overnight.

But then she smiled. Behind her, post lay in a pile by the front door, letters for tenants long gone, free newspapers nobody ever read.

I said I hadn't seen her before.

She said, no, she'd just moved in, just a few days ago. Her voice was heavy smoker deep. She was attractive if you looked through the gloom hard enough. And then she invited me to her party that night.

'Nothing big. Drinks. Music. My way of getting to know people and getting pissed at the same time. Christmas, and that. I know it's short notice but I did knock a couple of times last night, only you must have been out.' She raised her eyebrows. 'Yes?'

'No,' I said.

The eyebrows relaxed. I tried to guess her age. Thirty-five? Forty? Older?

'Sure?'

'Yes. Sorry.' And I said something about being tired.

'Not for just an hour?'

I said no again.

And she said something like, 'Oh well, if you change your mind . . .' and shrugged as if she really couldn't care less whether I came or not, and I watched her climb the stairs into the darkness until she was gone.

Afterwards, I lay on the bed with the orange glow from the streetlamp outside over me and drank Carling and listened to the radio, a carol service, which made me think of Eddie and me as kids in the choir at St Chad's. Tuesday night practices in the Memorial Hall when we'd test each other on how many of the gold-painted names of the war dead we could remember from the dark wooden plaques which lined the walls. Sometimes, without thinking, I would search hopefully for my dad's name, even though I knew he was no more dead than Eddie or myself, but living somewhere else with the woman called Ruth who'd once worked in the greengrocer's on the corner of Berkeley Road. Five shillings we were paid for weddings. Now and again, Mum would come along, even though she didn't know the couple from Adam and Eve, sit right at the back of the church, just so she could listen to Eddie and me and the choir.

And then there's the Bible, cold and heavy as a damp-course brick; Gran's and Great-Gran's property before belonging to our mum. The Bible that lay like a part of night on the sideboard. The Bible we had to swear the truth on. The Bible she hit us across the back of the head with if we lied or went where we shouldn't have or back-chatted or asked about Dad. Things Eddie was always doing. The Bible hitting the back of his head, knocking him forward into furniture, the walls.

The front door slamming made my window rattle. As footsteps climbed the stairs, I wondered if someone had arrived early for the party. I could hear traffic hissing past in the rain and in the next room the old man came to the end of a coughing fit and began shouting again.

I have this memory of Eddie and me walking through dusty grass that came up to our waists. I am ten; he is thirteen. The air is warm and sticky. Cabbage whites flicker in front of us. Smoke from Tyseley factories smears the sky. Mum is in Dudley Road Hospital. There's something wrong with her: she is thin now and doesn't look like Mum. She looks like someone's gran. She hasn't got much hair left and her face has changed shape. Before going into hospital she was tired all the time; one morning she fell asleep over the sink. We didn't get fed, Eddie and me, and so we took to feeding ourselves, cooking our meals rather than waiting for her to wake up. Before going to school, we'd creep into her room, bend over and kiss her on the forehead.

And so, stepping through the grass on that afternoon some time in the school holidays, I can sense that the world is going to change, and I start to cry. The noise makes Eddie turn and stare at me in a strange way, like I'm someone he hasn't seen before, a stranger. He carries on and I follow, and we walk to the edge of the clay pit and stare down, and it's like staring into the earth's bellybutton.

After the carol service there was some talk followed by someone singing that song about chestnuts roasting in an open fire, something I've never seen. I switched off and threw the empty Carling can at the wall separating me from the old man. Then I thought about the woman upstairs and her party.

I hadn't been upstairs before that night. The lights were on a timer. No sooner had I reached the end of the first flight of stairs than I was standing there in the dark, clutching four cans of lukewarm lager, sweeping my hand over the cold plaster to feel for the plunger. Along the landing, strips of light showed under some of the doors. From behind one, a woman's voice said, 'Nothing changes, does it? Nothing at all.' A television blared in another room. Further along, I paused to listen to 'Like a Hurricane', Neil Young's glorious guitar solo sounding tinny through cheap speakers.

On the second landing, part of the ceiling around the light fitting had come down, laying bare a mess of wiring, laths of wood and cobwebs swinging stiffly in the draught. The smell of damp was stronger than ever and there were no lights or sounds coming from any of the rooms.

I stood by the window, looking out at the surface of the wet road where the reflections of streetlights appeared like unfinished pictures; at the huddle of figures in the bus shelter; at the hedges, shadowy lumps in the darkness.

Hers was the only room on the top floor. I stopped on the last stair and listened, unable to understand the silence. I wondered if no one had showed up, thought about turning round and going back down. I could drink the cans on my own, in my room; throw them at the wall when the old man got started. But then the door opened and the small landing lit up, so I could see the wallpaper, old and stained and scribbled on and missing in places, and she was standing there in the same clothes as earlier.

I offered the cans.

She stepped aside and I went in.

There I was, in her room, seeing the reflection in the window above the sink, her placing the four cans of lager on the draining board next to a bottle of Haig and two glasses, seeing her lean forward to pour two drinks. The room was warm and smelled of heated tomato soup – the dirty saucepan soaking in the sink, the water inside orange and scummy. There wasn't a single Christmas card on show. I remember the books on a shelf, but not the titles or authors. I remember how she concentrated on pouring the drinks.

'Others will be along soon,' she lied, handing me my drink before going over to an old-fashioned Dansette, which was on the table. After a few moments, there were some clicking sounds and Diana Ross began singing 'Ain't No Mountain High Enough'.

I put the glass to my mouth, tasted washing-up liquid before the downward burn of the whisky.

'Well.' She raised her glass. 'Merry Christmas.'

I said, 'Merry Christmas,' too, because I had to say something.

And she said, 'I'm glad you came.'

'I thought there might be more here.'

She smiled, very, very slowly, like she was determined to reveal just one tooth at a time. Then the smile turned into a laugh which stopped suddenly.

She asked me my name and repeated it when I told her, eyes closed, raising the glass with the whisky moving about inside it to her lips. 'Dave. Dave. David,' she said, quietly, and it struck me that I hadn't been called David since Mum died. She'd hated people calling me Dave, said it was lazy.

I asked the woman her name, but she ignored me.

All the time, she kept looking hard at me, as if trying to guess what I was thinking. Then she asked me what I did for a job. 'Work, David. What do you do?'

I told her about the warehouse. I told her about having to check in all the boxes that came off the lorries, make sure everything tallied with what was on the pink sheet. (I'd managed to wangle Eddie an interview there a few months after I'd started. Only he hadn't turned up and personnel told me not to bother them again with his name.) I said, 'It's boring, but it's a job. And I've got ten days off, Christmas. But I won't be there much longer. There's things I want to do.'

She nodded her head to the music. 'Tell me.'

So I told her about all the travelling I'd planned to do,

the countries I really had intended to see, and she mumbled about not wasting my life, and I said I wouldn't. And I remember I repeated that: I wouldn't.

The music stopped, but the turntable kept going round. I watched the arm lift, tremble, then descend. After a few moments, the record started up again and Ross's voice, which I've never been able to stand, bleated out from the hisses and scratches. I looked, but there didn't appear to be any other records.

The woman came towards me, holding the bottle. 'More?'

I could hear rain on the roof. I stood there, not knowing what to do. 'You must like Diana Ross,' I said.

She sat down on the edge of the bed, crossed her legs and lit a cigarette. There were scuffs on her shoes.

'Sit down,' she said. 'Don't look so lost.'

'I was just wondering where everybody else was.'

'They'll be here.'

There was one chair, pushed under the table. I pulled it out and sat down. The woman poured herself another drink and offered me the bottle. I looked around. The room was filled with the same type of junk-shop furniture as mine. A large scratch ran down the front of the wardrobe. The walls were painted white. Above the draining board hung a mirror; over the bed, a print of a kitten playing with a ball of wool. The rug in the centre of the floor was greasy and full of crumbs and ash. I imagined the woman standing on it in the morning, brushing her hair in the mirror, getting ready for wherever it was she worked. Her eyes had been closed as she swayed slightly to the music, but she opened them when I spoke.

'There's no one else coming, is there?'

'No,' she said.

'There's no party?'

'No.'

Her eyes closed again and she went back to moving with the music until it finished when there was silence while the arm went through the process of lifting and jerking about before dropping once more and the song began over again. I don't know why I didn't get up and go. Perhaps I wanted to see what would happen.

I asked her, hadn't she got anything else to listen to? But she ignored me, drained her glass, poured herself another. Then she went over and switched off the light. Her face was paler than ever in the darkness, a tiny moon in the room's night. She sat back down, her face changing shape as she moved her head, the shadows turning her young and then old, as if showing me her as she was and would be.

I looked out of the window above the sink into the darkness that had filled the room, drawing it into the night outside. Somewhere out there was Eddie.

'Had you just got in from work earlier when I called?'

I shook my head.

'Been for a walk in the rain, had you?'

I looked down into my glass and rolled the whisky round inside it. I imagined Eddie wandering the streets in the rain.

'I was looking for someone. I was looking for my brother.'

'Oh?'

'Eddie. My brother.'

'And did you find him?' she asked. 'Your brother.'

Again, I shook my head.

'Why were you looking for him? Is he lost?'

'In some ways.' I don't know why I used those words. But, immediately, I saw a look pass across her face and she nodded, as if understanding. And then, for a long while, we fell silent and drank our whiskies and that bloody music played over and over and on and on.

Then, out of the blue, she said: 'Shall I tell you something, David?'

I looked up.

'I'm actually married, you know. Me. This thing here, in this chair, with this drink.' She laughed to herself, a laugh that belonged in that room, on that evening with the rain coming down. 'Quite recently actually. Late starter, me. Met him at work. Knew straight away. You do, don't you? Well, anyway. Age difference didn't matter, not to me, at least. We didn't hang about. "Let's not wait, girl," he said. Famous last words.'

She gave a long, tired sigh. 'Traded me in a few months ago for a newer model. Everyone running around saying, "Told you so. You wouldn't listen."' She sat, perfectly still, her eyes staring down at the dirty rug for a while. Then she said, 'I'd stay awake so I could watch him sleeping.' She went quiet again and I wondered if she was imagining her husband asleep, their faces so close she could feel his breath warm on her cheek. Then she shook her head slightly as if to shake a memory out.

'Still,' she said, standing up so the glass fell from her lap and dropped to the floor, but didn't break. She came towards me, arms outstretched. 'Dance with me, David,' she said, quietly. 'Dance with me, before you go.'

So I did. I placed my hands on her hips and we swayed to that music I'd begun to hate, while outside the rain poured down onto the city in which Eddie was hiding somewhere. I moved my hands over her dress, her waist, her shoulders, all over. I stroked her hair. I could smell her sweat. I kissed her lips and saw tears in the corners of her eyes, but didn't care. I don't know how long we danced, that same song playing over and over, so that by the time we were on the bed, I knew not just the lyrics by heart but the precise moments when the needle would pick out the scratches and clicks on the record's surface.

When I'd finished I lay beside her, smelling all the smells coming off her, not quite sure why it was I felt ashamed. I could hear her breathing into the darkness. I wondered if she was sleeping, but I didn't want to speak in case she wasn't and began talking.

I got to my feet and zipped up my jeans. The record was going round but had stuck. It clicked over and over again. I crept quietly as I could to the door. But just as I turned the knob, her voice, quiet, a whisper, stopped me dead for a second.

'Night, night, David. I hope you find your brother.'

The old man in the next room was shouting at himself when I got back. I turned off the light, undressed, had a piss in the sink and climbed into bed. I switched on the radio and moved the dial: Meatloaf; Bowie; another carol service; a melancholy voice lamenting how materialistic Christmas had become. I settled on some classical stuff I didn't understand, someone playing the piano, simply because I found it relaxing and enjoyed the way it allowed my thoughts room to move about so that soon I started thinking about Dad leaving, and Mum sitting in the front room with her head in her hands for hours on end. I thought about the Christmas, the last one before Mum died, and Eddie and I had to go and live with Dad and greengrocer Ruth, who didn't want us and made sure we knew it before she left Dad as he'd left Mum. I thought about the transistor radio Mum bought Eddie that Christmas. Just a cheap thing, red and cream plastic with an earplug, like an old-fashioned hearing aid. I remember that in the dark cold we forgot about the rest of the presents, slid down into the bed and took it in turns to move through the stations. We heard snatches of music, words, someone laughing, music again, and always, in between, what sounded like electric storms raging some-where far out in outer space. The slightest touch on the dial meant the station was lost, chewed up by static. We'd get it back only to lose it again, give up, move on. Voices would fade, as if their owners were being dragged away from the microphone. Now and again, we picked up two stations at the same time, a pair of simultaneous and incomprehensible voices straining out of the speaker, an argument conducted in two different languages, or speech drowning in the swirling sea of a symphony. Finally, we came upon the sound of church bells ringing and Eddie held the dial still. I could sense his concentration filling the darkness under the blankets as the bells rang and rang while we didn't move, just listened. And then the bells faded and I heard Eddie's breath pass sharply down his nostrils, and a click and the radio was off. After that, we lay there under the blankets not speaking, one of us occasionally peeping out to witness the room turning grey as the darkness faded into what we didn't know would be Mum's last Christmas morning. Even now, I can remember how warm we were.

Next morning, I climbed the stairs again to the woman's room. It was Sunday, Christmas Eve. The house was cold. There was no one about.

I knocked twice before I thought I heard her coming across to the door. I asked her quietly if she was all right. There was no answer. I could hear her breathing. She was the other side of the door and I put the side of my face to it so that just the thickness of the wood separated us.

I said, 'Look, would you like to go for a drink, later? Nothing . . . Just a drink.'

I waited there for a minute. Then another.

Finally, I turned and went back downstairs and out into the rain. I don't know for sure, but I suppose I must have gone looking for Eddie.

The Tonsil Machine

Annie Murray

'When you have your tonsils out, the tonsil man uses one of these.'

Her father extends a shiny gadget towards her, which looks strangely fragile against the hairy backs of his hands.

'See – it goes like this – slide, spike, chop!'

The tonsil remover is about seven inches long, with two loops of metal at one end lying flat on top of each other which slide apart so that one can fit over the unsuspecting tonsil. A slim metal shaft runs along the middle like a spine, also sliding, oh so carefully, so that the two prongs bite into the flesh. Then the second steel lasso is pushed back and clips into place snugly alongside its partner, slicing off the tonsil at its base and leaving it perched like some queer breed of sea anemone on the metal hoops.

Madeleine remembers this lesson of three years ago now she is about to have her tonsils out. Memory shows her father standing – of all places – in the workshop. He has been carrying the gadget in his tweed jacket pocket and brings it out, now they are all gathered on the wooden boards, which are covered with a down of sweet-smelling sawdust and ringlets of woodshaving. The air is speckled, shot through with sunbeams, and suddenly emptied of the sound of hammers and chisels. Certain of effect, he has

brought the tonsil machine out to show the men.
Madeleine has followed, pigtails swinging, too awed by
him to clutch his hand. Loop, slide, puncture, chop.
Finished in seconds. Willie, Colin and Mike guffaw and
marvel.

'What the 'ell's that for, then?'

'Shouldn't want that bloody thing near me!'

They all snigger suggestively, hands pushed down into
overall pockets. Madeleine looks away from the instru-
ment as her father explains, raises her blue eyes to the low
rafters, sees a spider shuddering in its web, curiously pale
like a brooding icicle, caught in the dusty rays of light from
the window.

Now she is eight, she remembers, betrayed by her father's
relish of the joke, running out of the workshop, across the
narrow strip of garden where her frock brushes against the
fuchsia bush and into the shop through the green baize
door, to Gordon.

'What's up, kid?' He swings down to sit her on his knee,
pushing the fringe back from his face. 'Are the bogeymen
after you?'

She nuzzles the scratchy grey of his jacket, hiding.
Gordon is the young manager of the shop. Too stupid,
though – a disappointment to her father.

'Nothing one of these won't cure.' He grins, and tears
open a crackly packet of liquorice allsorts. 'What's your
favourite today, then?' Gordon always lets her have the
sandwich with the pink and white sugary stripes and
night-tasting liquorice between. He tickles her under the
chin and she squirms and grins in spite of herself, her
mouth watering darkly from the sweet.

Gordon: always there with smiles and sweets, black hair
carefully combed, poring over the ledgers. He keeps tabs
on the ins and outs of antiques; anxious. Gordon, who
should be in the workshop, not doing the brainwork,

overtaxed, chewing his well-scrubbed nails. He asked for a transfer when the manager was sacked for filching, and Madeleine's father took pity. 'Gordon's slow, but sure and honest. I'll give him a chance.' Too slow, and getting slower.

Now she is eight, the edges of life are crumbling. Gordon has a brain tumour. There have been months of hushed conversations on the wide staircase, or in the office over mugs of tea during Gordon's absence. Much of this is generated by the two cleaners, Gladys and Em. Daily, without so much as a caress, their hands flick over the rich sheen of mahogany and walnut, miniature Japanese trees with stiff leaves, wrought silver salvers and what-not, in this restless spectacle which shifts with whimsical regularity. Gladys and Em are guardians of the shop's elbow grease and sparkle. They also reserve rights to custody over all the latest about Gordon.

They stand, often with an elbow resting on the high dresser in the office, chipped mugs in hand, and Em swirling the undiluted sugar grains around in her tea dregs. Their overalls – Em blue, Gladys pink – smell sourly of Silvo and Duraglit, which is daubed in grey patches down their fronts. Gladys, petite and peroxided; Em portentous, one leg always bandaged emphatically to cover a septic ulcer. Both are approaching middle age, both already grandmothers. They tease out the threads of conversation.

'His brain's going, bit by bit, you know,' Em pronouces.

'They say they bored a hole right through his skull,' Gladys chips in. 'It'd take anyone a bit of time to get over *that*, wouldn't it?'

'I don't know.' Em sighs, then makes a tight kiss of her lips. 'I just don't know.'

Madeleine sees Gordon in a regular pose now since his return, bereft of jokes. He rests his head on one hand, dousing himself with painkillers and, to combat the globules of catarrh which seem to be filling his head as well, throat sweets called Meggozones. They are minute black pellets, hard, almost metallic looking. Gordon's face is thinner, more pallid, and a half-smile plays round his lips, contradicting the perplexed furrow of his eyebrows as if he is constantly trying to recall a half-forgotten song. As Em says, there's nothing can be done. Madeleine feels walled out, at a loss. Before, Gordon would have helped her through the tonsils, but now . . .

'Gordon . . .' Plaintive, she tries to rouse him, pulling his sleeve. 'Gordon . . .' Asking the old Gordon to pop out like the cuckoo from a clock and tell her something funny to chase away the terrifying shadows which creep up on her, full of leering tonsil men.

'Leave him, Madeleine,' Em says, looking up from the brass fire tongs she is polishing. 'He's got enough on his plate at the moment.'

Gordon sniggers mirthlessly.

'He's getting worse,' she has heard her father say. She has seen the childlike grins Gordon gives when asked a question. He does not recall the answer, if he ever knew it, and gives a slurred laugh. He is losing control of language.

'I'll have to keep him on till he really can't cope,' Mr Kingston says. 'But he's turning into a vegetable.'

Madeleine pictures Gordon's brain like a great doughy cauliflower, shot through with Meggozones like the lead pellets in roast pheasant.

In a week she will lose her tonsils to the tonsil man. Gordon's companionship lost, the days are spent in a peculiar kind of solitude, interspersed, when Em takes pity on her, with bouts of cleaning. As they rub at the knobby brass poker handles, bulbous coal scuttles or the curling body of a French horn, Em, panting slightly from the exertion, harangues about the price of smoked kippers or cleaning fluids. Occasionally, without any apparent provocation, she smiles, motherly, pats Madeleine's head and says, 'Don't you worry about it all, little'un.' Madeleine feels comfortable with Em, like sitting in a vast armchair. Her real mother, meanwhile, is out temping for Mr Turner, the solicitor, and her father types as if his livelihood depends on it in the small office at the back. Or he deals with customers, sustaining a perky patter, not chancing leaving it to Gordon.

Em, on account of 'me legs', mostly does the downstairs, leaving herself the two main front rooms to dust, as well as polishing and tea making. In the course of this last pursuit she mutters dark prophesies over the simmering kettle as to what happens to 'them that does without it'. 'It' – the absence of which apparently detracts without compromise from the general current of existence – is by now well known to be sugar in a mug of tea.

'That's what's the matter with *him* – I'll bet you any money you like,' she diagnoses, jerking a gnarled thumb at Gordon who is bent, unfocusing, over the office reckoning machine. He moans softly. 'My mother used to say –' Em grunts, bending to pick up a dropped hanky and exposing a network of varicosity on the unbandaged leg and a layer of petticoat '– that those who don't get enough sugar ends up with spots in front of their eyes. Now –' she goes on, with a disconcerting change of tack, 'I wonder where *she* can have got to?'

Everyone knows that Gladys's birdlike figure can whip round the shop in a trice, flicking dust with an urgency only mustered by one whose sole desire is to retire, on apparent completion of the job, into a small cupboard under the upper staircase – where she hangs her coat and keeps a little folding chair – to knit sugar-pink bootees for a soon-expected grandchild. Frequently Madeleine encounters her there, with the cupboard open just a crack

161

to let the light in. She is routinely silenced by Gladys, finger pressed urgently to lips. The other fist presses a hard lump into Madeleine's by-now expectant hand, which is used to the feel of hush money in a currency of MacIntoshes' orange-wrapped toffees.

Madeleine gazes at Gordon, her eyes pleading for some sign of recognition and, immediately pierced by the expression of pained bewilderment in his face and sickened by the smell of catarrh sweets, she slips unnoticed into the hall. She spends more time out of the office now, the great rooms of the shop her expanding horizon. Gordon, she is sure, is afraid of hospitals too. And she knows the tonsil machine got Gordon in the head – the big metal loop sliding over his brain and *puncture, chop* – all in an instant.

The thin green carpet takes her to the front of the shop, where two spacious rooms divide off on each side. She wanders back and forth between them, counting her steps with half her mind. She has had dreams. Firstly she enters the left-hand room, her brown shoes sliding on the carpet. In the middle stands a gleaming dining table laid with a pink, white and gold flowered dinner service. The centrepiece is a huge tureen, arranged there as if full of sumptuous promise. Towards the edge of the room, away from the window, are ranged a pair of French chairs with brocade upholstery structured with an air of effortless quality. Between them are two dainty side tables on which rest a collection of Chinese snuff boxes and, from the wall behind, Madeleine stares back at herself out of a huge, gilt-framed mirror. Among other objects in this room of today, in front of the window, sits a beautifully proportioned spinning wheel with a few threads still dangling from the spindle.

She has had dreams. The tonsil man with his great hairy hand forcing its way down her throat, darkness like a rubber-smelling mask over her face and blood, stuck pig, spurting all over the hospital bed and the tonsil man . . .

Suppose, she thinks, moving over to the right-hand room, with its splendid chandelier sprinkling prisms of light about the off-white walls. Suppose I stuck a pin in one of the veins in Em's leg – I wonder what would come out? She imagines black treacle, the colour the veins look through Em's stocking. She is trying not to think about the tonsil machine, about Gordon. She circles the room. It is growing late and the winter daylight has almost gone. Faces pressed against the long windows for an instant, outside in the street, see her among the cabriole tables, the elegant couch and ivory-faced clock, like a tropical fish swimming around in coloured water.

She retreats to the back room opposite the office, which is more dimly lit, less of a showpiece room. The floor here is uncovered grey flagstones, no good for skating on, and the furniture is on the whole more sombre: heavy oak chests and a table strewn with a scattering of pewter mugs, old swords, brass hunting horns. There are also cobwebs. Madeleine shivers.

As she tiptoes into the room she notices, after a moment, something new on the table at the far end of the room. It is a small wooden chest with the lid flung open and in which various shiny objects, all strangely contorted, are catching the light from the dingy bulb. Moving nearer, her eyes begin to take in the shape of these items and she halts abruptly, and gasps. Then she moves forward again slowly, as if approaching a notoriously vicious animal.

She begins to rifle through the old medicine chest with mesmeric fascination. There are sharp-pronged instruments, hard and tarnished – not as shiny as the tonsil machine – and some flat-ended devices which appear designed for scooping. There are dull-coloured scissors with curved ends for performing heaven-knows-what, scalpels with the blades still on, a number of squat containers which she does not open for fear of what might be inside, and four large curved metal loops which, if she only knew it, are birthing forceps. One thing she is not at a loss to identify, which comes to light under a length of perished rubber tubing, is a huge glass syringe as thick as her wrist, still complete with a needle and generous measure of some solidified pale blue substance inside. There is no tonsil machine. The box smells ghastly to her, more because of its suggestiveness of a career of writhings and screamings and pullings out of bits and pieces quite other than tonsils in heads or throats, than because she can identify what any of the implements were for. She stands silent, gazing into the chest, too appalled even for sobs.

Someone is standing just behind her, has walked quietly across the stone floor and is watching. She turns abruptly and sees Gordon, his face expressionless, staring beyond her into the chest. The tonsil machine got him in the head.

After standing for a moment he moves forward, stops for an instant, as if to still the pain in his head, making a soft 'Ugghh' sound. Then he looks down into the box. He begins to lift out items solemnly, almost ritually, saying nothing. Madeleine watches, eyes questioning, but still afraid of the wall between herself and the old Gordon, whose head was not a peppered cauliflower inside. He examines one of the shiny forceps, turning it over in his hands, then lays it down on the table again, selects a scalpel and tries the blade against his thumb before placing it next to the forceps. Madeleine waits, torn between curiosity and fright. Doesn't Gordon know they've got him, got his proper brain in a glass jar instead of the cauliflower – in a jar like the one where they'll put her tonsils, leaving a gaping hole at the back of her mouth for the flies to go down?

She keeps very still, flesh up in goosebumps in the chill

room, while Gordon, his dark head bent, lays out his row of implements until he comes to the syringe, which he turns round and round in his hands, gazing at it. The contents have long turned to powder. He looks at the needle, and one side of his mouth twitches faintly. He jiggles the glass tube until he can budge it about half an inch, and keeps sliding it back and forth. Madeleine jumps as he turns to face her, still grasping the syringe. His strained face has broken into a broad, new smile. Without a word he takes one of her hands, then the other, and presses them round the end of the syringe, the needle pointing towards himself. As she holds her end, Gordon keeps pulling on the glass tube and between them they budge it further, managing to push and pull it along its little passageway of almost an inch.

Madeleine watches Gordon's expression, and suddenly feels a grin breaking out across her own face, and giggles fizzing and popping out of her like little corks. They are pulling the syringe between them now, like a tug-of-war, a dance, in which the tonsil man's neck is being tugged and squashed, tugged and squashed, until they are both gazing into each other's delighted faces while great gulps and guffaws from Gordon and Madeleine's peals of giggles echo across the stone floor of the shop's back room.

Special Strength
Alan Mahar

1

You'll be wanting an explanation. I'll take it slow.
Talking's not my strong point. As you know. Except with a
few cans of SS inside me. But I'm not dumb. Just because I
work with my hands. There are questions I'd like to ask
you. If ever I get to see you. I can tell you some more about
the decision I came to. You were clever, though. Or was it a
coincidence? I only recall that the night before he appeared
I was walking you home.

2

I'm walking her to a taxi office because outside it's not safe
for everyone. Buses are a thing of the past. She hasn't got a
vehicle herself. And sometimes I choose not to drive mine
round the city. When I get the chance at night I chase the
lights, stay awake a few hours longer. There are others who
do the same. I've seen them.

Just as she's stooping into a Toyota Corolla, perfume and
cushions, Mahmood her usual driver, she says innocently:
Why do you have to work nights? I'm shagged out and I
don't have to hide it with her. She touches my leather
coatsleeve with her hand. *Couldn't you drop the nights?* I
took it as a compliment. I enjoyed our time together too.
It's only every so often. I go over everything we said.

3

I have a season ticket for the swimming therapy. Courtesy of the Corporation. Hardly anyone else goes when I go. Nobody talks. And women have to go on different days. I stay under the water for a long time. Hold my breath for seventy-five seconds; I've practised. That's supposed to help the skin. The Baths Company is the only quiet place I can bear.

I first met her there. She checked the tickets and watched for accidents. Attendants are trained to inspect the skin at the small shower by the entrance. My patch is no more than itchy. She looks for livid signs. She told me not to hold my breath underwater too long. Bad for your heart. She said her father taught her confidence in the water. Trained me himself the different strokes. Lucky then, I said. And he took me walking along the river that wiggles between the factories, showed me balsam and rosebay willowherb. Not so fortunate, I said. Then he died on me. Heart-busted with the early-retirement option. All when I first met her.

I've seen the old men in the baths with their bloodless legs and all the grey veins showing. As soon as they hit water they're fish, ancient carp that understand the reason for their slowness and a long life. The water separates for them, and then zips back up when they take their leg kick up the pool, following the lines of the cracks in the tiles. Sunlight through the glass in the roof improves their appearance. I don't talk to them ever.

I thought I saw him there once, just above the stable door of one of the cubicles. He was towelling his eyes before he put his spectacles back on. Wet calf lick across his brow. He manages to stay younger. Some of them can. They have special interests and spend all day on the exercise machines, while the rest of us work. They haven't had to for a few years. But that's a minority that know what to do apart from clean away their scraps of rubbish. Dead time for most of them. I have the chance to work extra and I wouldn't think of refusing.

4

The size of this building though, that's something, and only me inside. An enormous box encasing great space and volume: all the waste at the centre of the processing plant. High walls without rooms, without floors. I sort through the rubble mounds, move mountains to the incinerator shaft. The grabber travels easy on a gantry above the expanse of the pit. Thick breezeblock walls, no windows: straight lines and rectangles. High white smoke-stack adjoining. Geometrical forms. We send the smoke over. Who knows in the night where it gets wafted?

I've never had a fear of heights. Surgical mask protects from the dust. White hard hat for cranium safety. Lager to sluice the throat. The stench that wafts up from below can even be sweet for a moment before it is nauseating. The rubbish. The convoys of container trucks unloading round the clock.

I've got the cab fitted out comfortable for all the long shifts. Four-packs of Special Strength: it doesn't alter my concentration. Headset playing trumpet high and loud. Freddie Hubbard, 'First Light'. I shake my head. Do the shout inside. With me it's the fast thing. Noises pinging in the brain.

What do I think about when I'm up there? Shapes. Lines. Parabolas. Swings. Angles. Distances. Nothing else. I'm guessing and gauging every pick-up and every drop. They pay me decent money for a good eye. I like being high up, and then dropping the grabber arms, opening them at just the right moment, cupping them around the object. Then I trapeze it gently over the chasm. Right onto the spot. It's a point of honour. I don't drop things. Not accidentally.

5

I can talk to her because with her I don't stammer. She didn't try to finish my sentences. Gave me time. I don't lose track of them at all. The ideas rattle out like trumpet fire. Speech always the impediment. Except in my apartment we can blather on in noughts and noughts about distances and planets. *You CAN talk when you're not half pissed*, she says. When we talk. When a meeting is arranged. We sit at the window. Fourteenth floor. No need for curtains so high up. We can lie around naked on the bed after a good fuck and look out. I put my music on. Trumpet time. She sits, hugs her knees. I'm not sure she hears it the same. We watch the winking lights on flight paths. The worming trails of tail-lights on motorways. Stars, planets, satellites. The drink works on me. Patterns I have chased on electronic games. Colours, lines. Everybody's reflexes need to be good.

And what about this planet that we're on now? The Rainbows would say there's some danger. I listen. In the next flat I can hear a vacuum cleaner going. I couldn't say I keep a tidy place. I've never seen my neighbours, but I know they're old, the way they mutter and clean.

She tries something else. *You see, anyone can go in the Baths Company. All the pestering old men I meet – not even a man with interests. Well, except I met you, didn't I?* I jump tracks on the CD, don't like the slow ones. *But the Environment Corporation is a different matter, isn't it? That whole area by the railway fenced off and patrolled. Creepy, if you ask me.* I listen to her observations. I want to lick her hips instead. I say: *It's not interesting to talk about. I transfer garbage in enormous volume. Same every day.* She pulls away from me. *OK*, I say, *have you any idea of the tonnage I shift every day?* I tell her some astronomical noughts. She laughs. See. No wonder I get a bonus. I offer her one thickish bicep to press. *Strength, stamina. That's why I get the special night job. Simple.* I stroke her leg skin: hardly a mark. My touch doesn't quieten her.

Might that have anything to do with the big marshalling yards? Heavy rail movements, large freight in the night. I have to be careful. Could be. I don't know from one week to the next. I just do the loading. No fuss. That's it. They don't give me details about the really special loads, do they? Nobody even says the N-word any more. They're hardly likely to give me the train timetables in advance. Simple security. I just get a phone call. And I don't talk about it. Even after a drink. They've tested me. *I don't ask.* All I know is lifting special loads requires special care. My eye, my hand, my strength. I see the official danger logos on the side of the bulk carriers. I know what it is. *Why are you so interested anyway?* She responds feebly: *I'm just trying to get you to talk.* The stammer starts up then.

6

He was pleased whenever I took a girlfriend home. Then he would talk affably about his garden herbs, and collect dandelion leaves and spinach for his salad bowl. Salads don't have to be so predictable. Then he'd use his infuriating modesty: We can but try. We drank his ginger beer and sipped his nettle wine. He discoursed on their properties and invited the girl in question on one of our Sunday walks. He would ask her if she had an interest in hedgerows. I lost different girls in either mild October or sunshine May. He charmed them all with information, learning worn lightly. They always lost touch nicely, though.

In the garden he worshipped at his compost heap. He liked to see the grass cuttings cause it to steam. Vegetable leaves in a separate boxed area, weeds always bagged separately, and secured with green twine for the dustbin collection. If it was operating; sometimes the Corporation deploys staff elsewhere, and people try to complain about having no collection. He took a pleasure in keeping a tidy garden, dutifully packed the waste bags into the van for the civic amenity. He never failed to sharpen his spade and his hoe after every Saturday 'tilling'. He wore a beret and Swiss walking boots. At one time he had an allotment he marched to; something was built over it – a garden supermarket.

Not the necessary curiosity for a scientist, I'm afraid. Never once picked up on the interests I put your way. Accused me of failing my exams on purpose. *Some childish revenge, is it? How could geometry be enough on its own?* That was an ancient battle. I wish it didn't matter. It doesn't. We could have come to blows. I developed a capacity for lager. In his collector's collection the record racks of steam engines, birdsong, Shakespeare formed one part of a whole wall – all the classical symphonies and the history of jazz. Young Armstrong, yes; I don't hate all the old. Otherwise I only listened to Clifford Brown's supple trumpeting. None of his other records was of interest to me. I discovered the video game arcades: *Star Wars*, *Intergalactica*, *SDI*, *Missile Attack*. I spent some money. Still do when I can find them. Test my speed.

7

I'd even forgotten that I'd been in this city before. Once I could operate a crane, every site seemed much the same, every Portakabin, every cab a home from home. The arguments, the brew-ups of tea, the little rolled-up newspaper passed round.

Don't imagine it was anything but the money brought me here. Not a question of coming back home. A section of a district of a region. That's all. A venue on a worksheet. Next year I'll be somewhere else. North Coast B.

Somewhere with spoiled beaches. No, I don't have any special feeling for this city. I memorize afresh the roads, the lights, the railway lines. And they're the same and different anywhere. But I'm privileged inside the Corporation complex: I can look down the railway line, past each bridge, all the way to the skyscrapers; and I'm not appalled by the waste space on either side. I only hear of the clearances there have been, and new uses for emptiness. The steam railway museum's another scrap yard, the BMX track redundant: no one can remember children being interested. Cleared space makes the view simpler. The railway leads to the city; these towers to those towers; the dilapidation located there and the dormitories somewhere else.

I had to travel away for the work. A disagreement over exams. My future. No qualifications. We couldn't be under the same roof, the two of us. Then the long wait in rented rooms for the chance of an HGV licence. Transport, warehousing, construction – I tried them all. Something about Environmental I found conducive: the shifting of massive weight; the special crunch of sizeable materials; good riddance to bad rubbish; no one wanting to talk. Don't ask me what it was. I showed an aptitude. I was quick, I was accurate at judging distances, I was available for work, and I kept my mouth shut. They ask me; I always say, Yes.

It was a special job. A train coming through the Midlands. A dangerous load has to travel slowly between power stations, and none of the protest people has to know. From South Coast C up to North West A. Our plant conveniently halfway between. I move the load from one train to another train waiting. Perfectly safe. The waste-processing plant is conveniently next to the marshalling yard. So I go from long hours on the waste disposal – that's my usual; then this extra work with the trains. In someone else's cab. But I take my four-packs to feel at home: my Special Strength. Nights, of course. Some loads have to be under cover of darkness. Floodlights to work in. Special care. I'm not frightened.

8

So when I see this Mitsubishi van pull into what used to be the public area, the civic amenity, I don't suspect anything. There's nothing different. Someone's tipping garbage, like they did before the checkpoints and the intercoms. I forget for a moment about the change in public access.

It could be wood in a pile, garden sods in fertilizer bags, crow's wing umbrellas, the polystyrene squares for videos and computers. It might be beer cans and ring pulls, pop bottles and tangles of audio-tape. Yoghurt pots and chip papers, burger packs and cat food tins, shiny foil freezer-meal trays and Embassy packets full of ash, dried tea leaves in eggshell halves, sodden balls of Kleenex, all toppling out of heavy-duty black bags. This is how it happens every day. I don't mind it myself. It gets tidied away. The grabber sorts it. Out of sight and up the chimney.

I'm in the cab and I'm looking down. I see the usual shape on the VDU, one of our chaps shifting something. Then I freeze-frame on the figure bending to unload the van, remember again the Corporation ruling cancelling the civic amenity. I don't know what made me look closer. The studied walk, the quiet confidence. And the flash of grey hair under the beret.

Woodshavings, privet clippings, wallpaper strippings and sump oil flagons, perished bricks and splintered guttering. Smashed-glass TV sets, opened-up video recorders, typewriters, transistor circuits, vacuum-cleaner bags spilling. The sparrows always at the new mounds, checking. I didn't see him coming. I'd forgotten. It wasn't in my mind that he lived here. He would have had a way of getting past the barriers. He could always talk people round. Security guards in booths, middle-aged pensioners in bifocals. He's one of those that waved the old survey maps at farmers. The politest of troublemakers.

9

She started asking again about this extra responsibility. I say I keep the headset whirring; I crack open the cans. Don't give it a thought. Was I at risk from these campaigners? she wondered. Rainbows had broken fences, left messages inside. But my skin hasn't got any worse. Anyway, I trust the security force at Environmental Corporation. They'd know what to do with cranks. *I expect they're what you call nice people*, I say to her. *The worst sort.*

She wants to contest my flippancy immediately, of course. She thinks I can't mean it. *I know lots of nice people who don't share your views. A whole group.* She was speaking of her allegiances more than she meant to. I should have guessed then, but I didn't. *An old man I know, he talks to me sometimes about wild flowers and garden vegetables after group meetings. I mean, no one knows that stuff any more. I love to listen to his quiet voice. He's not trying to prove anything.* She's been taken in by all that pretended weakness. Words that insinuate a power over you. *Well, I've met his sort before. Quite deceptive really.* Her gullibility was a disappointment to me; or else she was clever and needling me. Either way I sensed us reaching conflict. *I like him. The old ones are not all the same. He wears this curious beret.*

10

I lift him up so he can see me in the cab, face to face. See how he likes it. See if he realizes. All that time struggling. I draw him up level with me. So he can see me. Recognize me? Long time. Now everything could be equal, more or less. He could be made to understand. But I'd no idea what I'd do. Something just so he knew. I drop him down. I let him fall. Out of the grabber's arms. He tumbles in, a dust cloud rises. He's trudging in the shifting matter, he's struggling for a foothold. I'm watching. I finger the cab controls. I'm counting. Holding my breath for seventy-five seconds. Watched the sparrows gathering a safe distance from commotion. On the headset a fruity trumpet blast from Freddie Hubbard speaks up against sentences too sensible. There. An easing through noise.

I'm able to look down again: the man was speechless, pleading something. Perfectly powerless. I swing the grabber down to him. Speedy levers open out the hand for him, close round him, pick him up and deposit him on the parapet. He's back by his van brushing dust off his boots, pulling at his beret. One look up at my cab. That's all. He climbed into his van then.

11

I don't really want the Corporation to know who he was. It could go down as an accident, couldn't it? It was: he shouldn't have been there. They don't need to know.

I didn't find out till later: he collapsed on his way out. Trying to drive away. Wedged into his steering wheel at traffic lights. Face all contorted from the attack, the security guard said. I saw a Rainbow sticker on the back window of the abandoned Mitsubishi.

12

Every evening I've been to the hospital. Now I have a chair at my father's bedside. He can't talk the way he used to. Not yet. I study the blinking of the electrocardiograph. A new light for me to follow in the night. I find I am gripping his hand with all my strength.

13

Why would I connect him with you? Couldn't we meet again? I might understand more of your questions. You weren't using me to find things out, were you? I could tell you I've given up the night work now.

Homing Instinct

Maria Morris

I found another dead bird in the bin outside this morning –
its neck broken. My father, Pete, raced pigeons. Earlier
he'd squeezed the straggler, last week's lagger-behind. Slid
its neck sharply round and round in his swollen fingers
until he heard a soft click. The dead grey thing sat on top
of the other rubbish and when I saw the green numbered
marker-ring clasping its pink leg, I only felt a numbing
dislike. Well, it had been stupid enough to come back here,
hadn't it? But I felt nothing for it, nothing at all.

Unlike when I contemplated my father's bullet-like head.
My eyes must have been drilling small holes into the base
of his skull because his ripe beetroot face, with eyes the
colour of rusty wire, turned to me. Ignoring me, he cajoled
and click-clicked, 'Come on then, come on then,' to the
hapless birds which circled the houses far, far above the
squashed black and white box of the pigeon pen.

Clive, the real competition, sat next door. An altogether
grander affair, his birdhouse was topped with white spires
which towered high above our fence. He could have staged
an opera on this monstrous set and in his own way he did.
Clive sat centre stage. A chorus of friends crowed out the
names of this season's races he had already won – Stroud,
Wincanton. Today's was Penzance. Feeding tub in hand,

Clive threaded wheat and maize through his fingers, which flittered like restless moths. The big clocking-in clock sat by his side awaiting the first arrival.

Then, like a plane with one engine on fire, our neighbour's bird landed. Clive grabbed its spindly leg, tore off its ID ring and clocked in. The show was over. A chorus of approval came from those gathered – except from this side of the fence. I replaced the frayed bin lid softly or else he'd accuse me of trying to scare the birds away. Just looking up was enough to trigger Clive's smile again. 'Ben,' he shouted across the fence, not bothering to conceal the satisfaction in his voice.

My father wouldn't even look at me and the sun kept needling the patch of sunburnt skin at the back of my neck. Under pressure from the heat all the worst smells had ganged up together. The hunched-up, defeated-looking black rubbish bags that I kept forgetting to take out front. And white pigeon shite everywhere, even on the crisping leaves of the lavender trees at the bottom of the garden. Almost lost were the specks of purple dislodged onto hard clumps of soil, the softer greyish clay beneath which had preserved all the childish things I used to bury there – vinegar-dipped George VI pennies, leather wristbands and even the blank faceless discs from the railway trucks.

Whoostle – wings over the roof, turning, heavier, closer, bluish-grey feathers thick with broad shadows. Unaware, my father groped inside the nesting boxes for his favourite racing hen and, gathering her crudely in his hands, fanned out her white wing feathers before the strained light.

So soon summer had become moribund, dwindling until all the light seemed squashed out of these oblique days. I watched my mother through the big window that opened out onto the garden. Listlessly, she watched television. Never even looked up as I slipped, half guiltily, into the living room. Large dark circles seemed to extinguish all light from her face. And still wearing that white nightdress, the one that always crackled with static whenever she moved. Today it was silent. I'd got eyes in my head, but every day I always asked, 'How are you feeling, Mom?'

'Better than yesterday.' But that wasn't saying much, as she kept rubbing the flat of her hand over her swollen belly which, in the last two months, had become enormous. And it wasn't a baby growing in there, either.

'Are you in pain?' I watched her face carefully: whenever I asked that question she always lied.

'It's more discomfort, really.'

'Mm,' I said under my breath. 'Your appointment's on Monday, isn't it?' I knew; of course I knew.

'You don't have to worry, Ben. Your father's got the day off work.' She smiled at me as though I was still ten years old. 'Where's your father?'

'Oh, still licking his wounds I expect.' And I made no effort to conceal a smile. But her eyes flashed disapproval and I couldn't understand her loyalty. Well I couldn't, not after the way he'd treated her over the years.

From tight, pale lips: 'Did you apologize to your father, Ben?'

Looking out the window: 'Oh, Mom.'

'Ben!'

'But it wasn't my fault . . . he treats me like shite . . .' *The way that he's always treated you*: I thought it best left unsaid.

In fact, I just let it drop as soon as I realized that we were both going through the motions and I couldn't have said no to her if I'd tried. One look at her face was enough for me. How could I say this? But she was starting to scare me and Dad as well, although he thought he could hide it. I couldn't remember the last time she'd slept a whole night. Always a light sleeper, I could hear her downstairs before it was even light, shuffling about, anxious and restless. And last night, when she said goodnight, she hugged me too tight . . . and I knew. The little finger on her right hand never rested flat and I just wanted to take that hand in mine, but I didn't.

'Have you thought any more about Israel?' she surprised me by saying.

'How can I? I mean . . .'

'You don't 'ave to stop here because of me, you know,' she said, her look steady.

It was me who faltered. 'Mom . . .'

'Right, I'm off to the Pigeon Club.' Dad bulldozed in. 'The lads 'aven't turned up,' he said, his voice competing with mine. 'So, I've got to carry all them bloody pigeon baskets myself.' He looked at me.

And I would have ignored him if Mom hadn't said, 'Go on, give him a hand,' in a cajoling voice.

'Well, perhaps I could . . .' Reluctantly I got up.

That was good enough for Dad. 'Why don't you come for a pint when we're done . . . if it's not interrupting your busy social life?' And because I didn't say no immediately, he took it as a yes.

Anyway, before I'd had chance to say anything he disappeared out into the back garden. And I must have had that look on my face because Mom said, 'Go on, it's the nearest you'll get to him sayin' sorry.'

No response.

'It won't hurt you, Ben. He hasn't had the opportunities you've had. He might not show it, but he is proud of you, you know.' But her eyes said, just do it for me.

'Your sister will be here soon, anyway,' she said, then regretted adding, 'You're not going out like that, are you?'

'Why not?' Annoyed. She never knew when to back off. But I still glanced at myself in the big frameless mirror over the fireplace. Automatically I straightened up whenever I looked in a mirror, but I could never stop my shoulders looking lopsided for long. 'But I always look like this,' I said, and she managed a smile as I kissed her on the palest of cheeks.

Before he started on at me again I loaded up the rusty red Fiesta with wicker baskets full of pigeons with their plaintive *Er-woo, Er-woo, Er-woo* sound, which seemed to come right from the stomach. Hundreds of other birds at the transporter all made that sound. And, in this light, the birds no longer looked ordinary as they stretched their necks, which glistened green and pink iridescent in the sunlight. Soon, the lorry would take them to their new destination for tomorrow's race. The furthest – France.

All the way to the club, Dad was either singing or talking too loudly. 'If my luck's in I should be second today.' Simultaneously his left little finger whirled around inside his wide nostril, his right hand gripped the steering wheel and he always forgot the words to the songs, every time. Busy island. Forward, back, forward, the car heaved. Dad's hand wouldn't move from that horn until someone else gave way. 'Arseholing scrawls' was his general term of abuse (as opposed to 'idle scrawls' reserved for the unemployed).

'All right?' he asked. Ratchet-like sound. Dad's St Christopher chain was being slowly wound through his fingers, which always meant he'd drifted. Finally, he looked up expecting an answer.

'Mm,' I said warily.

As soon as Dad flung open the bar door they started:

'Call yourself a pigeon flyer, Pete!'

'I thought you was gonna be first, this week.'

'That's ten quid you owe me.'

And my dad beamed at his mates in the corner, but the smile dropped right off his face as soon as he saw Clive, at the far end of the pub, a look of self-congratulation on his face. But then he knew we were watching him. I could tell by the way he turned his head to talk to a flurry of red-faced men with tobacco stains on their teeth, and by the slightly stilted jerking motions of his neck. Without a doubt, I could tell you what Clive was holding up in his fist – today's racing result sheet. I tried not to smile, but Dad was put out. It didn't take much to deflate Dad's ego. Despite his big mouth and brusque manner he was as thin-skinned as a balloon. This was why, I suppose, he refused to share anything with Clive, even friends.

This was a plain pub for plain men – the creamy walls were bare, except for charcoal drawings of the local landscape before the houses hid the fields and before the fields hid the mines. The red tiles were uncovered and the bar stools too hard to sit on for long. Some men at the next table were playing a noisy game of dominoes – white hollow dots pressed into fat calloused hands. Their heads uniform (black with blobs of white), and smoky as newly lit matches. An elbow lobbed a pint from the table. A fist left an ear looking redder than usual. Strange and muted, they sat back down and started a new game. But my father was still egging them on, posturing, arms stretched over the back of a bench, legs wide like a cowboy's. He thought he was being impressive but, in the past, I'd known him pick a fight with a little runt of a man. Someone whom even I could knock out with my fist, which was about the length of a library card. At heart he was a coward, why else would he need to hit a woman?

'How are you, Ben?' said one of my dad's saner friends, whom I recognized by his fifties rock 'n' roll hairstyle, complete with sideboards. It looked exactly the same as when I was a kid. 'Are you going to stay around 'ere . . . now you've graduated?' The man seemed to sense my discomfort.

'Well, I'm thinking of accepting an offer to do a year's voluntary work in Israel,' I said. Dad was giving me one of his looks.

'First I've heard of it,' he said.

'I only found out the other day,' I said, but I'd told my mother as soon as I got the news. I knew what his attitude would be, so I'd said nothing.

An oversized hand suddenly rested on my shoulder and I was worried until I recognized Jason's younger brother. But he looked too big now – unnatural. The way those biceps just hammed it up in a white T-shirt with cut-away sleeves.

'Right, mate, can't stop,' he said.

'When's Jason back from South Africa?'

'Next month, I think.' No smile. Didn't do his moods much good, either. The bar window tried to absorb the sound of several impatient fists. Jason's brother looked up. Cricked his head goodbye at me and disappeared with a group of men who were even bigger than him.

'Who was that?'

'Jason's brother. You remember Jason, funded his own dig to Africa?' Unheard of for someone our age.

'Oh,' he said and I didn't go on. All he'd say was that you could earn more in a factory and he was right. But then I thought about Lee, my mate from Bristol, who'd already started his MA – Conservation at Camberwell. What had I done with the last year?

Awkwardly, I lied and said I had to leave soon. Dad was secretly relieved I was going, but he offered to buy me another pint all the same.

'No, really,' I said, too quickly.

It was still early on this warm summer's evening. Light until ten o'clock most nights. As the sun set, the light fell at an angle through the plate glass door and made green and yellow patterns on the bare walls. Wherever the light moved the colours moved too.

I had to say it. 'What do you think's up with Mom?' I almost whispered.

'I don't know, son. Honestly, I don't.' But Dad wouldn't

look at me; he was being evasive. He didn't want to be forced, not just yet, to put a name to his fears. But I noticed all the brusqueness had gone out of his voice and he had a muted, faraway look.

I knew, despite his bravado and bar-room banter. In spite of the fact that Dad always seemed to be travelling on a different course away from Mom, almost living his own separate life: drinking, working and flying pigeons. Still, he desperately needed the *idea* of my mother in the house waiting for him, even if he didn't go home at all some nights. He needed her like a ship needs a lighthouse – in the distance, always in the distance – to orientate himself, to steer him away from the rocks, or he really would be lost. And it was then that I saw it – that choked-up look – and, just for a second, I glimpsed the eyes of a drowning man.

'I have to go now.' Dad barely noticed as I left.

Tall grasses brushed my jeans. Behind my house, the open fields led nowhere and the ground was so soft, in some places, just like walking on sponge. Now I knew what they meant – from here the precarious, downward-sloping gardens all looked like they were going to fall into the fields. Some had already started to crumble and sand had been dug into the soil, but it didn't help. The old mines were supposed to be capped but a great crater had opened up in the middle of the field – now it was full of old fridges, prams and last year's trainers.

The closer I got, the more I churned – a light in my parents' room, already.

Thin curtains closed. I didn't want to leave Mom, but I couldn't live with Dad any more. And the way she always said, 'Don't let me stop you,' that just made me feel worse.

So quiet in that house. My mind like an uneasy bubble inside a spirit level.

Later, Dad appeared, swaying and swearing in the doorway of our living room.

'Shh,' I said.

He gave me a filthy look. 'Where's your mother?'

'In bed.'

He stumbled into the kitchen and I heard the fridge door open and close, and when he came back into the room some of the doornails popped up out of their hinges.

'Where's my supper?' he boomed.

'You'll wake Mom up,' I said, but he was too drunk. No way was I going to budge, not for him. This was why both my sisters had already left home. 'I'm going to check on Mom,' I said, and after some thought added, 'You should sleep in the spare room tonight.'

He swore at me and said at the top of his voice, 'I don't know what you've got to be so high and mighty about – you're never bloody 'ere!' It was true: I stayed at my girl-friend's whenever possible, but what with Mom being the way she was I tried to be home as much as I could.

When I got upstairs Mom was already up and in her dressing gown, but I managed to persuade her to go back to bed. All she said was, 'Tell him to be quiet, will you?' And it pained me to see how old she suddenly looked.

Downstairs, he was still moaning. 'Your sister could 'ave at least done my supper before she left.'

I hated everything about him, especially the way the chicken fat shone on his lips and the feather in his hair. 'Why don't you get off your arse and do it yourself, you selfish bastard!'

I'd gone too far. He had that look in his eyes, like a dog before it's going to go for you. By the time Mom came down my lip was split, my mouth raw with blood. I felt very shaky on my feet. But he would have hit me again if it hadn't been for her. Mom did what she always did when-ever it got nasty with Dad and me, she sandwiched herself in between us. Only now, I could feel her belly pushed up against me. Whereas before I had wanted so badly to hit

Dad, now I just felt ashamed and nauseated. I couldn't put her through this. So – when my father shoved me out the front door and slammed it in my face – I stopped protesting. The decision, it seemed, had been made for me.

That night it couldn't even be bothered to get dark, instead the buildings turned black, while the sky retained its purplish uneven look. I watched the housing estate opposite with its boarded windows and torn fences, where sagging horses were tethered on sloping banks. And I waited a long time before my girlfriend got back, until the houses finally merged, blackly unbroken as railway tracks.

Dad, who didn't like phones, rang me the next night. Just as I arrived home a nurse was leaving, a box of sharps clutched under her arm. That figure, motionless on the sofa. I could only think of Mom in terms of movement, not this awful stillness. Those large, bony, matter-of-fact hands. That sheenless wedding ring, always covered with blue tape on the days she'd worked at the canteen. When it went quiet, Dad and me just looked at each other – all you could hear was the Walkman-sized machine pump its intravenous mix of painkillers. A side valve allowed Mom to increase her dosage.

After that, she started to disassemble, and you had to search for fragments of her old self – something you could recognize. Her eyes didn't seem to focus properly on you any more. That starey look I'd only seen once before in my life. Hand, sore and bruised from all the drips, but I was afraid that if I didn't take it now . . . I squeezed it and asked, with futility, if there was anything I could do.

She looked directly at me and said, 'I can still fight the lot of you.' And that was it; I'd seen my last bit of her.

Shadows of wings cross over my hands and I know it's time to stop work – when the sun is brightest and the shadows longest. I like to work because if I don't I just sit and think. It's hit me harder here, for some reason. And sometimes it seems the only difference on this site is that I'm wiping red clay from my hands instead of grey.

Artefacts are just artefacts wherever you are. But it's comforting, in a strange way, that in my parents' garden, in the bluish-grey clay, is the worn George VI coin and next to it the smooth, silver disc. I like that contrast.

The Incident Room

Mike Ramsden

Lately, I've felt my influence over Sean diminishing. Another voice is threatening to out-voice mine. He's come under the influence of a woman and he's due to marry her in a week's time. What's more, in a church of some sort. I've advised him not to bother, think of the fuss and expense, but he says she expects it, the marriage bit; and the relatives, good church-going people, wouldn't hear of them marrying outside the Church. The wedding business has become like a barrier between us. It's not only the woman. The other voices, of family and conscience, are strong and clamouring, transcending his desires. There's still the one from childhood attempting to whisper pieties in his ear. I've never managed to silence that voice.

That evening, I tell him he needs a break, needs to get out of the house. It's not difficult to persuade him. I monitor his conduct and whisper advice. What I advise usually elides with his own desires. I can sense he's feeling restless and I know him well enough to know why.

He gets ready and comes into the kitchen, the only warm room in the house, where Susan's reading. She's got copper-coloured hair, worn down to her ears, not so very different in colour from Sean's, except his is darker, cut short and looking as though it needs a good comb through it, but he tells me it's fashionable. Her face is pale and freckled and her eyes greyish-blue. I think she looks anaemic but I suppose he must find her attractive.

I like the way he tells her he won't be long. – Just a half *or so*. I smile at the addition of 'or so'.

She witters on for a while. – I wouldn't go at all if I were you, Sean. It's late already, and you do have that interview in the morning and we've little enough money as it is.

He gives her a look. – Just a half. *Right?*

I know what she's thinking. It's the neighbourhood. Not all that safe. And the drinking.

– You're going to regret this. I can only take so much. She shakes her head and exhales in her exasperated fashion.

This brings him up short. – I told you, *I won't be long.*

So off he goes. It's a cold night, December. He's well wrapped up, thick jacket, cords, scarf and flat cap.

I give him a mental nudge as he heads down the street. – *No, not the Clarion tonight, Sean, you've been in there enough.*

He begins to argue. – Does it matter? I'm only going for a half.

– *Yeah, well, try somewhere different like the one on the corner. Might be some interesting people.*

He's slowing down, weighing up the prospect, how he looks, his clothes. Can't do much about his face – that straggly red beard, accentuating his blue eyes with their 'inquiring' look. Puts people off, turns them belligerent: *What yer staring at, then?*

I tell him he looks OK. Should blend in nicely. Yeah, he does like to rub shoulders with builders and that. I'm all for it. He has these fantasies when he's in his incident room, like he's packing it all in and joining them. I don't advise it (hell, the condescension, the ups and downs of the trade), and besides he's better off with the tensions in him. He has more problems like that. And that's good. I think he used the word *paradox* or something once. One of those types who are happy with problems to mull over.

He walks straight into the Dog and Whistle, looking neither to right nor left. (That must mark him down as a stranger for a start.) He stands at the bar and begins to adjust himself, elbows on the bar, so he's less than his six foot three, eyes slightly down. I know he doesn't want to give the impression he's any different from any other bloke in the pub. The barman approaches and he straightens up. He's about to order a half of bitter when I draw his attention to the pumps.

– *Your favourite's on draught. You know what it does to you.*

– A pint of cider, please. That deep voice of his. I hate it.

People stop talking and stare for a second. He nods at the thin guy with the ponytail to his right. I know he wants to strike up a conversation, what d'you do and where're you from and all that crap. Like he's standing at some bar overseas. Like an interrogation. The thin guy grunts and looks at him heavy-eyed and empties his pint and walks out. Looking at the other blokes, I can see his clothes aren't quite right after all. I think it's the red woolly scarf.

Someone's playing golden oldies on the box. Sean likes these. The Kinks, 'Waterloo Sunset', 'Sunny Afternoon'; The Byrds, 'Mr Tambourine Man'. Joe Cocker comes on: 'With a Little Help from My Friends'. The music makes him feel warm inside. I tell him he'll feel even better with another pint of cider.

He begins to look at the reflections of people behind him in the mirror. There's about half a dozen tables and a banquette along the opposite wall. A couple of middle-aged women, three younger women with them, but the rest men, young and old. You get the feeling of locals, not your transient trade. I think he's going to move from the bar and sit at one of the tables, but then at the same time something's going through his head. He's getting twitchy, envisaging a bollocking from Susan. It's got noisier as everyone gets tanked up. Sean hasn't found anyone to talk to, so he's retreated to his incident room. He's not thinking of his marriage – good – instead he's off on a trip to the future, a future of unspecified events and unknown people.

I like it.

Then, hey, it all goes quiet. There's a presence in the room. Sean can see what it is in the mirror but he looks round nonetheless, as though not trusting a reflection, and sees a cop has come in. He turns back to his pint quickly and lowers his head. It's his fucking conscience again. When cops come close he always wonders if he's done something. He has, like, *in his life*, but nothing the cops can get him for. He's watching in the mirror and then he really does look as guilty as hell with his head down, but still able to see the mirror. The cop is coming straight for him. He doesn't look up, but waits for the hand on the shoulder.

– Can we have a word with you, sir? Outside if you don't mind.

So out they go; Sean first, the policeman following. He hasn't taken a look at the cop, but does it matter? It's a uniform with a cap. The uniform takes his arm and guides him to a patrol car.

– In here, sir.

And so there he is, in a cop car, back seat with the officer, another in front.

– What's your name? The 'sir' has gone. The voice is harsher.

– Sean Fitzgerald.

– Irish, eh?

– Kind of, yeah.

– Barman's not seen you before.

– How d'you know?

– Been away, have you?

– Yeah. Now look . . . OK, Bahrain.

– In the building trade, are you? Painting and decorating?

– No, I'm a teacher. English as a foreign language.

– So, it's a foreign language, is it? You've got white paint on your hands.

– So? I've been painting.

– Painting what?

– Well, a picture if you must know. Painting as in 'art'. I use my fingers as well as . . .

The cop in front leans over the seat and goes, Jesus, Pete, what we got here, then?

– So, Mr Fingers, where's your, erm, attic?

– Twenty-four Paget Terrace. Up the road. Now what the fuck's all this about?

There's an odd silence. The uniform in front takes off his cap and rubs his forehead. The one in the back moves an inch or two away as though he wants to look at Sean from another angle. The one in front wants to know the name of the woman living at 24 Paget Terrace.

– Susan Fallon. She's a teacher too.

– Living with her, are you?

– What the hell's it got to do with you? We're getting married.

Oh dear, there he goes, justifying himself to the police.

– Is that so? Miss Fallon phoned in to say she opened the door to someone fitting your description. He had white paint on his hands. Foolish, she admits, to open the door that time of night. Thought it might be you and yeah, looked like you. Anyhow, he gained entry. Must have seen you go out and him looking like you . . . She says she had to give him her valuable jewellery.

Valuable jewellery? He laughs. – That's rich.

– A few hundred quid and then in her words he 'pushed her violently'.

Pushed her violently? Sean frowns. Something's not right here.

– And then made his getaway.

– Hang on, when was this?

– You're free to go, sir.

He hesitates at the kerbside as the car drives off. He looks at his watch. I know what he's thinking. He turns his head in the direction of Paget Terrace. Then round again to the pub. I'm not sure what he should do.

– *Got to think this through*, I tell him. – *You do this better with a pint. You could be in there another forty-five minutes before chucking-out time.*

– Yeah, but I'll be pissed in no time. That's not the way to think.

– *But you'll enjoy the process, won't you, snug in your little room, going over the ins and outs, the pros and cons.*

If anyone were to ask me what I like to see him doing, it's just that – standing at some bar, going through the motions of thinking, never bringing any results, never moving him forward. But he's happy doing that and I care about him being happy.

So in he goes again. Up to the bar. And it's a pint of cider. I'm not sure he's gained any street cred from this encounter. They stare, yeah, but he's been with the police for over half an hour and now he's back and the way he wears that scarf and his clothes, he doesn't fit.

– What they want, then? This is the beefy type to the right of Sean.

– Thought I'd burgled someone. Breaking and entering, he adds.

– Don't look the type, does he, Pat? This is to the bloke standing next to Beef.

– I'd say not.

– Sure you weren't having a chat about something else?

– Like what?

Sean's staring at Beef. His lips are pursed. There's a hint of fear mixed with aggression on Sean's face and I tell him he should get out of here but he wants to finish his drink and now he's back in the incident room. Has Susan set him up? Teaching him a lesson? Phones the police, concocts that story and says he'll be boozing in the Dog and Whistle.

No, a pub near by. Can't know where he is exactly. What kind of police would believe that a burglar would hang around the neighbourhood after a job?

Possible, he supposes. The barman gets a phone call. Check this description.

He should get back.

He's got his head down, fists on cheeks, leaning on his elbows. He can see the hand of the man on his left wrapped around his pint. He can't take his eyes off the hand. Sean looks in the mirror and sees he's got a red beard and blue eyes and he wasn't there before Sean went outside with the police. I'm giving Sean as forceful a mental nudge as I can. – *No, please, don't do it.* But he does, talks to this guy.

– What d'you do, then?

– Not a lot.

Someone sniggers behind him.

He can see in the mirror he's being hemmed in. Pat and Beef have shifted position, detached themselves from the bar and there are three other blokes, about his age, donkey jackets spattered with mud. Something's about to happen, some unvoiced plan to be put into action, like they're all thinking the same thing, no need to have discussed this among themselves, almost an instinct with them.

He puts his drink down on the bar counter and turns round. – Excuse me, please.

He's off now. Definitely. The group part ever so slightly, giving him just enough room to pass. Someone imitates him, adding a lisp. *Excuthe me, pleathe.* But he's not going straight out. I implore him to do it outside, down an alley. But he's bursting.

He stands at the stall. He feels his cap pushed over his eyes. I'm powerless to save him. I can't say *Duck!* or anything. It's too fast. The wall, and the pipe coming from the cistern slam into his face and he's down in the urinal.

I don't know why they did that. It wasn't something I envisaged happening when I persuaded him to leave the house. It's what you get with staring at people, out of his league, his depth.

Then the landlord comes rushing into the Gents. – OK, lads, throw him out, take him well away from the entrance. Gets us a bad rep this kind of thing. He started it, didn't he?

– Found this on him.

– That's drugs, innit? OK, hold him. Might be the one they want. Put the packet back in his pocket. Watch he doesn't get shut of it.

He keys digits into his mobile. Sean has his mouth open. Blood drips from his nose. I am powerless. I know he's never done drugs in his life – OK, a few tokes here and there, but booze has always been his drug of choice. I'd convinced him very early on that if he wanted to retain some sanity, he shouldn't tax his mind with anything other than alcohol.

They take him away in the same police car he'd been in before, except this time they have the cuffs on him.

– Well, then, Mr Fingers, been a naughty boy, have we? I wonder what the missus is going to say about this? She know English as a foreign language as well?

Pete chuckles. – Could be a pair together. She in Bah-rain with you? Made a few trips further east when you were out there?

*

They have him down at the police station and hold him in a bare room and a couple of suits start on him and want to know who his 'associates' are.

He babbles about a man with white paint on his hands but they don't seem interested in white paint any more. They examine his arms, looking for needle tracks, but it's a pretty desultory check. Their heart isn't in it. I suppose they think that with his 'foreign' connections they might come up with something.

Then the pager of the officer with the largest gut and the most raddled face sends him out of the room. When he comes back, he says to his colleague, OK, cut him loose. He's nobody. Oh, book him for D&D. What about the white powder? Is it what I think it is?

– Powdered paint. He paints with his fingers.

– Can't afford a brush, then?

Susan goes ballistic when he arrives home by taxi in the middle of the night, reeking of urine and booze, his eyes all shades of red and purple.

– It's all your fault. You had me picked up.

– Was it my fault you started fighting?

– I was beaten up for no apparent reason. But hang on, I suppose it was you who slipped a packet of white paint –

– Why should I do that? Think they're stupid, do you, Sean? It only takes a fingertip of it on the tongue. You don't know what you're doing half the time. Your mind's addled, you live in a fantasy. I can't reach you, Sean.

– Well, at least admit you phoned the police about a break-in. Someone looking like me, white paint on his hands, wanted your jewellery?

– What break-in? What jewellery? I don't have any. You should know that.

*

I know he's not going to speak to me for a while. He'll go inside his little room, indulge himself in some endless monologue, standing at some bar, knocking back pints of dry cider. He'll start early. He likes drinking in the late morning, over lunchtime. He'll lick his wounds. Then he'll start planning, where to go, what to do – his CV's badly compromised now – and then we'll start our dialogue all over again. In the incident room, until all desire has left him.

Looking for Aimee
Polly Wright

Angela is sitting on the edge of my bed. She wears a yellow towel wound round her head in a turban the same colour as the bedspread. She runs her hand down the length of my body, feeling the curves and crevices beneath the blue checked nylon.

Why are you wearing a jay cloth? she laughs. When she gets to my feet, she bends to kiss them. I try to sit up to stop her looking at them. I haven't cut my toenails for weeks. She pushes me back down again and her turban falls off, but her hair isn't wet. It is backcombed and stiff and the colour of cake.

I whisper, *I'm sorry about Marie*, and she doesn't say anything. She makes her way up my body again with her hand and a flame snakes up me as if I'm laid out to be lit like a firecracker. When she gets to my shoulders she rocks me in her arms, and I can smell talcum powder and soap and lemon.

And I can feel her skin, soft as her own baby's.

When I wake, I hear Mum coming up the stairs. She'll try to persuade me to come downstairs for supper. I can't get up. I have to lie still so I can get my breath properly. I have to concentrate. If I go down they'll both watch me while I hold my ribcage and gasp my breath. I can't bear their anxious, kind faces.

She taps at the door. 'Rachel. Are you coming down?'

I lie very still and watch the sun sink behind the bristly horizon of trees and telegraph poles. I need to gulp air, but I can't. She might hear, and know I'm not asleep. At last, I hear a bump as she puts the tray down outside my door.

'Don't let it go cold.' *Oh go away, Mum. Leave me alone.* 'It's spaghetti Bolognese.'

At last she goes. I listen to her soft steps on the stair carpet and then the clip-clop of her shoes on the parquet floor downstairs. The dining-room door opens and closes, and I can hear low muffled voices start up again and the high squeak of knives and forks on plates.

I lie flat, put my hands on my sides and open my mouth for air. Like a fish.

The next day, Mum wakes me. I have known it is morning for a while, but I hold onto sleep. As she sits down on the bottom of the bed, I shift my feet out of the way. The sheets in the new place are cold.

'Doctor Swain's here,' she says. 'He's talking to Dad in the front room. Politics, of course.'

Mum never allows Dad to get onto politics if she can help it. She's playing for time to get me to have a wash. I'm not sure I can get to the bathroom without passing out. I gulp as much air as I can and pull myself out of bed. The spots come and my heart flutters. I fall heavily onto Mum.

'Just a little wash, darling, please.'

She fills the bowl for me, still with her arm around me, and when she has finished with the taps, she uses her free hand to rummage in the airing cupboard to get out one of her clean nighties. The material is like the stuff they make jay cloths with and it has a broderie anglaise flounce at the top.

'*Mum.*'

'*Please,*' she whispers, unbuttoning my stinking grandad shirt. But she has to leave me to it because she can hear the doctor on the stairs.

'Hurry! He's coming up.'

The doctor is standing at the end of my bed with his back to me. He turns round as I come in. He has a sad face, but nice. Like Trevor Howard in *Brief Encounter*.

I can't tell him I'm dying. They said it was nothing at the hospital. He'd probably say the same.

'Just been to the toilet,' I say and he nods. Implying he understands bodily functions. I fall heavily into bed and try not to look at Mum. She's furious that I'm not wearing her hideous nightie. Nobody says anything for a minute. He breaks the silence.

'Well, let's have a look at you, shall we, young lady?' He already has his stethoscope around his neck. He doesn't look at me. That's understandable. It must be embarrassing looking at young girls' breasts in front of their mothers at three o'clock in the afternoon. But he still doesn't look at me when he takes my pulse and feels the glands in my neck. He stares out of the window at the beech trees with such intensity that I'm sure he's going to say something about them when he shifts his watery eyes back to me. But he says: 'Everything shipshape there.'

Perhaps they suggested nautical phrases for certain bedside situations at medical school. I can't imagine he's ever been on a boat.

'There's nothing wrong with her heart.' He clicks open his briefcase and rummages for a thermometer. 'Let's pop that in, shall we?'

Now we all look out of the window. After a moment he takes it out and looks at the silver line without interest.

'A little above normal. Nothing to worry about.'

'I get dizzy. I get black spots in front of my eyes when I stand up.'

'I thought, perhaps, anaemia?' Mum says hesitantly.

He sighs. 'She'll have to come into the surgery so I can take some bloods.'

He gets up and stands by the other window – where the blind is still down. 'May I?' he says as he pulls it down so it will go up. 'Pity you've no view of the cathedral from here.'

'No, but we've got a good one of the water tower.' Mum giggles as she says this. *Does she fancy him?*

'How old are you?' There's a pause and then I realize he's asking me.

'Nineteen.'

'You'll be going to university soon, or something?'

'Art school. I hope.' Why is he asking me all this? There's another long pause, while he looks steadily out of the window. Is he determined to see the cathedral?

'What were you doing before you got . . .' He can't say ill.

'I was an au pair.'

'She was living abroad?' he says, turning to Mum for explanation.

'Oh no. Here. Well, not here – in Littlebourne with a woman called Angela Didier. She was looking after two children. She was going to go to Paris but, well, it didn't work out.' Mum is nibbling the back of her hand while she talks.

Hearing Angela's name suddenly makes me feel like crying.

'It didn't suit me,' I say, my voice shaky. Mum looks at me sharply. The doctor still keeps his eyes on the water tower.

'Is there anything troubling you?'

'I don't think so.'

'Is there anything you'd like to tell me?' He clears his throat. '*Alone.*'

'Oh, yes,' says Mum. She gets up, fussily, picking up a

pair of dirty tights from the floor as if she's only just spotted them.

'No.' I'm almost shouting.

'All right.' He sounds a bit relieved and puts his briefcase on the end of the bed to open it. The catches click. 'Don't keep it to yourself. Talk to your mum about it.'

I feel hot with embarrassment and mumble, 'OK.'

He lifts the stethoscope from his neck as if he's removing a garland, folding its tubes carefully. He puts his thermometer in its silver case and fits it somewhere into the briefcase's padded lid. A place for everything. Shipshape.

He takes his prescription pad from a fold in the lid and a pen from his jacket pocket, but he doesn't write on it. He still looks sad. I feel responsible, somehow. As if I should have cheered him up.

'You say there was a man. French, you said?' I hear him asking Mum, as they go down the stairs.

Madame Didier was not at all what we had expected. For a start, she wasn't French. Mum and I had imagined a thin, stylish woman with dark hair, cut sharp along the chin, getting English phrases wrong and shrugging a lot. In the letter arranging the interview she'd signed herself *A Didier*. We decided that the *A* probably stood for Aimee.

So, when this big blonde woman waved her rolled-up *Kent Messenger* at us in the Koffee Kup, neither Mum nor I took any notice. We hovered in the doorway, looking for Aimee.

The Koffee Kup was on the top floor of a department store in town – next to the beauty salon. It smelled of perming solution and nail varnish and was packed with women. They sat in pairs or threes at tables, their stilettos digging into the zigzag black and white lino, trying to drink their frothy coffee without spoiling their lipstick. They all had either honey-blonde or chocolate-coloured hair backcombed high off their scalps and plastered into huge flick-ups.

In the end, Madame Didier had to come up to us and virtually shout over the clatter, and we kept apologizing as we followed her back to her table. She strode through the groups of people quickly and cleanly, while we stumbled over feet and bags of shopping. She motioned us to our seats and put the newspaper down on the table between us. For a moment we all looked at it, as if to remind us of what had brought us together:

> Au pair required – to look after two children and some household duties. Required two months' trial period in the Old Rectory, Littlebourne, Kent, followed by nine months in Paris.

'So, Rachel. Tell me why you want to do the job.' To my surprise, she seemed to be looking at me with something like approval. But then I remembered – Mum had got me out of my usual rugby shirt and jeans and into costume: brown velvet skirt, neat white shirt, American Tan tights and shining shoes.

'I want to go to Paris,' I said.

Mum looked horrified. 'She loves children. Don't you, Rachel?'

'Oh yes. I love children. And cleaning. I love cleaning, too.' Mum stared at the floor. Madame looked suspicious.

'I *am* very house-proud,' Madame said.

I nodded. As if I too polished and sprayed my house and body until everything was lacquered and nothing stank or moved.

My first night in the Old Rectory, I couldn't sleep. I got up at about two and laid all my jumpers and shirts on the bed. I folded the arms behind the torsos like they did in shops. I wished I had tissue paper to make a really good job of it. I laid them back in the drawers again. The insides were lined with waxy paper and smelled lemony. Mum always lined ours with newspaper.

The next day, I missed the alarm and was up late. Madame had started making breakfast and from the way she was banging around it was clear she thought it was my job.

'Wash this lot up, will you? I'm late and I still haven't done my hair.'

Her hair flopped disobediently over her eyes. She was a large woman. Like a Rhine Maiden or a grown-up Heidi.

'And, in future, you should be down at seven,' she tossed over her shoulder as she went. She always delivered judgements on the hoof.

I piled up the dishes and poured away orange juice from the kids' plastic beakers. I turned on the transistor on the windowsill. *Hey Jude*. I stood for a moment with my hands in soapy water, humming the tune.

Suddenly I was aware of Madame behind me.

'You should rinse after washing. That's what the other sink is for.' I'd noticed that there were two sinks, but I hadn't thought to ask why. I just thought it was part of being rich – like having two cars and two bathrooms.

'Look.' She pushed me out of the way. She demonstrated – using one of the children's Beatrix Potter bowls, lifting it out of the bubbles and filling the other sink with clear water to plunge it in. 'See?'

I nodded dumbly. She turned to the mirror and applied her orange lipstick. When she'd finished, she blotted her mouth on a tissue. Mum hardly ever wore lipstick and when she did she was always in a hurry and it smudged.

'The kids are in the playroom.' She kept her eyes on her reflection as she turned her head from side to side and patted her hair. 'Make sure you never let them out of your sight. And they're not to have their elevenses till eleven o'clock.'

I smiled. She looked at me sharply. It wasn't meant to be funny.

'Understand?'

Mum's planning something, I can tell. She and the doctor have been talking. It's about six o'clock and she comes in with her sherry. No knocking again, I notice. I seem to have forfeited all rights to knocking now. She plonks her so-called sewing basket on the end of the bed and plunges her hand into the tangle of cotton and loose needles. Mum never looks for anything – she just feels. Eventually she pulls out the wooden darning mushroom and stretches Dad's sock tightly over it. The way she does it, it reminds me of Danny pulling that slimy membrane over his thing – and I feel sick.

'Shall we have some music?' she asks, after a moment. I don't answer. All the same she puts the transistor on.

'*Hey, You. Get Offa My Cloud.*' She twiddles the controls till she gets what she wants. 'Ah, the *Messiah*, how lovely.'

I lie, curled up, staring at her cream sherry. It is ruby red in the lamplight. In the shadows it is the colour of dried blood.

'Darling. This man. Madame Didier's husband. What did he do?'

'Some sort of business.'

'Rachel! You know what I mean. You said – in the hospital. He came back for the weekend and he did something.'

'He . . . just . . . you know.'

'Made a pass?'

I watch her pushing her needle hard through the grey woollen sock. 'I don't want to talk about it,' I say.

*

The children's playroom was as big as a primary school classroom. Neither Peter nor Marie looked up as I came in.

'Your mum's gone out for the morning,' I said.

'We know. She told us,' said Peter. He was playing with his cars and Marie was taking her shoes and socks off.

'Would you like me to read you a story?' I asked Marie feebly.

'Shoes off!'

'I think you should keep them on,' I said.

'Off!' She stuck her chin out and kicked her fat peachy legs at me, as if she wanted to get rid of them as well as the shoes.

'She should keep her shoes on, don't you think?' I appealed to Peter, who was six.

'Keep them on, stupid.'

'No!' She managed to work one of her sandals free. The force of her kick propelled it across the room into a plant pot. The sock went with it. I gripped both her ankles.

'No. No shoes off,' I said. She screamed and kicked.

'Let her have her shoes off,' said Peter without looking up from his Dinky cars. I put her down and let her kick the other sandal and sock off. She stopped crying and started to run around the room on tiptoes.

I couldn't think what to do with them.

Then I remembered elevenses. Although it was only half past nine, I let them eat and drink as much as they liked. When they had finished, Peter asked for cake. I said I hadn't got any, but he led me into a sort of larder and showed me a yellow sponge with pink icing and drifts of hundreds and thousands all over its top. It had a silver frill with a frayed red border round its waist. Peter and I stood in the cold room and shivered.

I knew it was not for eating now. 'We can't eat that now,' I said.

'Just a little piece,' he whispered, touching my hand seductively.

'Another time. When Mummy says so.'

He looked at me, coldly. He seemed to be planning what he was going to say next. 'You're ugly,' he said.

It was as if he had hit me.

'You shouldn't say that sort of thing to people,' I said in a shaky voice.

'Why not?'

'It hurts their feelings.' He shrugged. I squeezed his arm very tight and yanked him away. He cried out.

Back in the playroom, I sat dully on one of their little chairs. I knew I wasn't beautiful, but no one had said I was ugly before. If it was true, there was no hope. No one, apart from Danny, would ever fall in love with me and my life would never change. I wanted to squeeze the breath out of Peter.

When Madame came home Peter ran up to her and whispered something. She looked at Marie's feet and her face distorted. 'Where are her shoes?' she bellowed.

Mum pulls a plastic tube triumphantly out of her cardigan pocket. 'Doctor Swain left this.' She gives it to me.

I turn it over. It has a label wrapped around it and a screw top.

'You know what it's for, don't you, darling?'

I shake my head even though I do.

'You do a pee into it, then Dad will drive down and drop it into the surgery.'

I see Dad getting into our rattly van, holding the bottle upright in one hand and driving with the other. I feel hot and my ears burn.

'Doctor says we need to take a urine test, you see.' Because he thinks I'm pregnant. 'Pop into the loo now and do it. There's a good girl.'

'I don't want to go. I've just been.'

'You haven't, dear.'

Does she know everything?

'If it's difficult to go, run the cold water tap. The sound will make you go.'

In the bathroom I sit and stare at the running water while I hold the bottle under me. I can hear the 'Hallelujah Chorus' from my bedroom, with Mum joining in, in her high quivery voice. At last, warm liquid gushes over my hand and misses the tiny mouth of the tube – which is, in any case, pressed up against the wrong place.

'I told you. I can't do it,' I tell Mum when I snuggle back into my warm bed.

'What happened?'

'I missed.'

'I'll come in with you.'

'No! Mum!'

Back in the bathroom, she firmly plumps me onto the loo seat. She turns her back on me and rummages in the corner cupboard.

'Yes. I thought so!' She almost falls over in her effort to reach something at the back. 'It's still here.' She turns round, red-faced. She's holding a powder-blue plastic potty with a picture of Peter Rabbit on the front. 'This should do the trick. Pee in here, and I'll transfer it to the tube.' She's looking pleased with herself.

'Mum, no! I can't,' I shout.

'Yes you can, my girl. Now, I'm going to go and make us both some tea – and when I come back I want that potty full.'

After she has gone, I lock the door and slowly lower myself onto the cold plastic.

Angela was girlish in the evening. After her bath she got out of her smart day clothes – a polo-necked jumper and slacks – and put on a sort of Indian kaftan affair which she told me Gide had bought for her in Paris.

'Just slipped into something more comfortable,' she said, giggling. We were sitting on her huge flowery sofa and eating our dinner on our knees. I heard Dad's voice, scoffing: *TV dinners. So American.*

We watched the news.

'Holding the country to ransom,' she said when a man from the unions came on. 'Listen to that accent. I can't understand a word he's saying, can you?'

I concentrated hard on not spilling my tomato soup.

'Really, you'd have thought she'd have done her hair before she went on television,' she said about a woman whose house was flooded.

The phone rang. She skipped out into the hall like a big schoolgirl. Angela never walked.

'Ah mon cher.' She obviously thought my French was much better than it was, because her voice suddenly became muffled. She must have stretched the cord into the broom cupboard.

When she came back, her mood seemed to have changed. She turned off the TV and sat looking at the fire. Then she picked up a magazine and flicked through it aggressively. I finished my dinner with relief, and sat back so I could take a good look at her.

She had what Mum called English Rose looks. Pink and yellow, like Battenburg cake. I felt an incredible urge to stretch out and touch her golden haze of hair. I had to grab my left hand by the wrist to stop it moving.

'Have you got a boyfriend, Rachel?' she suddenly asked, without looking at me. I'd supposed everybody else thought Danny was my boyfriend, so I said that I had, while reminding myself to chuck him.

'What's he like?'

'He's OK. Just someone I knew at school.'

'Is he good looking?'

'Not really.'

She laughed. 'Why d'you go out with him?'

'Because he asked me.'

She turned and looked straight at me. 'You could do better than that.'

I was dumbfounded.

'You'd be quite pretty really, if you did something with your hair,' she said, leaning towards me and pushing my fringe aside. I froze. 'Let me do it,' she said, standing up.

Angela's bedroom carpet was white and there were drapes all round her bed like an old-fashioned four-poster. She motioned me to sit on a white and gold seat in front of the mirror, which was designed like a box stage so you could see yourself from three angles. I couldn't meet my own eyes while she picked up handfuls of hair and dropped it, rubbed it into a fringe right over my eyes, then gathered all of it in both hands and pulled it so hard off my face it hurt.

The circle of gold hairspray cans was multiplied three times in the mirrors. Angela picked out the tallest. Then she shook the can, which rattled as if there was a single bead inside it, and made huge circles with her arms as she sprayed my head. She stepped back, like an artist, to judge the effect.

Suddenly, she seemed to come to a decision and frantically backcombed my hair. She sawed away until it was sticking out round my pasty face like Struwwelpeter. The hairspray smelled like aniseed and I struggled not to sneeze.

'Much better,' she said, through tight lips, full of grips. She crammed my hair into a French pleat, the way she sometimes did hers. When she finished, she picked up one of her hand mirrors and showed me the back, like they do at the hairdresser's.

'Very nice,' I said, wanting to cry. I couldn't believe how

old and pale I looked beneath my hair which had become a wig.

Upstairs, in my room, I tore out the grips and brushed and brushed till my scalp hurt. Afterwards, I lay for hours, looking up at the shadowy triangles of the attic ceiling, unable to get the sweet synthetic smells out of my nostrils. At last, I drifted into sleep.

Angela and I were staring at our multiple reflections, while she brushed my stiff hair. Sparks of static electricity crackled and flashed. Suddenly she lifted it all off, and underneath my head was bald and wooden, like a puppet's. Then I was lying in bed, with the bedspread pulled right up to my mouth like a security blanket and Angela was leaning over me – like Mum used to when I was ill. She pulled me up and rocked me. She smelled of lemon and aniseed and her skin was as soft as a baby's.

'Angela,' I whispered. And she kissed my forehead and my nose, like a mother. And then my mouth, like a lover.

The kiss was the kiss I had lain awake and dreamed of, before my first kiss.

When I awoke, I couldn't breathe. I couldn't get enough air in my lungs. I pushed the bedclothes aside and lunged towards the window. I wrenched the handle off its spike and pushed myself half out. I gulped and gasped air into my lungs, as if I'd just been underwater. Deep breaths weren't enough – so I snatched lots of shallow ones. Then I felt so dizzy, I thought I might fall out of the window. I gripped the flaky frame until my hands hurt.

When at last I got back into bed, numb with cold, I couldn't sleep. Afraid of what I might dream.

After that, we settled into a sort of a pattern. In the day Angela chided me like Cinderella but, in the evening, she confided.

Gide never came home all the time I was there, but he rang every night. One time, after the call in the broom cupboard, she came into the sitting room, crying. I sat back in the armchair, stiff with embarrassment, longing to disappear into the chair's blowsy pattern. Eventually, she stopped, and slopped wine into her glass. I hoped for a refill, but didn't like to ask.

'He's having an affair,' she said. I couldn't believe that she was talking to me as if I was one of those women in the Koffee Kup. 'Occupational hazard of being married to a Frenchman.'

'Are you sure?' I'd seen a picture of Gide and thought he was very lucky to have anyone as pretty as Angela. He was losing his hair and seemed to be shorter than her.

'Oh – of course – he doesn't tell me in so many words.' She adopted a sort of ironic nasal tone, like they did in television plays. 'He doesn't say *I'm having an affair.*'

'No, of course,' I said.

'You just know, don't you? Woman's instinct.' She knocked back the wine as I'd seen Dad do with spirits. *Don't let it touch the side of your mouth – straight down the hatch.* A trick from his Navy days.

'Who . . .' I trailed off, not knowing at all. I couldn't think how to phrase the sentence.

'Oh, his secretary, of course. Who else? Little tart. Don't trust them an inch.'

'Who?'

'Men. What about Danny?' She was suddenly looking at me. 'Your boyfriend.'

I was amazed that she'd remembered.

'What's he up to, while you're here?'

I had no idea – and cared less. 'I . . .'

'You watch him. He'll be off, soon as your back's turned.'

She sloshed more wine into her glass and fumbled for her cigarettes. I hadn't seen her smoke before.

'Men. They're all the same.'

The cigarette packet wasn't made of card like the Embassy and No. 6s we smoked at school. It was floppy and blue. I watched as she tapped the end and a fag popped out, smooth as a dispenser. She inhaled glamorously and the exotic smell filled the room. It was as if a fox had entered a perfumed bedroom.

I love her, I thought, and tried to breathe.

That night she was there. In my dreams. This time she was more bold. Her hands stroked my breasts and my thighs. She didn't seem to need to breathe; her kiss was continuous. Her breath tasted of wine and musky smoke.

When I woke I ached between my legs and I could feel how wet I was without touching. She seemed to have sucked the air out of me. Clutching at the window frame, the cold night jabbing my lungs, I thought: I am probably dying.

Then I thought, how can I tell her? How can I go downstairs and part the curtains on her four-poster to say: *Please, Madame. I am dying. Get me to hospital now.*

'She had long, long silver hair and was sitting at a spinning wheel. And when the princess looked up she saw that the blue ceiling was painted with millions of tiny stars. But then she realized that there was no roof and she was in fact looking up into the sparkling night sky.'

Marie's eyes widened. I held my breath. How long would she be like this?

'Draw me. Draw me stars.'

I put my lips to her plump arm and made a sort of farting noise so the gesture was funny rather than affectionate. I couldn't risk displays of love in case she pushed me away again. 'Don't you want me to finish the story?' I asked.

'Stars!' she demanded.

I got out their paint box and glue. I didn't have any silver so I slapped blue and grey and white onto some roughly drawn stars.

Peter was running round the room with his arms stretched out, making loud aeroplane noises. He stopped and looked at what I was doing. 'That's rubbish,' he said.

Marie started to lose interest. 'Want Mummy,' she said.

'No. Stars,' I said urgently. 'Look – look at this.'

I drew two people as fast as I could: a girl and a boy. With underwear, to avoid awkward questions. I was good at drawing – I could get likenesses really well. I did cartoons for people's birthdays at school. 'This is Peter and this is Marie.'

Even Peter stared. The pictures looked just like them. He had a proper boy's haircut and sturdy legs and she had a chubby face and wispy curls.

'Shall we make some clothes for Marie and Peter?' I drew trousers and a dress with cutout tabs like I'd seen in *Honey*. 'Now, you colour them in.'

To my amazement, Peter was really excited. He sloshed his brush into the jam jar of water and scrubbed it into the thin paints. Soon his hands and face were spattered with every colour in the box.

Meanwhile, I stuck the paper figures on cardboard and made them stand up on a little table holding hands. I lay down to make myself disappear, like a puppeteer, so they saw the dolls without me.

'I say, Marie. Let's go for a walk, shall we?'

'Oh yes, brother Peter. It's a lovely sunny day.'

Now, I'm good at voices too. At school I was always picked to play men or old people or characters with strong accents. I could just think hard about the person and the voice would come.

I couldn't see Marie's face, because the puppets were in the way. Peter came and lay down beside me.

'Say, *Let's go into the woods*,' he whispered conspiratorially. 'And say that we're going to find the gingerbread house.'

'Let's go into the woods, sister Marie. Ooh and look, there's the gingerbread house,' I said in Peter's voice.

'And the wicked witch,' he hissed.

'And here's the wicked witch and you children look good enough to eat.' I put on an old hag falsetto voice.

I could hear Marie whimpering. I looked up, over the puppets' heads and saw that she had tucked both her wrists under her chin and was clenching her fists.

'No! Wicked witch! Want Mummy!'

She started to scream and kicked the jam jar. The water went flying all over the beige carpet – the plastic paint box was kicked into the air and landed face down on the carpet.

Peter stood up and put his hand over his mouth. 'Ummm,' he said.

'No wicked witch!' Her face was screwed up and bright red. She lay on the floor, thrashing her bendy legs and arms. I bent over her and tried to get hold of her wrists and her ankles to get some stillness.

'There, there,' I said hopelessly.

'Hate you! Want Mummy!'

She was tiny, really. A bundle of plastic and cotton. Squealing like a pig in a frock. Like in *Alice in Wonderland*. I put my hand over her mouth. Not hard. Just to stop the noise.

'Shut up! Shut up! Fucking shut up!'

Madame was at the door, with Peter. Her face was crooked. She pushed past me, knocking me so I fell over. She lifted Marie onto her shoulder and rubbed her back, making cooing sounds.

'Pack your things,' she snarled, without even looking at me. 'Pack your things and get out.'

I held my ribs and tried, *tried* to fill my lungs, but I couldn't get enough air, and then my heart started to do jumpy things like a trapped bird in my chest and I saw black spots ringed with light like a kaleidoscope and I said, 'Please, Madame Didier. I am dying. I need to go to the hospital now.'

The room tilted and went dark.

Clouds move fast. I never noticed before. This one coming at me is going really fast. It's huge, like a deep blue ocean liner. The cream puffy ones behind it are stiller, though. They seem painted on, like a stage set, lit from below.

Mummy is different now she knows I'm not pregnant. Neither of us has said anything, but we both know that was what the urine test was for. She comes and sits with me every day now and I like it. She doesn't ask me questions any more.

Yesterday she brought a bottle of pills with my tea. She shook out two blue and red capsules onto her palm and gave them to me. She said the doctor prescribed them. I took them. I don't ask questions now, either.

Mummy brings me special things to eat. Like today she brings Battenburg cake. I love the crumbly pink and yellow squares and its heavy marzipan coat. It reminds me of Angela.

Angela came to me again last night, though I wasn't quite sure it was her. She seemed thinner and her hair was dark and well cut. She still smelled of lemon and aniseed, but she tasted of French cigarettes.

This time I made love to her. She whispered to me what to do.

I don't get any of the breathing now, when I wake up.

Mum asks me what I am smiling at. I say it's a private joke. She looks worried.

*

Today there's a letter on my tray. I can see it's from the art school. I don't open it. She asks me if I want her to do it. I say, OK.

'They're offering you a place,' she says.

'Oh,' I say. 'Put the radio on, Mum.'

She lets me listen to Radio Luxembourg now. 'In Dreams'. *Only in Dreams*. Like me and Angela.

She turns it down. 'D'you want to go, darling?'

'Where?'

'Art school.'

I don't answer.

'In London?' she says, very quietly.

I still don't say anything. I'm too tired. I'll have a little sleep first.

It's getting dark. Mum puts the light on, but doesn't draw the blind down, so you can see the whole bedroom reflected in the window.

She's cutting up last year's Christmas cards and sticking them onto new card to send this year. I think how shocked Angela would be if she sent one to her.

'Madame Didier rang while you were asleep. You left your red jumper there. She's sending it.'

I picture the jumper, nestling in the lemony drawers, and I wonder if she was surprised by how neatly I folded it. I think about whether I would like to see Angela again. In the flesh.

'She was pretty icy. I suppose she's embarrassed about her husband's behaviour.'

I pull myself up and lean against the pillows. I watch the raindrops sparkle like thin strands of tinsel on the window and the streetlights hanging like orange lozenges in the blue night sky.

'D'you want to talk about what happened, darling?'

'No.'

My face is reflected in the window. And now I see Angela's spectral face on top of mine. Like a doubly exposed photograph.

We both smile.

What Friction? Which Factions?

Stuart Crees

It was a Sunday, one of those depressing nights wrapped in fog and drizzle that take all the fun out of the football season, when there's nothing better to do in Woodbridge than hang about in the Social Club, drinking in the cosy light of the pool tables while raincoats steam on radiators. I was looking at the notice board as I waited for a game of pool, when Clancy came in, and said hello.

'Evening. The football team lost one nil again.'

I was only being chatty but Clancy cursed. 'Typical. We need a new striker. I keep telling Cleggie to give young Kevin a try, but he won't have it.'

'Well, Cleggie's an arrogant sod. Thinks he knows it all.'

Clancy was incensed: 'It's his fault the darts team is doing so badly. He keeps picking himself and Arnold Baker. Dougie's better than either of them, but he can't get a look in. And what's this rubbish?'

Clancy stabbed his finger at a sheet of paper near the bottom of the board. I read:

INTER-CLUB GENERAL KNOWLEDGE QUIZ
Round One: v. Southley Conservative Club (Away)
Dec 4th
The team will be:

J. Clegg (capt.)
A. Baker
A. Williams
S. Crawley
A minibus will be available for supporters.
Please sign below if interested.

The rest of the paper was blank. 'He can't be serious,' I said, incredulously. 'He can't really reckon that team to be the four best brains that Woodbridge Social Club can offer. We'll be plastered.'

Clancy nodded sagely. 'Not that I care if we are. Come on, I'll get you a drink.'

My turn came to play pool, and I had to play Clegg on table two. He fancies himself at pool, as well. I was three balls in the lead when Clancy brought my pint over. By then, I'd told Clegg what a rotten quiz team he'd picked. His reply was typical: 'I'm activities organizer and chairman of the team selection committee. If you think you can do better, get yourself elected at the AGM.'

I told him I was planning to nominate Clancy: that scared him, and he missed an easy pot. Clancy and Clegg hate each other. Clegg collected redundancy money from the car factory at just the time a Tory council offered to sell him his council house. A week later, he wangled himself an office job in Arnold Baker's motor-repair business. Overnight, he became a middle-class Tory diehard, and Clancy is everything he's come to hate; Clancy having been born into a successful business family, only to desert university and a bright future to work in a paint-spray shop – a passionate union and Labour Party activist. The two of them argue about everything. The only thing they seem to agree on is the weight of each point of view is dependent upon the relative positions of Liverpool and Manchester United in the Football League – and Clancy has had the better of that for a very long time. With Villa doing so badly, I don't have political opinions.

'So who would you pick for the quiz team?' Clegg demanded, as I pocketed another ball.

'Well, Alan Williams is fine, but I'd get rid of the others, and put in Dougie and Clancy.'

'One more. Come on, one more.'

Clancy was listening now. He stabbed a finger in my direction and said, 'Him.'

I potted another, and played the white safe on the bottom cushion.

'Listen,' Clegg said, waving his cue belligerently at Clancy. 'Dougie's a loudmouthed piss-artist, you're a troublemaker, and he's stupid.'

'I'm not stupid, Cleggie. Watch your mouth.'

He paused before taking his shot and rolled his eyes upwards. I was so mad, I could have hit him – but I didn't.

'He's beating you at pool,' Clancy pointed out. 'I'll lay a fiver to a pound that he wins. And I'll give an even tenner that your rotten quiz team gets slaughtered.'

'You're on. Both of them.'

Clegg promptly missed his shot; it took me four to end the game. Clegg paid out gracelessly. 'I'll have that tenner off you next week,' he seethed.

'Can I have a tenner's worth?' I said quietly. His face bleached, but he put out his hand and shook on it.

Clancy bought me another drink. I beat him at pool, then bought another round. Clegg eyed us miserably, muttering to his cronies – poisonously, no doubt. The bar had closed, and we were all getting ready to go home, to bed, television, and the gloomy imminence of Monday morning, when Clegg came over and tugged on Clancy's coatsleeve. 'I think it's time for a showdown,' he announced loudly.

Everyone within earshot gathered around. Sunday nights in Woodbridge aren't often so exciting.

221

Deadpan, Clancy answered: 'Six guns at noon, or swords at dawn?'

That got a laugh. Clegg didn't like it. 'Listen, I'll back my teams against any you can pick at a fiver a time.'

Clancy grinned: 'I hate to take your money.'

It took them twenty minutes to argue out the details, and agree on Alan Williams as umpire, referee, quizmaster and stake-money keeper. Side-betting had already begun.

Clancy selected his teams carefully, losing a couple of useful footballers known to be betting against him.

I led the snooker team for him, and we did him proud. Clegg declared that the chess would be the real test of intelligence. The chess match was a draw – all bets void – but Clegg lost all three of his games, and Clancy beat him in seventeen moves.

'I'm worried about the darts, though,' Clancy admitted, while we celebrated over a game of crib. 'The only decent player I can pick is Dougie. I've put myself and Sid Glossop in, but I don't fancy either of us. No offence meant, Sid. If I were you I'd have a fiver on Clegg's lot for the darts.'

'I can't find anyone who'll take the bet,' I answered lugubriously. 'Where is Dougie, anyway?'

'Over at the bar,' Sid Glossop said. 'Getting his raffle prize.'

We looked, and saw Dougie coming over with a bottle of whisky in each hand.

'Who draws the raffle?' Clancy asked, his eyes narrowing.

Sid and I answered together: 'Clegg.'

'Nobbled,' Clancy concluded, his voice as bitter as my pint.

Dougie couldn't be persuaded to part with the whisky. He promised faithfully to be sober for the darts match. He wasn't. The outcome was never in doubt. We went home early that night, leaving Clegg explaining to anyone who needed a free drink badly enough that darts required greater co-ordination of hand, eye and brain than any other game.

Clancy dropped Dougie from his quiz team, and substituted Sid Glossop.

Alan Williams seemed to have a very odd idea of what was general knowledge. His first question was: 'Name any four of the amino acids essential to protein.'

I don't think any of us knew what amino acids were. His next seven questions beat us all, too. Clegg was first to score, naming both teams and the result in the 1927 Cup Final.

'This is for two bonus points, then,' Alan continued, obviously enjoying himself. 'In what year did Drake defeat the Spanish Armada?'

'What sort of question is that?' Clegg growled. 'Christ knows.'

'I'll throw it open for one point.'

'1588,' Sid Glossop said quietly.

'Correct. The next question is for your team. Who invented Frankenstein's monster?'

'Frankenstein,' Clancy answered, but he didn't get the points.

About ten questions later, though, he knew the winner of the 1962 Derby. We went into the lead. 'Your bonus question for two points. In what year was the penny post instituted?' Clancy tried a guess. He was wrong. 'I'll offer it for one point.'

Sid Glossop said, '1840.'

Much to my surprise, I knew the speed of light in kilometres per second. Barlow answered a boxing question for Clegg's team, and Clegg picked up the bonus points by naming four members of the Cabinet at the time of the Suez crisis. But there were four more history questions, and Sid knew them all.

Clegg appealed for a void match because the questions

had been too difficult. Alan Williams was adamant. Clegg took a long look around, saw no sympathy and paid up. Sid Glossop stood quietly at the bar, beaming over a queue of gin and tonics.

Saturday afternoon's five-a-side football was played on a pitch which had been rained on almost continuously for a week. Sid Glossop and I, the only spectators, chased seagulls away while the teams were getting changed. Sid watched the entire game in freezing rain without moving or speaking, a huge grin plastered on his round red face. The teams blundered around ankle deep in mud, chasing a ball that would neither roll nor bounce. Clegg's team won by nine goals to eight. Clegg was sent off halfway through the second half after savagely chopping Clancy's great hope, Kevin Driscoll, in the penalty area. Kevin scored from the penalty. He scored all the goals for Clancy's side, and Clancy paid up cheerfully.

Clegg was too busy sneezing to gloat. 'You're getting a cold, Cleggie. You should go home and go to bed,' I told him.

Creepy Crawley, who had played a fine game in goal for Clegg, had nothing better to do than gloat. 'You're looking cheerful, Clancy, considering you lost.'

Clancy grinned: 'It's only a game, innit?'

Clegg growled: 'I don't know why you're smiling either, Creepy. You're out of the quiz team tomorrow night. Sid Glossop's in.'

Clancy thought this out over a pie and a pint in the club, and decided it didn't matter. 'It's all over now, anyway. Let's have an end to all this friction between factions.'

Dougie asked: 'What fiction? Which fractions?'

Clancy gave him a hard stare, then turned his attention to the *Sporting Life*.

We assembled outside the club at six fifteen, sharp. Clegg arrived in the minibus, twenty minutes late, complaining of

flu. 'Is this all the support we
climbed in. 'Three yobs?'

He meant Clancy, Dougie and me
did you expect? The sedentary septu
supposed to be running the club?'

Clegg ignored him, and turned on
drunk!'

'You gave him the whisky, Cleggie.'

'Well, I don't want any of the team catc
habits.'

'I'll not waste good booze on your soddin' br.
Dougie muttered, wrapping his arms around th
empty bottle.

'Come on, Clegg. Drive! We're already late.'

Clegg's driving is awful when he has time to spare.
hurry, he becomes an animal, spitting and cursing w
brake, gears and accelerator curse back, locked in mor
combat, howling, screeching and stuttering. I was greatl
relieved to arrive.

Clegg was enraptured, entering the Conservative Club
with an awe that most people reserve for the Grand
Canyon, Canterbury Cathedral or Liverpool Football
Club. 'Look! Bridge Nights! We don't have Bridge Nights.'
They had better snooker tables, too. Clancy pointed out
half the local Labour Party, playing doubles.

The blue-rinsed, fastidious refinement of the ladies
behind the bar was written on their faces: presented with
Dougie in his Sunday Best, they simply refused to serve
him.

'They're me gardenin' clothes. I've been doin' me
gardenin'.' Dougie's argument failed to impress. Clancy
bought him a drink, and he sat in a corner, grumbling into
his beer.

The quiz was a farce. Half the questions concerned television programmes that nobody on our team ever watched.

oney was looking safe enough. Even Sid Glossop
ered. The Conservative Club was leading twenty-
to four when the quizmaster asked who won the
Nobel Peace Prize. No one on either team knew.

airead Corrigan and Betty Williams, founders of the
rthern Ireland Peace Movement,' the quizmaster told
m blithely.

Clancy was on his feet immediately. 'That's wrong,' he
houted. 'In 1977, they were awarded the 1976 Peace Prize
n retrospect.'

The room went silent, and all eyes turned on Clancy.
Dougie and I rose to our feet, prepared to fight if we had
to.

'It doesn't matter,' the quizmaster yelled back. 'Sit down.'

'It does matter if you don't know the answers to your
own questions,' Clancy retorted.

Clegg yelled: 'Shut up, you fool!'

'All of you shut up,' the quizmaster said, standing up.
'And, for God's sake, sit down.'

Dougie flopped heavily into his chair, which collapsed
noisily beneath him. Nobody laughed. He climbed to his
feet, tugging at pieces of broken chair, and met a roomful
of silent stares. He grinned broadly at them, and said
loudly, 'I thought it was a safe Tory seat.'

The silence cut like a razor. One of the bar staff quietly
ushered Dougie out.

Clancy and I saw the contest to Clegg's ignominious end,
but the sparkle had gone. We found Dougie in the nearest
pub, nursing a double whisky and an urge to kill, and led
him back to the van, which Clegg was trying to start.
Clancy lifted the bonnet and put the rotor arm back. Clegg
glared, started the engine, then suddenly leapt down and
hurled a bottle at Clancy, which sailed past his nose and
through a window of the club with a satisfyingly impressive crash.

For a moment, everyone froze; but before the last tinkle of glass had died away, we were on the bus, and Clegg took us out of the car park at about forty and rising. Clancy said brightly, 'That was a silly thing to do, I expect there'll be trouble about that.'

Clegg screamed back: 'If you breathe a word of this, I'll –'

'You've got nothing on me, Clegg,' Clancy said quietly. 'If you're going to make threats, make sure you can deliver them.'

Clegg took a deep breath. 'I work my balls off for this club. It's yobs like you that cause all the trouble and do nothing for the club. What bloody thanks do I ever get . . . I've a good mind to chuck it all in. I've had enough . . .'

The van was veering all over the A38, at about sixty. Sid Glossop interrupted to point out that this wasn't a good time to attract the interest of the traffic cops. Clegg slowed, but continued his tirade: 'I really have. That's the last straw. I shall resign tomorrow.'

Clancy said quietly: 'You do that, Clegg. Then we'll say no more about tonight.'

The van veered again. I could see Clegg shaking as he drove. I was drunk on gin, the night was bitterly cold, and a maudlin mood was stealing up on me. Clegg seemed a pathetic figure, stubbornly proud in a world which conspired to humiliate him for no other reason than that was all he expected from it. 'Leave it out,' I told Clancy softly. 'He really has had enough.'

I could feel Sid beaming in the darkness as he offered cigarettes around and suggested brightly, 'Why don't we all go back to my place for a nice cup of tea?'

Huddersfield versus Crewe

Alan Beard

'Pools? God. Yes. Years since I did those. Frank never bothered. It's a man's thing, isn't it, the pools? The lottery's more women.'

I reassured her: lots of women on my round. Single women, too. She gave me a sharp look at this.

'I wouldn't know where to start with filling it in.'

I could help her. I wouldn't mind showing her.

'I'm just going out.' She was dressed up, plenty of eye make-up, a necklace catching streetlight. A long, long neck. 'Call next week, could you? I'm Kath and you?'

'David. Dave.'

How things start. I nearly didn't call. I was drumming up business on a second round I'd just taken over. I wasn't having much luck among the narrow rows of terraces whose sloping streets always seemed to be in fog that autumn and winter. It was the last house I tried before I trudged back under the motorway home.

I've always kept up the pools round, all through the other jobs I've had, mainly factory work, but also shop assistant, maintenance man in a block of offices, supply postman. Itty-bitty jobs my wife Liz called them. But that's not quite right: the maintenance job lasted six years until the firm relocated to Scotland. The pools always brought in that little bit extra. It also got me out of the house.

The way I saw it, towards the end, that's what they wanted – me out the house. It seemed to me they were ganging up on me. My wife would say, 'You're just short of useless.' (Just being the money I brought in – she often earned more with her part-time nursing.) 'Why do you bother pretending to take an interest? You're so full of yourself,' she'd continue. 'Apologies for breathing,' I'd say.

My daughter Ruth was no better. When I talked to her there was this sneer on her face the whole time. As if she couldn't quite believe what she was seeing. If she could she'd lie in front of MTV all day. An essay she wrote, on 'My Dad': 'He shaves in the sink and Mum is sick of him.' I pointed it out to Liz. She said, 'And?'

The cat was held in more esteem. I'd come home weighed down with shopping and park the stuff in fridge and cupboard, the kid's chocs, her yoghurts, my beers, and not say a word to either of them busy anyway with TV watching, hoovering, on the phone. Of an evening we'd shuffle past each other between fridge and sofa. There didn't seem much to look forward to; I was sitting on the toilet reading pension leaflets and working out sums. My hair getting wirier, more like a wig each day. My latest job didn't help, forklift driving in a warehouse and a lot of it was waiting about between deliveries. I looked at the days in my life and could see no difference in them, unless we won the pools. I'm sure Liz thought that as a poolsman I should have been able to arrange that.

The night I first went into her house I smoked so much I silently vowed to smoke no more. 'Blimey. No doubt you can keep up then?' She wanted me to catch the doubleness of her words.

We sat on adjoining sofas in this small room. The former

tenant's heavily patterned wallpaper – she hadn't bothered to decorate though she'd been there three years – made it seem even smaller. We pored over the coupon I put on the coffee table, our hands and knees close. Her hair smelled of tea; it was the colour nicotine leaves on the fingers. I explained the green panel, the blue panel, the booster entry. I could see how her eyes smiled – not quite her mouth – at that. She thought the crosses were like marks on a treasure map.

Every week she found some excuse for inviting me in. *Top of the Pops* on the television while she searched her bag for change. She always asked advice. 'Shall I go for Huddersfield versus Crewe, sounds like a draw to me.' I told her to stick to the same numbers, the same pattern. 'It's the best way.' She wouldn't. She'd come to the door and say she was on the phone and to come in and I'd watch her squat in a position she must have assumed hundreds of times she looked so comfortable. All the time I looked over the planes and corners and curves of her face for the beauty I saw there.

Sex with her was like dishes being served, one after the other, and all tasting new, ingredients you recognized but a new mix. She quite liked me to eat off her. I spent a long time gazing at her pale, rounded, marked skin, like a hoard of gold in the light from the anglepoise. It was a lazy, dabbling kind of sex, but occasionally she clung and dug into me hard, kneading, as if to make something new of my flesh. After I was tingling, felt the blood reach right down to my fingers and toes.

By now I was always late in from the round and told Liz I always would be – meeting a mate down the pub. She took this with a shrug – 'Enjoy yourself.'

Thoughts of Kath cut through the week, far-off lights calling through the fog as I stomped around the house. 'Wotcher strop-features,' said Ruth. 'Villa losing, are they?'

Liz finally noticed. I was spending too long in the bathroom looking into the mirror trying to figure out what it was Kath saw in me. 'You got a woman?' Her dark eyebrows arrowed. 'Yeah – you,' I said, but soon after I left, Kath had been saying I could, I should, and moved three quarters of a mile away under the always roaring motorway to the other side.

We'd eat cheese on toast and do little. Didn't go out much. It was a relief to come home to such quiet. She liked me for the oil on me, the way I talked apparently. My steadiness. I was 'handsome in a way'. 'What way?' 'A way I like.' I liked her for the difference she presented. She was a Brummie but had spent time away and lost – almost – the accent. She was so pale after Liz's dark looks. 'My ghost,' I called her.

'You can save me from going under in this place,' she said, nodding towards the window. The fog was a mixture of weather and fumes from the battery factory, she said. She said she could hardly breathe out there and nothing would grow in the garden, a short one backing onto the motorway embankment. (She was later disappointed to find I didn't have the green fingers she wanted, but I made up for it in other ways.) She said the neighbours stole her catalogue parcels. She talked of moving out, somewhere 'nice' – Sutton, for example, but we couldn't afford that.

I didn't think it was so bad. True, when the motorway cut our district in two when I was a kid it was deemed the rougher part. Liz in particular didn't want Ruth mixing with the boys from here. But on my round I found little difference in the people – some were friendly, I got a kiss and a tenner from someone who won a couple of thou third dividend; others guarded their property as if you had a second job as a burglar. I had to admit it wasn't as pleasant with the high sagging factory walls, the shunting yards and the huge weathered billboard (a fading 'It Could Be You') welcoming you, but then the other side wasn't exactly Solihull either.

Kath was an actress. 'An actor,' she'd say, 'an actor. I am an actor. Or at least I was.' We watched the videos that proved it. In one she opened the door to police, in curlers, a shrugged-on dressing gown, and was pushed aside. An ageing moll. (I got her to play that role later, and I was a policeman who stayed to interrogate her.) A speaking part in the Cable company ad. No, she couldn't tell the difference between a BT phone and this one. Except when the bills came in. Behind her was Central Library and the glugging fountain in Chamberlain Square. I saw that a few times, and noted again how she was cast as ordinary, hair blowing in the wind looked almost grey, and yet she seemed young to me. She actually got her phone installed and bills paid for a month as part of the deal. 'I made so many calls I ran out of people to call. My daughter got sick of me.'

Her daughter, Bernadette – Bernie – was going to be the one that did it. Actually be an actor. She was tall, brilliant, her face so expressive, camera friendly. I asked her how she knew since she hardly saw her now. Bernie, at fifteen, had decided to live with her father after the divorce, and took his side always. 'All right it's true at that time I was a bit messed up. I was seeing Frank who I later moved in with, and doing drugs, a bit.' She regretted not fighting for custody through the courts. That would have sobered her up and Bernie would have seen her how she could be, straight, responsible. Like now. On top of things. Bernie would have stayed and by now Kath would be visiting her in London, seeing her perform. Standing by her in photographs.

Kath told me it was she who did all the work with the

baby and her bringing up. It was she who made Bernie what she was. How could she choose the father who left her to her own devices all those years? Neither was he the saint he made himself out to be. I sat and agreed with her word for word, because I felt too how children can be so heartless, unthinking.

One night in spring I came in from the job and she was listening to Virgin Classic Album Tracks – U2's 'She Moves in Mysterious Ways'. Doing a little dance. Sunlight was squeezing in from the tiny shred of sky visible above the embankment.

'Do you think I'm mysterious?'

'Yes, very.'

'I used to think I was an alien. Or been abducted by aliens. But maybe I just dreamt it and you know some dreams are so real they become real.'

Again I looked over the paleness of her face, the tiny red marks – neck creases – under her ear, her hair tied back gold in the late slanting sun. I wanted to get to the bottom of her.

'So you're an alien. I always wondered. Your slippery skin. Your bug eyes.'

'No, I mean it. I mean I'm not me.'

'Possessed maybe.'

The whole room was gold and she golden in it. I moved towards her.

She told me how handsome Frank was: 'All he had was nice black hair and a good couple of eyes. When all's said and done it's the eyes that get me on a man every time.' And how she missed her ex – a steady type like me – and although it brought a bad taste to my mouth, I understood it, it was a kind of accounting for herself. And because a similar thing was happening to me, thoughts of my wife, soon to be my ex, had begun where for long years when she was right beside me I'd done nothing but try and block her out.

Little things: finding Liz's photo-booth picture, the one that didn't make it into the passport fifteen years ago, in the inside pocket of a jacket I'd hardly worn and picked up on a forage back there. When Kath played music it was seventies stuff – T. Rex and Roxy Music. Her favourite single was Hawkwind's 'Silver Machine'. Liz had similar tastes, only Kath liked the treble high and Liz liked it low, more bass.

I thought it was to be expected really and it needn't be a problem, but one night during my first summer here I lay awake watching Kath undress. To cool us we had the window open behind drawn curtains. Her skin was still pale but glowed from the warmth of the day. I recalled a scene from an early holiday with Liz. Torremolinos in June. She took off her bikini in the hotel room. The evening light and her deep tan made it look as if she'd put on some bizarre skin-tight costume that left her private parts exposed. Through the night with Kath snuggling close but not wanting sex, I seemed to hear the sea breaking outside the window: maybe the noise of the motorway.

No one seemed to call on Kath, the phone never rang. The people on my round didn't know much about her, though they remembered Frank. I asked her where she was going the night I first called, all dressed up. She said some function, she couldn't remember, as if she went to them all the time.

One night though when I got in, still thinking it strange to get my key ready on the corner of this street dominated by the motorway that rose above it, she was on the phone. She was crying, the receiver in her lap. Bernie was on the other end. I took the phone from her, despite her protests.

'Can't you be nice to your mother for once?'

'Who are you?' said the voice. 'Where's Frank?'

'Frank's gone. I'm here now.'

'But who the fuck are you?' And she put the phone down.

After that was our first argument. Because she hadn't told her daughter about me. How was that going to make me feel? I said she should write to her explaining I wasn't some fly-by-night. But she was still wet-faced from the call and I stopped and put my arms wide. 'You've got to believe in me. We've got to stick together.' She agreed and came close and kissed and promised everything would be all right. There was nothing wrong.

I was still doing my old round. Which is how I found out my wife was no longer there, nowhere in the district. A former neighbour said something about her going. Sure enough I called on our old house, even though Liz had cancelled the pools when I left, and a tall Asian in white robes and waistcoat opened the door. I asked him did he want to do the pools but he wanted to get rid of me and didn't give me a chance to look through, past him to my old world.

I didn't go back. I gave up my round there. I knew she'd have to contact me soon, for the divorce to progress. She did and she said she didn't require maintenance any more, they were all doing quite nicely now.

In her letter, which was almost friendly, she said I should keep in contact with Ruth, and that I should want to, and I did, although at one time I hadn't of course. Ruth came to our house a couple of times, nodded disdainfully at Kath and sat and watched television until it was time for me to take her back. So instead I met her on my own, once a month, and we'd go out, to the cinema mainly, the latest blockbuster – she liked special effects, *Independence Day*,

Total Recall, and so did I – and a McDonald's after. More recently she wanted to go for a meal, she introduced me to Greek food, or a new balti at some place across the city. For many years, I told her, our diet had had to be as bland as possible because otherwise she wouldn't eat it. She said she was grown up now – she'd be sixteen soon.

She tells me of her new life, how Liz has changed – brighter, more relaxed apparently from the burden of me being lifted, and of Robert, her stepfather. I was glad to hear her say that though he was 'all right' and worked hard he was a bit of a creep. But then anyone over twenty-five was a bit of a creep to Ruth.

She pointed out that what I was doing, had done, was nothing new. Just the same as thousands of others, like her friends' parents, middle-aged prats running after younger women. But she's not, I said, only a few years. Same as your mother. (I turned it into a compliment for Kath when I got back but she didn't want to hear anything Ruth might have to say.) Anyway, I added, your mother's no angel. I was referring to a brief (I think) affair she'd had years before which Ruth wouldn't have known about, but she nodded as if she did.

We – Kath and me – went to see *The English Patient.* I practically had to force her out of the house. I thought she'd want to go. 'You're the actress,' I said. She didn't correct me. Before she went she read up on the film and during the screening she told me the critics' opinions.

After we dropped into a nearby bar, across from the Hippodrome. I thought she'd like to be near a theatre. When we'd settled in a corner by the window I asked her if she couldn't refrain from telling me what everyone else thought of the film during it, so I could make up my own mind.

'Oh,' she said, sniffing, and looked out at the crowds

leaving the theatre. It was nice to be out among people. I'd thought about going back to the Villa again. I knew Kath wouldn't want to come, but she wouldn't mind me going.

'No, I don't mean I don't want to hear, but after the film.'

'No, you're perfectly right,' she said, still looking away. I gazed back towards the bar. I had been sat in a corner like this once, out with Liz. She was at the bar and I watched as a few men glanced across at her, some not so slyly. How she stood on her toes in strappy shoes, waiting to be served, then dropped back on her heels. The backs of her knees bent in, one a deeper hollow. How she moved steadily across the room holding the two pints and not spilling a drop underneath her narrow, lopsided smile. A man was singing as we came out and for once it was a good, strong voice. A small mob who had been shouting and chucking things stopped to listen. His voice became larger, only drowned out by a passing bus, and he got on his knees for the finale. Me and Liz clapped and whistled for the man in the padded sleeveless anorak with his arms wide.

Me and Kath got the bus back to the motorway inter-section and stopped on the corner by the billboard to light cigarettes. She had been quiet on the way home despite the rowdy passengers trying to get everyone to sing 'Three Lions'. She turned, she was smiling, she was trying hard. 'I'll get a job. Do something useful with myself, you see.'

'That's great,' I said and apologized for what I'd said in the bar. For some reason we didn't carry on down the street, but stayed until we'd finished smoking. We watched lights arc into the sky as cars went up slip roads. Then we put our arms round each other and hugged for what we'd done in this life, and what also we had no control over.

She did get a job. At the local supermarket on the one till. But she didn't like the customers, got flustered with special offers and always feared armed robbery. She came home jittery. She took more and more time off and in the end I told her she should leave the job if it was getting her down so much, we could cope. (I thought she'd get the sack soon anyway.) But then we'd definitely have to stay here. She didn't care, she was grateful I'd said the words, and she rang up, went to get her wages and never went there again.

She hardly ever went anywhere again. One Sunday afternoon with fog again at the window she cried at *Oliver* the musical, as much at Bill Sykes and Nancy's twisted relationship as over Oliver's plight. During the film I'd laughed at the mock-cockney and now wished I hadn't. I'd say that was the beginning.

She started spending days in bed, or wandered downstairs in her dressing gown. (I said was she auditioning for her old role but she didn't seem to know what I was talking about.) I'd say, 'What you been up to?' 'Not a lot,' she'd say. She always had excuses – 'If I'd gone out I'd have drownded.' (Mimicking my accent.)

She got a cat, I don't know where from. It didn't like me; it scratched me. 'It's only a kitten,' she said. It wasn't. She put a dirt tray in the kitchen. 'You have to train it to go outside,' I said. She wouldn't. Her fingers started smelling of cat food. Her breath was fags, but then so was mine.

At night with Kath in bed I zapped through cable channels (as Kath did in the day and evening: where's the zapper, she said once, things are no good without the zapper). I watched the weather in Norwegian, *Exotica Erotica*, Tommy Vance and MTV which I imagined Ruth would be watching. You had to hand it to Liz she had turned out much better than I would have imagined – I looked forward to seeing her now. I thought of her early life, not so much babyhood because that was just a whirl of broken nights, mopping up, feeding, bathing. But of later when she grew into who she was. How she couldn't get enough of learning. The phases she went through. I remember her doing the Ancient Civilizations: copying the alphabets of the Egyptians and Phoenicians (the trouble she had with that word), and writing messages in hieroglyphics. She made her bedroom into a museum, with a sign on the door and exhibits (bits of broken plates, paintings she'd done), and charged admission. Her Bugs Bunny teeth, her shining face, the freckles beginning that she would hate later. The singing of hymns, trying to do handstands in the kitchen, her rending cries if she was hurt. When she was reading *The Lion, the Witch and the Wardrobe* she said I was like Mr Tumnus (something to do with my wiry hair). Telling me off about smoking even though I was doing it outside in the yard, in all weathers, wind and snow whirling about me.

Even though I'd lived here for a couple of years I couldn't get used to the place. Even though people would shout hello across the street, stop and chat about the Villa and whether Stan Collymore was any good, I didn't feel part of things here. I'd grown up just down the road but it could have been another city. Ironing one Saturday afternoon, listening to the football on the radio, I was looking out into the back garden, the bare laburnum framed in the window above the low square hedge. A leaf scraped along the path in a light wind, I could hear the cars and lorries moving always just beyond, out of sight. It seemed wrong. I couldn't get it to seem familiar to me.

She was ill, she had a pain in her chest. She called it her 'fear' pain. She was on the verge of being sick all the time. She wouldn't go to the doctor. I started to feel coming back from work like I did with Liz in our last years together and wondered whether all relationships ended up heading this way; this one had got there much quicker. I stayed out longer on the pools round. Started attending matches. Stan Collymore wasn't any good.

Two years almost to the night she came out of the house all dressed up like that first time. I was just arriving home. Even from my distance I could see she wasn't as expert at applying the make-up. She didn't seem to see me and walked off down the street. I followed her but she just walked down to the land underneath the motorway and wandered among the pillars holding up the rising road. I went back. She returned about an hour later, said nothing.

I wondered should I get help, call a doctor or something. Instead I called Bernie. The number I eventually found on the back of an envelope wasn't London, but a Coventry one. There was no reply but I left a message. Could she just come and see her mother, could she just come and talk to her, it would mean so much.

'Hello, Dave,' I heard as I came in, dripping wet from the round.

I wouldn't have known it was her daughter, must have taken after the father, except for the pale skin which brought out roses in Bernie as opposed to her mother's milder, more mottled colouring: age.

Kath was watching the television, Michael Barrymore (early on she'd wanted us to apply to go on that show but I hadn't wanted to have the piss taken out of me), and keeping her eye on her daughter. I dripped, took my coat off, ran my hands through my wet hair, went to the kitchen, and came back. I thought they must have had the big conversation, or Kath was so pleased to see her she could hardly speak, beyond the usual exclamations – well, look at you! Actually Bernie wasn't tall and didn't look glamorous to me. She wore trainers, dull green tracksuit bottoms, splashed with rain. She chewed gum, and looked around frowning at the room. When Kath went upstairs she leaned forward and asked what tale Kath was spinning now.

It turned out she wasn't a drama student, though she had applied once. She was working in a hotel. Assistant Manager, she reckoned. I thought of Ruth who I was seeing at the weekend (Imrans, Balsall Heath), as Bernie went on to detail her mother's crimes. She was lazy, selfish, nuts. Hadn't I noticed?

'You could try being sympathetic,' I said.

'Tried that,' she said, 'so did Dad, and look where it got him. Wrecked his life. Probably Frank's too – but who gives a toss about him?'

We heard the toilet flush, movement upstairs.

'Are you going to visit her again?' I hoped not, I was bristling, could have smacked her, but I was thinking of Kath.

'Nah,' she said. 'Don't see much point. And you? You going to stay the course?' She got up, stretched herself.

'Yes,' I said, feeling a last raindrop run down under my collar. 'I'm starting on the decorating next week.'

Help the Aged
Julia Bell

'It's too hot,' Anna grumbles, playing with the handle on the window.

'Don't do that! Can't you see it's broken?' I say, sharper than I mean. I know I should try to bite my tongue more. I've been on my own too long.

'But it's boiling.' She's whining now.

'It's an old car,' I say, patting the steering wheel. I love my MG, even though it's inconvenient and cantankerous and doesn't have a soft top. 'Have some respect for it.'

We're going away for the weekend for the first time since we started going out. I'm taking her to the coast to visit my gran.

Anna's younger than me – by ten years – nearly a generation gap. She's bright, full of energy. Makes me wonder what I've been doing with myself all this time: getting older, rustier, stiffer.

'Look. I'll open my window, all right?' A rush of wind blows my hair across my face.

'That's better,' she says, wriggling in her seat.

We've been together six months, seeing each other mostly at weekends. I let her do all the running – last Sunday, after sex, she said she wanted to move in with me, marry me. I laughed and said maybe. I know what can happen when it all gets too close. In fact, since then, I've been thinking of cooling it a bit. Perhaps after this weekend. Tell her to do her own thing for a while. Y'know, nothing serious, just casual, just good friends – that kind of speech.

'What's she like then? Your gran?'

'Old,' I say.

'That's not very inspiring.'

'She's kind of, uh, eccentric. You'll like her.'

I haven't been to visit Gran since I started seeing Anna, and I feel guilty. I used to try to get down once a month. It's an easy route into Devon from my bit of Chiswick, an excuse to unwrap the car from its tarps, give the engine a good run out.

I look at her slyly, she's tapping the black vinyl dash-board with her slender fingers, nodding to a tune that's she's humming under her breath.

'What are you singing?'

'Guess.' She hums a few bars. It could be anything.

'Give up.'

'Oh come on.' She hums again. Then sings, '*Will the* real *Slim Shady please stand up*. It's Eminem.'

'Oh.' I haven't got a clue who or what she's talking about. 'I couldn't hear you over the engine.'

'Well, get a quieter bloody car, then,' she mumbles.

'There's nothing wrong with my car.' I can feel my voice starting to get shrill.

'Jesus. Don't be so defensive.'

'I'm *not* being defensive.'

Here we go, I think. Just like all the others. Relationships just *disturb*. Rake up muck that's been settled for years. Better to be on your own, keep everything casual, than have to explain yourself all the time.

She makes a face and flips open a pack of Marlboro. She doesn't ask before she lights one. I want to tell her that I'd rather she waited. The smell still gives me cravings and it was hard enough giving up in the first place, but I don't say anything. It's not her fault I'm being vile.

Once we get off the dual carriageway, it's B roads all the way and winding single-track lanes. The roads are clogged with fat BMWs blocking up the passing places, their drivers shouting at tractors for getting too close to their immaculate paintwork.

'What do they expect, bringing those tanks out here?' Anna says, frowning at the driver of an especially flash Merc who's refusing to back up for me. 'Wanker.'

As I reverse closer into the hedge, I tell her that it isn't surprising, it's a sign of how much this part of the country has changed in the last thirty years. Village life overtaken by rich Londoners with a taste for country living, expensive delis and Michelin-starred restaurants.

Anna gives the Merc the finger as it passes and its middle-aged contents look gratifyingly shocked.

I laugh. It's the kind of thing Gran would do. Shout, and insult the tourists. She's always spoken her mind, my gran. Won't hear of pussyfooting: 'It's so much better when words are out in the open. Your mother has never quite understood that.'

Mum lives in Scotland now, too far away for day trips. Once a year she'll get the train out of Glasgow and spend all day rattling towards north Devon. She'll stop for a week and then phone me up to tell me what a terrible time she's having and how impossible Gran is being.

They always row if they spend too much time together – Mum complains that Gran is ungrateful, stubborn, that she'll end up having an accident and no one will find her for months. That she should start thinking about sheltered accommodation. 'Her hips are beginning to go,' she said, when I told her I was going to visit. 'She's got a lot slower.'

Gran says that Mum needs to leave her alone. 'I've been to Cliff Side, and I'm not ending up like them, dribbling into their bibs in front of the TV, being roasted alive by the central heating. It's undignified.'

Mum went to live in Scotland after Dad. Her life is split into halves: With Dad and After Dad. With Dad she says she was always unhappy, that he didn't give her room to breathe. After Dad she went to live with Gordon, a property developer she met on the internet. 'I'm fifty-six, I've got nothing in my life. I might as well go for it before I turn into your grandmother,' she told me.

Gran's house is set back off the road, in a clearing on the top of the cliffs, overlooking the estuary. The river is just a narrow creek that emerges from beneath a tangle of tree roots and turns twice a day into a lazy, tidal pool. Boats list in the muddy sand, waiting for the incoming tide to make them buoyant; they are sheltered from the open sea by a curve of headland that houses the best part of the village. The house is old, wooden; built chalet-style as a holiday home by Gran's father. After Mum got married, the last of their children to leave home, Gran and Grandad sold the old house in Exeter and moved here full-time.

I park the MG by the back door.

'Very pretty,' Anna says, swatting away a swarm of aphids hiding from the sun under a chestnut tree.

The grass is overgrown, and I wonder if Gran's had anyone in to help her with it. She's silly about things like that: 'I'm not being nannied by anyone. And if I end up in a wheelchair I want you to shoot me, you hear?'

Hobart, her little Scottie, emerges from the bushes, sniffs around our shoes. I pick him up, tuck him under my arm. 'Where's your mummy then?' He smells of old dog and freshly dug dirt.

She's out the front, on the lawn that faces out to sea. I

can see the bulk of her body stretching the striped material of the deckchair.

'Hi!' I say, loud enough to wake her.

Nothing stirs. She's lying in the deckchair, the *Daily Mail* spread across her face. Her legs are strangely askew, her dress hitched up indecently high over legs that are beginning to burn.

For a moment I panic; my mouth goes dry, my palms sweaty. This is it then, I think. It had to happen, but why now? And then, absurdly, that tragedy always happens on a hot day. I look at Anna, she's slouching with her hands in her pockets. I want to tell her to stand up straight.

But then Gran moves, lets out a little snore. Pages of the *Mail* slip onto the grass.

Anna smiles. 'She's drunk.'

'She's not. Gran.' I shake her. 'Gran.'

'She bloody is.' Anna picks an empty Jameson's bottle out of the grass and waves it at me.

I don't want Anna to see her like this. 'She's not usually this way,' I say. 'I mean, she likes a drink but . . .' I look at Anna, but she's arching her eyebrows at me like she knows that this is the lamest excuse. 'I mean, she *knew* we were coming.'

Gran stirs, lifting a puffy hand to pull the paper from her face. 'Essie? Is that you?' She blinks into the sun.

'No, it's Cath.'

'Oh. I was having such a lovely dream. Isn't it hot?' She giggles. 'I'm ever so glad you're here. I don't think I can get out of this chair by myself and I need to pee.'

She grins like a kid, her eyes twinkling, but I can't look at her without thinking that she's too old for this. I wish that we hadn't come.

Anna just laughs and threads her arms under Gran's.

'Ooh it's a boy!' she squeals. 'It's a boy!' She pauses for a moment and squints at Anna. 'Still, looks like a girl.'

'I thought you were dead,' I say, foolishly, before she can say any more.

She laughs. 'I was having such a lovely dream.' She giggles again. 'That's what happens when you get old like me, the dead come back to you in your dreams. It's lovely to see you, girl, lovely. Come on, give us a hand up.'

It takes the two of us to heave her out of the deckchair. We hold onto her as she stands, swaying slightly.

'Can you manage?' I ask, not wanting to let go.

'I got out here, didn't I?' she says, taking a baby step forward. Slowly, she creeps towards the house. Tortoise pace; me and Anna on either side, holding her by the elbows.

We go in through the back door. Inside it's even hotter, the air dank and slightly rotten. A bowl of bananas are blackening on the kitchen table, and piles of paper slide on all the surfaces. There's even newspaper on the floor to save the lino while she's cooking, except it doesn't look like she's changed the torn and crumpled paper for months.

'I'd've tidied up if I'd known you were coming.'

I tell her not to worry, although I'm trying not to breathe through my nose. She shrugs us off when she gets to the corridor. 'We'll go and put the kettle on then, shall we?' I say, letting go of her arm so she can lean against the wall.

Her hearing aid squeaks. 'Don't be cheeky, dear, there's no need to shout.'

We leave her, Anna closing the kitchen door politely behind us. 'Sorry about the mess,' I say, as I stand at the sink filling the kettle for the stove. The whistle's missing, but I can't find it amid the mess. There's a muddle of mouldy loaves, used tea bags, open cans of dog food. It doesn't look like she's thrown out her rubbish for weeks.

'Ugh.' I shake out a bin bag and start filling it.

'Don't apologize.' Anna is sat down at the kitchen table, looking at the photos on the dresser. 'It's a bit like my house.'

I've never been round to her house. It's always seemed

more convenient to end up back at mine, seeing as I'm the one with the proper job and a mortgage, and I have to get up early for work on Mondays.

'Is it?' I say, surprised.

'Well, what did you think a squat would look like? What's wrong with this? It won't take much to get it tidy.'

I shrug. 'When you're your age maybe, but she's nearly eighty-five. She's just not taking care of herself properly. Look!' I hold up a tea bag that's grown blooms of green fungus.

Anna shrugs. 'What does that prove? That she's not very house-proud?' She picks a photo off the dresser, wipes the dust off it with the hem of her T-shirt. 'I thought you liked her because she's eccentric.'

Blood rises to my cheeks. What does she know? When she's older the idea of this kind of lonely decrepitude won't attract her, it will terrify her.

'Is this her?' She points to the photo, black and white turning sepia. In the picture, Gran is young, smiling, her hair pulled back off her face making her look boyish and handsome. She's leaning against a small sailing boat that's beached on the sand, wearing three quarter-length trousers, deck shoes and a man's loose shirt, sleeves rolled up to the elbows. Next to her is another woman, dressed almost identically, apart from a checked necktie, knotted at a chic angle. They've got their arms tightly round each other's waists and they're squinting against the sun. Wisps of hair, moving too quickly for the camera to catch exactly, make them seem windswept, weather-beaten, like they've just stepped out of the surf that boils into focus behind them.

'Yes, it's her and Essie Staunton.' I point to the woman with the necktie. 'They were best friends.'

Anna smiles. 'Oh, cute.'

'They were in the WRVS together. Gran's still got that

boat,' I say. 'She repainted it when she died. Renamed it *Essie*.'

Gran pushes the door, holding onto the doorknob for balance. Any moment, I think, she's going to fall. She looks sunburned and pissed; her eyes are red and watering.

'You won't mind if I go for a little nap, will you? I think I got a touch of the sun.'

'No,' I say, relieved. 'We'll take Hobart out for a walk.'

She looks at Anna who's still holding the photo. 'Oh Essie,' she sighs. 'She'd be eighty-six today, you know. If she was still with us,' she adds quietly.

We walk over the cliffs to the village with Hobart panting in the heat. He's slowed down too, his coat is duller and the hair around his ears is turning grey.

'It's beautiful here,' Anna says as we round the headland. The sea is dotted with sails; boats tacking lazily around the coastline. 'I think if I was your nan I'd be really happy to live here till I died.'

I look at her in her parachute trousers and sleeveless T-shirt. Age hasn't really touched her yet. 'What, on your own?'

She frowns. 'With you, of course.' Then she gives me that smile, full beam.

I don't know what to say. I bend down, pretend my laces need retying. It was what Lynne always used to say: 'You and me, we'll end up in an old folks' home together. I'm not leaving you.' Promises, promises. Better to be on your own than suffer the heartache when they leave.

'Well,' I say, 'well, none of us can see into the future, can we?'

But she's already gone on ahead, Hobart snuffling along behind her, starting and grunting at the shadows only he can see.

*

Anna insists on buying fish for tea. Even though I tell her that very little of it is caught locally any more.

'Doesn't matter. It still tastes better by the sea. C'mon, we'll tidy up for her, have a proper meal. I thought that's what you wanted.'

I do, I think, you've just stolen my initiative. You're being romantic. I feel cynical and boring.

And when we get back she insists on cleaning. I tell her that it's too hot for cleaning. But she just laughs at me. 'I can see where you get your moodiness from.'

And I don't know where you get your good mood from, I want to say. If you knew what I was thinking about you, would you be so happy then?

But she smiles, whistles to herself, keeps catching my eye as she scrubs the floor, bleaches the sink. She's trying to please me, but it makes me want to turn away, to shield my eyes, as if someone is shining a bright light directly at my face.

'Did I tell you,' Gran says, looking at Anna again and grasping her hand, 'that I taught this girl to sail.' She nods at me. 'I taught *all* my grandchildren to sail.'

'Cool.' Anna nods.

'You're a pretty little thing, aren't you? And so kind,' she sighs, a little over-dramatically, 'to come and visit an old soul like me. I knew something had to be up, Cath hasn't been down here for months.'

'I'm sorry –' I start, but she holds her hand up.

'No you aren't, dear,' she says. 'So don't even pretend. It doesn't suit you.' She's in her element now, the meal over, two bottles of wine empty on the table. 'You got any cigarettes?'

Anna reaches in the pocket of her jacket.

'Oh Anna, don't,' I say.

'You know you're not supposed to,' I say to Gran. 'The doctors said –'

'Bugger the doctors!' She takes the offered Marlboro. 'You know, Cath, you really are beginning to sound like your mother.' She flicks me a glance from the corner of her eye and makes a big deal out of letting Anna light her fag, cupping her hands to shield the flame, turning her shoulders away from me.

She's right, I *am* beginning to sound like Mum. Perhaps I was turning into her, as surely as the wrinkles were starting to pucker around my eyes. 'Oh, God, let me have one of those.' I lean over and pluck a cigarette from the pack.

'I think we should go out in the boat tomorrow,' Gran announces, taking another slug of her wine and shifting in her seat to face me. 'For old times' sake. It's what Essie would have wanted.'

Last time I saw the boat was on a weekend down here with Lynne. The *Essie* is moored up against the wooden jetty just down the cliffs, at the bottom of the garden. Only forty-three of the fifty-four steps that snaked down the side of the cliff were still functional. Under its tarps, the boat had spreading damp patches. The sail was mildewed and rotten, so I rowed Gran around the inlet a few times, the boat creaking and complaining while Lynne watched from the shore. I doubt if Gran's been back since. It was enough of an effort then, when she could still walk properly. It took us over an hour to get back up the steps again.

I open my mouth to protest, but Anna butts in. 'That's a great idea! That would be such a treat.'

Gran looks at me. 'Well, what d'you think, Cath? It'll be fun, eh?' She hunches her shoulders like a naughty child, and I know that if I object she'll accuse me of being like Mum.

'Yeah, I guess,' I say. 'If the weather's clear.'

*

'She's too old,' I say, as we make up our bed in the living room, clearing a mountain of newspapers and books so we can get to the sofa. 'She can hardly walk, let alone climb in a boat.'

'Who says? Surely you should be able to do what you want when you get old.'

'I don't know about you, but the prospect of struggling down that cliff in order to have a sentimental moment over an old boat doesn't exactly fill me with enthusiasm, not to mention the risks involved.' I tut at her, frustration building behind my eyes. Lynne would have bloody well agreed with me.

'Could you try any harder to sound like an old fart?' Anna says, turning away from me to spread a sheet across the sofa bed.

We don't say much after that. Anna falls asleep with her back to me, blankets curled around her. I lie awake and think about Lynne. Why did she have to leave? It's like, without her, everything inside me has gone sour and mean.

She wakes us at dawn.

'Come on, girls!' She switches on the light. '*Carpe diem* and all that. I've made some sandwiches.' She has an old canvas satchel strapped across her chest and a faded floppy cap on her head. 'I thought you girls could carry the chairs and the picnic table. I'm leaving Hobart in the house. He's too old to get down there in one piece.'

'OK, Gran, OK.' I look blearily at my watch: six thirty. That's another thing about getting to her age: you need less sleep. 'Give us a minute.'

Anna looks like she's sleepwalking. It always takes her ages to wake up in the morning. 'Not so enthusiastic now, eh?' I say, pointedly, regretting it straight after. She tenses, but doesn't reply.

I know it's why Dad left. *Pick pick pick* until he couldn't stand to think of his retirement being full of her voice. He's happy now. He's lost the pinched furrows in his face, put on a bit of weight and got his golf handicap down to twelve.

The bottom of the garden gives way to brambles and then to the remains of a fence. To get to the steps we have to negotiate a stile, which is too high for Gran to climb over. I break what's left of the fence and tread down the brambles so she can walk round.

The drop to the jetty is at least a hundred feet. The steps are still there, snaking in a zigzag down the side of the cliff, although at intervals the grey, weathered planks are smashed or missing.

'It's a long way down,' Anna says, biting her lip.

'Nonsense!' Gran says, turning to face us. 'I'll be fine if I go down backwards.'

The first step cracks as I stand on it. I grab onto a tuft of grass – it comes away in my hand. The soil is loose and full of shale. I take another step forward, concentrating on keeping my balance. The next step feels a little more solid.

'OK,' I say, 'let's go for it. Careful with the first step.'

We sandwich her between us. Me first with the picnic chairs folded uncomfortably over my arm, then Gran, then Anna holding her hands. I try not to look down.

'Your grandad built these steps,' she says. 'And the jetty. Me and Essie helped him best we could, but he said it was a man's job. Wouldn't let us carry much more than a nail.' She tuts and moves her leg, feeling gingerly for the next step. 'He was a silly man, your grandfather.'

Anna's face is red with effort. I can see her clenching her stomach muscles, trying to keep her body upright. As Gran comes down, two steps, now three, it's clear that she's relying almost entirely on Anna for balance.

It takes ages to get down the first flight. By the time we

get to the little platform where the steps change direction the sun is way above the headland. I change places with Anna, giving her the stuff to carry. 'Let's take it in turns,' I say.

The steps are narrower now, dug into the side of the cliff like a ladder. I can see the granite outcrop below where *Essie* is moored against the jetty. She still looks intact from up here, the green tarp bleached almost white by the sun.

'Steady as she blows!' Gran shouts, taking a nip from her hip flask. 'Come on, girls, let's get this over with.'

I can see Anna struggling to climb down and hold the chairs at the same time. 'Hang on a sec! There's a step missing –' she shouts, dropping one of the chairs. It slithers down the side of the cliff, the metal frame bouncing on the ledge beneath, then it launches itself into the air, blue nylon flapping, and drops with a clatter onto the outcrop below. '*Shit!*'

'Not to worry, dear,' Gran shouts. 'At least it wasn't one of us.'

I laugh nervously as she takes another step backwards.

We make it as far as the broken step, but the gap is too wide to negotiate without dropping down by holding onto the step above.

Gran is sweating now; her cheeks pink, her breath heavy. Even if we do get her down in one piece, I'm not sure how the hell we're going to get her back up again.

'Look,' I say. 'It's OK. If you want to go back. We don't mind.'

'Don't be patronizing, dear.'

'I'm not being patronizing, it's just –' *Impossible*, I think, this is impossible.

And then she steps backwards.

'No!' I shout.

But she lands safely on the step beneath; the wood cracks, but doesn't break. 'See?' she shouts up. 'Nothing to it!'

*

I look back up the way we have come; there are gashes in the soil where our feet have skidded and slipped. Gran wipes mud from her dress and takes another deep swig from her hip flask. 'Thought we'd never make it,' she says.

You're not the only one, I think.

The tide is in, the boat rocking gently against its mooring. Anna walks gingerly out onto the jetty.

'Take the covers off,' Gran says, 'see if she's still seaworthy.'

I open one of the picnic chairs for her to sit on. 'Here,' I say. 'Have a rest.'

She doesn't complain and grimaces as she sits down. This is taking more out of her than she'd like to admit.

'I loved her you know,' she says quietly.

'Who?' I ask distractedly, watching Anna jumping, confident and lithe, from the jetty to the boat.

'You really are quite dim, aren't you, dear? Your mother always said you were in a world of your own when you were a child.'

I can feel myself blushing. 'You mean Essie,' I say.

Mum refused to call her by her name. It was always 'that awful Staunton woman' or 'that lemon Staunton always hanging around like a bad smell'. I think she was jealous. Essie made Gran happy. She died when I was six; all I remember is a tall, bustling woman who smelled of yeast and vanilla and gave me packets of Parma Violets. Mum said it was Essie who drove Grandad to his grave: 'He couldn't cope with the shame of it.'

'Do you think it runs in the family?' I ask.

'Does it matter, dear?' She looks up at me. 'You love Anna, don't you?'

I watch as Anna pulls the covers off the boat and gives us a thumbs-up. I smile and wave back. 'I guess,' I say.

Gran sighs. 'You're still mooning after that Lynne, aren't

you? Give it up, love. Life's too short.' She drains her hip flask. 'Right,' she says. 'You'll have to help me get into that thing.'

I help her out of the seat. 'It's my knees,' she says, struggling to her feet. 'They took a bit of a battering coming down. I want you to promise me something,' she adds. 'You'll look after Hobart for me, won't you, when –'

I don't let her finish her sentence. 'Of course, of course,' I say. 'But he might go before you do.'

'He might.'

When she's sat down in the boat, she tells Anna to get out: 'I want a private moment.'

Anna jumps out and stands on the jetty next to me, looking at her, skirt spread over her lap, trying to get the oars out of their clips.

'Cast off, sailor!' she shouts. 'At the double!'

As Anna reaches for the rope, I put my hand on her shoulder. 'We'll only have to go in and get her,' I whisper. 'She won't get more than a hundred yards or so in that old tub.'

Anna shrugs me off, and begins to unwind the rope from its mooring. 'Bon voyage!' she says, touching her forehead with her hand in a mock salute.

'Look after Cathy, won't you?' Gran says, as she pulls on the oars. She's drifting out now, too far to jump. 'She's a miserable old boot, just like her mother, but she means well.'

'I can still hear you,' I shout.

'I know,' Gran says, grinning.

We stand there watching as she crosses the inlet. I'm expecting her to turn round and come back towards us, but she doesn't, the boat swings round and, before we realize what she's doing, *Essie* turns out to sea.

'Shit,' I say. 'Shit! What does she think she's doing? Silly old fool! Anna? We've got to do something!' I clutch her arm. 'Come back,' I shout. 'Gran! Come back!'

Anna turns to look at me; she's got tears in her eyes. 'And for what? They'll just put her in a home. Let her go, Cath.'

The boat rocks from side to side as Gran pulls on the oars, but she's still strong; very soon she'll be out of sight, rounding the headland, striking out for the open sea.

'We should call the coastguard or something,' I say. 'We can't let her do this. I *won't* let her do this.'

I start back up the cliff but it's like my muscles won't work properly, my whole body's stiff, unwieldy. Fuck fuck *fuck*. I can feel my chest tightening, my breath coming in panicked bursts.

There's a scrabbling noise behind me, and before I know it Anna is there beside me.

'Come on then,' she says, jumping up a step and offering me her hand. 'Let me help.'

The sun is almost directly above us now, the sky blue and cloudless. I stumble slightly on the rough surface, my hands flailing as I try to balance. I steady myself, and reach up towards her, into the light.

Biographical Notes

Gaynor Arnold has been a member of TSFG for sixteen years. She was born and brought up in Cardiff and lived in Oxford and Exeter before settling in Birmingham. She is married with two grown-up children and works for the City Council in the Adoption and Fostering service. She has had short stories published in various magazines and anthologies.

Alan Beard's stories have appeared in many magazines (e.g. *London Magazine*, *Panurge* and *Malahat Review*), anthologies (e.g. *Best Short Stories*, *Neonlit* and *Telling Stories*) and on BBC Radio 4. His collection *Taking Doreen out of the Sky* was originally published by TSFG and subsequently by Picador (1999). He has won the Tom-Gallon Trust Award for a short story. He has lived and worked in Birmingham since 1982.

Julia Bell is a writer, editor and tutor. She teaches MA Prose Fiction at Birkbeck, University College of London. Her first novel, *Massive*, was published by Young Picador in 2002, and her second, *Out There*, will be published in summer 2004, also by Young Picador. She is the co-editor of *The Creative Writing Coursebook* (Macmillan) and the anthologies *England Calling* (Weidenfeld & Nicolson) and *Hard Shoulder* (Tindal Street Press). She is very grateful for the encouragement and support of the Tindal Street Fiction Group, of which she was a member from 1993 to 1996.

Steve Bishop lives in Moseley, Birmingham, working as a comedian, musician and writer. The author of several published short stories, he is currently working on a novel and two screenplays.

Gemma Blackshaw was born in Essex in 1976. 'Going the Distance' is taken from a collection of short stories which are all based in her hometown of Chelmsford, entitled *The Promised Land*.

Leon Blades was born in Trinidad in 1930 and moved to England in 1963 where he studied drama at Dartington College of Arts, Devon. As a student there he wrote an unpublished novel, *The Prediction*, about life in Trinidad and also published 'Black Unity' in a local Devonshire magazine, later published in *Fingerprint* by Trinity Arts.

Michael Coverson was born in Birmingham, and has been a member of Tindal Street Fiction Group for ten years.

Stuart Crees, born, bred and buttered in Birmingham, is a poet, musician, writer and journalist. He has been a member of Tindal Street Fiction Group since it started.

Godfrey Featherstone has published short stories, poetry, art criticism, and articles on literary criticism, war, the media and third world issues. He has taught FE and HE courses in literature, cultural studies and sociology in London, Birmingham and the Black Country. He lives in Kings Heath and has two daughters, twenty-seven and twenty-nine. A member of TSFG for eighteen years, he has had a new transplanted heart for the last eleven and savours every moment of his new life.

Jackie Gay was born in Birmingham in 1962. She has published two novels, *Scapegrace* and *Wist* (Tindal Street Press, 2000 and 2003), and co-edited three anthologies of short stories including *England Calling*. She currently works as an artist in healthcare and community settings, and is writing her third novel.

John Gough is originally from Liverpool but now considers himself a naturalized citizen of the West Midlands. John's previous writing has been professionally based, and it is only since joining TSFG in 1998 that he is taking his long-held writing aspirations seriously.

Barbara Holland grew up in the 1960s. She has lived in Handsworth, Birmingham, for over twenty years with her Pakistani husband and their two children. Still active in politics, she has tried to keep alive the dream that people have the power to change things. She works as a Russian teacher and is currently writing a book about the fate of one of the Bolshevik women.

Joel Lane lives in Birmingham. He is the author of a collection of short stories, *The Earth Wire* (Egerton Press); a collection of poems, *The Edge of the Screen* (Arc); and two novels, *From Blue to Black* and *The Blue Mask* (Serpent's Tail). He is writing a third novel, *The World Turned Blue*. He has edited an anthology of subterranean horror stories, *Beneath the Ground* (The Alchemy Press), and has co-edited with Steve Bishop an anthology of crime and suspense stories, *Birmingham Noir* (Tindal Street Press). He has been a member of TSFG since 1995.

Sidura Ludwig is a Canadian writer currently living in Birmingham. She has been a member of TSFG since autumn 2001. Her fiction has appeared in *Pretext*, and *Birmingham Nouveau* (Tindal Street Press, 2002). In Canada she worked as a radio journalist for the Canadian Broadcasting Corporation.

Alan Mahar is the author of two novels, *Flight Patterns* (Gollancz, 1999) and *After the Man Before* (Methuen, 2002) and has recently completed his third, *Huyton Suite*, for which he won an Arts Council Writers' Award 2002. His short stories have appeared in, among others, *Critical Quarterly* and *London Magazine*; his book reviews in *New Statesman*, *Literary Review* and the *TLS*. He founded Tindal Street Fiction Group in 1983 and is Publishing Director of Tindal Street Press.

Maria Morris is originally from Wolverhampton but also lived in Leicester and Northamptonshire before moving to Birmingham in the late 1980s. She studied English as a mature student and now works as a proofreader. Maria has been a member of TSFG for three years, and 'Homing Instinct' is her first published story.

Annie Murray has been a member of TSFG since 1987. Her stories have appeared in *London Magazine*, *She*, *Pretext* and in the Tindal Street Press anthology *Her Majesty*. She has published seven novels with Macmillan, of which the latest is *Chocolate Girls*. She now lives in Reading with her husband and four children.

Mike Ramsden hails from Manchester but now makes his home in Birmingham. He has taught in East Africa, Yemen, Egypt and Brunei, and he currently teaches in the Language Centre, Sultan Qaboos University, Oman, where he edits

Language Centre FORUM. He has been published in a variety of UK magazines and is working on a novel set in Southeast Asia. He has been a member of TSFG since 1985.

Penny Rendall taught English at the University of the Andes in Venezuela in the 1970s and returns to South America regularly. She works as a freelance editor and translator and lives in Birmingham and Spain.

Polly Wright, born in London in 1950, is a lecturer, writer and actress. A founder member of the Birmingham-based theatre company, Women and Theatre, she has co-written and performed in many plays and cabaret sketches. In 1999 she joined TSFG, and started to write short stories. Polly runs Hearth, which is a centre for health, education and the humanities mediated through the arts.

'For the past twenty years the Birmingham-based Tindal Street Fiction Group has provided a rallying point for dozens of talented writers. The stories assembled in *Going the Distance* are a splendid showcase for its achievements'

DJ Taylor

'Tindal Street Fiction Group, as *Going the Distance* demonstrates, has been a hotbed of talent for twenty years'

Peter Ho Davies

'This anthology represents the best of Tindal Street Fiction Group over the past twenty years. While others pontificate about the sorry state of the short story, Tindal Street Press continues to seek out and publish some of the best writing in the form the UK currently has to offer'

Laura Hird

'Tindal Street Press is to be admired and encouraged for championing the short story at a time when its neglect is as perverse as it is uncultured'

Sebastian Barker, London Magazine

Tindal Street Fiction Group

Thanks to all members past and present:

* GAYNOR ARNOLD * ALAN BEARD * JULIA BELL * STEVE BISHOP * GEMMA BLACKSHAW * CHRIS BLACKFORD * LEON BLADES * LUKE BROWN * WENDY CARTWRIGHT * MYRA CONNELL * MICHAEL COVERSON * STUART CREES * MARY CUTLER * GUL DAVIS * GODFREY FEATHERSTONE * JACKIE GAY * CLARE GIRVAN * JOHN GOUGH * BARBARA HOLLAND * MAGGIE HOLMES * PAUL HOUGHTON * LYN JENKINSON * JOEL LANE * YANN LOVELOCK * SIDURA LUDWIG * ALAN MAHAR * MARIA MORRIS * ANNIE MURRAY * JAN PAGE * MIKE RAMSDEN * PENNY RENDALL * MICK SCULLY * BARBARA VINEY * POLLY WRIGHT *

Acknowledgements

The following stories in *Going the Distance* were first published elsewhere:

'Going the Distance' was first published in *Pretext Vol. 1: Salvage* edited by Julia Bell and Paul Magrs (Pen&Inc, 1999)

'And Weel No Wot to Do' was first published in *Mouth* (Tindal Street Fiction Group, 1996)

'A Walk Across the Rooftops' was first published in *Signals 2: 25 London Magazine Stories* edited by Alan Ross and Jane Rye (London Magazine Editions, 1999)

'The Country of Glass' was first published in *Dark Terrors 4* edited by Stephen Jones and David Sutton (Gollancz, 1998)

'Flowers for Doña Alicia' was first published in *The European*, December 1994

'The Glumbo Glisae' was first published in *Tindal Street Fiction* (Tindal Association for School and Community, 1984)

'Heart Trouble' was first published in *Raw Edge Magazine*, Issue 3, Autumn/Winter 1996/97

'Sinners' was first published in *Mouth* (Tindal Street Fiction Group, 1996)

'The Tonsil Machine' was first published in *Nutshell No. 4* edited by Jeff Phelps and Roger Pearson, April 1989

'Special Strength' was first published in *And God Gives Nuts to Those Who Have No Teeth: Heinemann New Writing* edited by Heather Godwin (Heinemann, 1990)

'Looking for Aimee' was first published in *Groundswell: The Diva Book of Short Stories 2* edited by Helen Sandler (Diva Books, 2002)

'What Friction? Which Factions?' was first published in *The View From Tindal Street: Nine Birmingham Stories* (Tindal Association for School and Community, 1986)

'Huddersfield versus Crewe' was first published in *Neonlit: The Time Out Book of New Writing Vol. 1* edited by Nicholas Royle (Quartet, 1998)

Also available from Tindal Street Press

HER MAJESTY
edited by Jackie Gay & Emma Hargrave

'Teeming with life and truth and with a rare quality of intimacy' Nell Dunn

Ali Smith, Liza Cody, Amy Prior and Helen Cross, plus unsung voices from across the UK, offer 21 majestic stories: adventures of the spirit that illuminate the everyday splendour of *Her Majesty*.

This bold anthology casts a crystalline light on contemporary lives. Modern dilemmas jostle with ancient themes: fertility, loneliness, survival. Stylish stories from some of the UK's best women writers told with an energy that will dazzle and delight.

'The strength of this book lies in its diversity – from cocaine nights to Saturday stews, daytime talk shows to Italian holidays – and the sense of women's lives documented and celebrated' *Big Issue*

'Short, sweet instalments of reality . . . Like an album of heartfelt songs, you are in there somewhere' *Pride*

'The short story is on the rise. The ones I read of these were excellent' *Bookseller*

ISBN: 0 9535895 7 9

Also available from Tindal Street Press

BIRMINGHAM NOIR
edited by Joel Lane & Steve Bishop

'*Cold, dark and very brutal*' Stella Duffy

From the industrial heartland comes an anthology of moody urban thrillers by John Harvey, Judith Cutler, Nicholas Royle and twenty other crime writers.

From hazardous canal towpaths to love on an orange summer's night . . . from cut-throat gangsters in the little Moscow bar to childhood ghosts igniting the terrors of today. Perfect for enthusiasts of crime fiction everywhere, *Birmingham Noir* will entice and chill.

'This is lightning in a bottle – dark, smoky tales of a city's underworld lit by starkly illuminating prose and genuine insights into the human condition. A brilliant collection' *Joolz Denby*

'Lock up your daughters, sons and the family cat until you've learned from these stories of crime in the city' *Carol Anne Davis*

'The heart of Midlands darkness evoked in bleak but fascinating stories by British crime authors of a particularly realistic bent' *Maxim Jakubowski*

ISBN: 0 9535895 9 5